TIME TO
RUN

TIME TO RUN

SUSAN C. MULLER

Published in the United States of America by
Stanford Publishing Company

ISBN: 978-0-9960797-8-5

Cover design by
Najla Qamber Designs
http://www.najlaqamberdesigns.com

Editing by
Carla Rossi Editing
Joyce Mochrie, One Last Look

Interior Design and Formatting by:
www.emtippettsbookdesigns.com

For Andrew, Sam, Caroline, and Bode
You are always in my heart

CHAPTER ONE

The April evening was mild for Sacramento, and the setting sun announced its departure by painting streaks of blood red through the darkening sky. Jax Duncan paused to take in the scent of camellias in hopes their fragrance would still the nagging voice in the back of her head that insisted she was about to make a fool of herself.

As she threaded her way carefully up the shadowy sidewalk to Cory Sheppard's home, the sight of the popular California state senator's crimson front door gave her a jolt of courage.

Her mother had always claimed a red door invited good fortune to enter. It certainly seemed to have worked for the senator. Everything he touched turned to gold.

If she could pull this off, she'd head straight back to her apartment and grab a paintbrush. If she couldn't, no sense painting the door. She was too broke to keep living there.

Jax shifted the stack of documents she carried to her other hand and knocked. The door swung open, allowing light and voices to spill out. The unlocked door sent a chill down her spine, but it was the voices that caused her heart to sink.

She hadn't counted on the senator having company. What a mess. She couldn't take his personal papers home for the weekend, and she certainly wasn't driving back to the capital building this late. She was so screwed. If he came out now, what would she even say?

Hi there, Senator Sheppard. I don't know if you remember me, but you set these papers on my desk at the State Budget Office when you received a phone call that sent you flying out of the building without them. I thought they might be important, so I drove over here, uninvited, on my own time, to bring them to you with absolutely no ulterior motive of hoping you might realize how much you needed someone dependable to work in your office when you run for governor.

Maybe she could set the papers on that little table in the foyer and slip out unnoticed. He could just wonder how they got there. No, she'd come here for a reason. She needed to face him.

"Hello, is anyone home? Senator Sheppard, are you here?" No one answered. She took several steps deeper into the house. Angry voices echoed from a back room.

This was bad. He'd never give a job to someone who lurked around, eavesdropping. Her only hope was to go back outside, pull the door closed, and start over.

She scooted backward until the heel of her Jimmy Choo's hung on the doorsill, dumping her on her butt with a loud *ooof.* Loose papers shot into the air, then rained down on her head. The contents of her purse skittered across the marble floor.

The voices continued unabated, the senator's deep baritone easy to recognize. "Get the hell out of my house if that's the best you have to offer. Go back to your boss, and don't show your face around here until you have something worthy of my position. Remember, you aren't the only game in town. My signature's not on that paper yet, so come back with the money or don't come back at all."

"Think again, Senator. There are forty senators in Sacramento. We only need one, and it don't have to be you. If our association is over, then it's completely over."

The answering voice carried a heavy, East Coast accent. Not Boston. She'd have placed that after all the summers she'd spent in Cape Cod.

Could be New York. No, more like New Jersey.

Jax climbed to her knees and madly swept papers into a pile. The salty taste in her mouth surprised her, and she touched a finger to her lip. It came away bloody. She must have bitten it when she fell. That would look attractive tomorrow. She wanted out of there. *Now.*

She'd wait an hour and act like she'd stopped to eat on the way over. She could even carry one of those gigantic sodas with her. The ice might keep her lip from swelling.

New Jersey spoke again, this time softer. "You're wrong about something else, too. I don't need to talk to Mr. Avendondo. He gave explicit instructions on what to do if you gave me shit about this deal."

Jax froze, her toes outside, her knees inside, her hands on the cold, marble floor, and her heart in her mouth. The New Jersey mob boss's face had been all over the news for the last week as his corruption trial neared, and the prosecution searched for *anyone* willing to risk testifying against the last of the big-time mob guys.

If the senator was in bed with Benedetto Avendondo, that explained how he could afford this house and the Porsche she'd seen him drive to the courthouse. And those tailored suits that made his shoulders look so big and his waist so small. Suddenly, he didn't seem nearly as desirable. Or intelligent, if he was thinking of double-crossing the guy.

Even toned down for TV audiences, rumors of the sadistic revenge Avendondo extracted from traitors and their families sent chills down her spine. One witness refused to testify after his sixteen-year-old daughter was found in an alley, almost beaten to death, all her teeth kicked out.

"You can't touch me," the senator blurted out in a much less confident tone. "The Sacramento police are on my payroll, and CHP will provide round-the-clock bodyguards any time I ask."

If she hadn't been so frightened, Jax would have laughed. With their budget cuts? CHP officers guarded the state capital and government office buildings. Sure, they'd protect the senator at an official rally. Maybe even follow him home. But wait outside his house all night? Not hardly, unless he admitted who was after him and why.

Which would send him straight to jail . . . where the mob could reach him whenever they wanted.

New Jersey chuckled. "Then the cops are double dipping. How do you think we heard about your 'secret meetings' with an Asian triad concerning the waterfront project you're supposed to be helping us with? There ain't a police department in the country that don't report back to Mr. A. And he outright *owns* the FBI."

Jax pushed to her feet, ready to bolt.

First one shot, then a second filled the foyer. The entire house vibrated from the sound. A whiff of gunpowder hung in the air. Her ears rang, and she grabbed the table for support.

As she started toward the doorway, the senator fell half in, half out of the back room. His sightless eyes gazed at her as blood pooled around his head. When his body began to move, she felt a scream build in her throat. Slowly, in jerking motions, the senator's remains slid out of view.

She clamped a hand over her mouth, afraid to breathe or move. An enormous man, his dark hair in a ponytail, appeared in the hallway with Cory Sheppard's body draped over his shoulders. She couldn't hold her scream any longer.

The man closed the distance between them in seconds, the senator's head bobbing with each step. A huge hand closed on her wrist as the strange man's lips pulled back in a growl. The scream died in her throat, taking all the air with it.

Blood dripped from the senator's body and coated Jax's hand, making it slick. Her mind fixated on a single word. It started small and grew louder and louder until it filled all the available space. *Run. Run. Run.*

One yank and her wrist pulled free.

She kicked off her heels and vaulted over the porch railing. Five years of gymnastics finally good for something.

"Bitch, I'll find you." His voice guttural, hateful, sent an electric current of fear charging through her limbs, spurring her to move faster.

Her head swiveled, first one direction then the other. He'd see her if she ran down the street to her car, although he couldn't chase her while carrying the senator.

With no time to analyze the situation, she sprinted for the neighbor's backyard and hoped like hell darkness would hide her movements. Edging from one source of cover to another, she made her way to her Audi, parked three houses away. Still, she waited behind a bush for half an hour, watching for any movement, before dashing toward her car. Thank goodness her keys were in her pocket.

She unlocked the door, dove inside, and sped around the corner, keeping her lights off until she was out of sight.

Nick Ross—Dominic Rossini to the few who knew him well—kicked a hole in the grass, sending a clump of fresh sod sailing across the yard along with a string of curses. What a clusterfuck. All his careful plans ruined in an instant.

He couldn't afford to let the woman get away, but he couldn't leave the senator's body in the front hall, either.

Apparently, anyone could walk into the man's house.

His job had been simple. If the senator didn't agree to the new terms, see to it that he disappeared without a trace. With Sheppard missing, but not dead, no new election could be held, and the county commissioner would decide who got the contract. And the commissioner worked for half the price Sheppard did.

Then the senator started to spew blood like an overheated can of beer before Nick could get his body to the plastic tarp he'd hidden behind the settee.

Mr. A wasn't going to like this. First, he'd screwed up the hit and now that damn woman. Nick used his shirt to open and close the front door. He hadn't left any prints so far. No point in making any more mistakes.

Nothing had gone right since he rounded the corner and saw the blonde, standing in the hallway, screaming. He should have dropped the body and grabbed her with both hands, but he'd taken down grown men twice her size one-handed without a second thought.

She must have the luck of the devil to have broken loose from him. And that vault over the railing was like something out of a spy movie. If she was a civilian, stumbling in by accident, it would be messy, but his contacts in the police department would find her for him.

If she was a professional from another syndicate, he was in trouble. Mr. A didn't forgive.

One problem at a time, as his father used to say. The senator was his first priority. Dispose of the body, then find the woman.

He'd finished rolling the senator's body in the plastic tarp when his eyes fell on a red purse, open and spilling its contents, half-hidden under a corner table.

He grabbed a towel from the nearest bathroom, sopped up as much blood as he could manage in one swipe, and headed for the door.

Maybe he'd be able to clean up this disaster without the boss ever being the wiser.

AT HER APARTMENT complex, Jax circled the block twice before parking in the spot assigned to 402. She'd been using that space since Mr. Wong died months ago. It was more convenient than hers, so why not? No one lived there, and she had as much right as anyone else.

For once, she was glad management had ignored her complaints about the broken lighting. Her Jimmy Choo's were lost, grass stains and blood covered her best suit, her lip looked like she'd lost a fight. According to her rearview mirror, at some point, she'd touched her face and left a smear of blood down one cheek. She didn't want anyone to see her like this and ask questions she couldn't answer.

The image of Senator Sheppard's sightless eyes staring at her replayed over and over in her mind. He'd been so alive only a few hours ago. She felt paralyzed. Unable to make any decision. All she wanted was to curl up in a ball and let someone else take over.

As soon as she got inside her apartment, she'd have a cup of hot tea and call her father. He'd take care of this mess for her. He always had.

She reached for her cell phone. A wave of panic caused her heart to skip a beat when her fingers found no familiar bulge in her pocket. She pushed the fear aside. The phone didn't matter. She couldn't call Gavin Duncan anyway. Not now, not ever.

She may have called him *father* since she was six years old, but he wasn't really. That honor belonged to her bio-dad, and he'd disappeared when she and her sister were still toddlers. Gavin was only her stepfather. And after last Christmas, no power on earth—not even witnessing a murder—could make her contact him again.

Once in the elevator, her hand shook so badly, it took two tries before her finger connected with the button for her floor.

The sight of the lighted elevator button—a red smear now coating the number four—caused violent shivers to race up her spine. She tried to clean it with her thumb, but that made it worse. Her whole hand was covered in red goo. Bile rose in her throat. Her entire body shook. She took a deep breath, trying to calm her racing thoughts, but the odor of fresh blood made the nausea worse.

Whatever happened next, she had to get warm.

First, she'd take a hot shower. Scrub every inch of her body. When she was warm and the blood was gone, she'd be able to think clearer. Make a plan. Figure out what to do, who to call.

The elevator doors opened in front of what should have been her apartment. It *was* her apartment. She could see straight inside. Her door lay flat on the floor like a gigantic welcome mat.

No point worrying about painting it red now.

The reflection of the ponytailed man flitted across the antique mirror on her back wall. A crash sounded as her flat-screen TV toppled onto the floor.

He swung his foot and kicked something small and round against the wall.

Another crash followed, and broken glass covered the floor. She eased back into the elevator before the doors closed, afraid to breathe in case he heard her.

A picture of her purse sliding across the floor unrolled in slow motion before her eyes. He had her wallet with her name and address. And all her credit cards.

Even her stepfather, with all his money and influence, couldn't fix this.

NICK UPENDED A jewelry box and pocketed an amethyst necklace. *The bitch lived too well for a city clerk. She must be in bed with the syndicate.* That knowledge might help him with Mr. A.

Maybe.

His foot crunched on broken glass as he surveyed the room.

Nothing. Not one thing to tell him who she worked for or where she'd gone. She was good. He'd give her that. But the Asians always hired the best.

She couldn't have gotten far in those bloody clothes. Not without help.

If she'd gone to any police department within a hundred miles, he'd know about it already.

He'd put off calling his boss while he thought he could take care of the situation by himself, but he couldn't wait much longer. Every minute he left Sheppard in the trunk of his car, unattended, this shit got more dangerous.

If he called his contact in the SPD first to help locate the woman, Mr. A would find out about it the moment he ended the call. And Avendondo hated being the last to know. He'd always preached knowledge was worth more than money.

Nick wasn't sure he believed that, but Mr. A did and that's all that mattered.

Shit. This was supposed to be his last job. He was ready to move out of wet work and into management. Now he'd never get a promotion. And it was all that woman's fault.

He needed to leave her a message. One she couldn't mistake.

His eyes fell on a pet crate in the corner, and he remembered the story of a woman who'd been locked in a fish trap and lowered into a lake.

He stepped closer, and a calico cat darted from under the bed and tried to hide behind a curtain.

A smile creased his face. The solution to two problems had just run across his feet.

JAX HUNKERED DOWN in her Audi and watched through the spokes of her steering wheel as the elevator doors dinged open. Ponytail stepped out, one hand balled into a fist, the other clutched to his side. His dark T-shirt hid most of the senator's blood, but some was visible on his powerful arms and thick neck. He studied the empty parking space with her apartment number stenciled on the concrete and stomped off into the dark.

She waited five minutes, then ten. A car engine started in the distance, its sound growing increasingly faint in the still, night air. She held her breath as she cracked open the door to her Audi.

Shit! She slammed the door when the overhead light came on and fumbled for the on/off switch before trying again. This time the light stayed off, and she slid out into the darkened garage.

She crouched beside her car, peering over the hood. There was no way to be sure that was Ponytail's car driving away. He could still be hiding somewhere in the dark. Maybe she should drive straight to the nearest police station—wherever that was.

Ponytail's words ran in a loop through her mind. *There ain't a police department in the country Mr. A don't control. And he outright owns the FBI.*

If she couldn't go to the police, and she couldn't go to the FBI, and couldn't stay in her apartment, what could she do? Maybe she should lay low for a few days. See what happened. Give the police a chance to solve the murder. If they found enough evidence to convict Ponytail without her, she was home free. Ponytail probably wouldn't mention her name—he would only incriminate himself if he did. They might never know she'd been there.

She tried to blink away the sight of the senator's home. Surely, with all that blood and gore, Ponytail had left some trace of himself.

Meanwhile, she needed a place to hide.

She had nothing—no shoes, no phone, no credit cards. No friends or lovers since she'd run out of money.

Only the clothes on her back, and they were filthy and bloodstained.

There was one thing in her apartment she couldn't leave—Cleo. She'd only adopted the cat from the shelter a week ago. They hadn't even bonded yet. The poor little thing had been abused and was frightened of everything. She barely came into the same room as her. She would have been terrified when Ponytail kicked down the door.

Cleo was probably hiding under the bed. She'd grab her crate and take her someplace safe.

Five minutes. That's all she needed.

Keeping to the darkest areas of the garage, she treaded her way between cars to the far edge of her building where a nondescript door hid a set of stairs. She'd never used them, but the manager had pointed them out the day she moved in. In case of fire, he'd said.

As if fire was the worst thing that could happen.

Even in her high-end building, the stairs were dark and creepy. The cement was rough and cold on her bare feet. The air smelled dank, as if no one had passed that way in weeks . . . months. She hugged the wall and listened for any sound as she edged her way up.

When she reached the fourth floor, she cracked open the stairwell door and peered down the hall. No one had come to investigate the disturbance. Why would they? When Mr. Wong died—leaving his apartment and his parking space vacant—she became the only one living on the floor.

Her apartment was exactly as Ponytail left it—TV smashed, end tables turned over, the contents of drawers dumped and scattered.

All the hours she'd spent picking the perfect furniture, color coordinating the drapes and throw pillows. Destroyed.

The door to her microwave hung loose, suspended from one hinge. She'd ordered it special, wanting the red one to add a pop of color to her stainless-steel kitchen. That was in the days when she'd had an unlimited credit card. Today, she'd have bought the small, silver one and eaten all week off the difference.

In the bedroom, Cleo's crate sat empty in the middle of her bed. She searched everywhere, but her cat had vanished. The shivers had calmed when she decided on a plan. Now they returned with a vengeance.

Ponytail hadn't been looking for anything. Mob or no mob, she'd witnessed *him* murder the senator. Now he was sending her a message. And poor Cleo had paid for it.

For once in her life, she needed to pay attention.

CHAPTER TWO

L ight from the hallway poured into Jax Duncan's demolished apartment through the shattered door.

Lincoln Montgomery pulled a pair of paper booties from his pocket and slipped them over his shoes. He held out a pair to his boss, who ignored him.

"She has a fifteen-hour head start on us. Why the hell didn't somebody notify us sooner?"

Lincoln picked a path through the worst of the debris. "Wasn't our case, sir. A missing person—even if it is a state senator, and even with that much blood—is local. It didn't fall under FBI purview until the money laundering aspect showed up. This has Benedetto Avendondo's fingerprints all over it. He likely sent one of his men to take out the senator, and she got in the way."

"Her fingerprints were all over the papers we found on the floor, and there are traces of Sheppard's blood in her apartment. She's the only one we know was there. So far, whatever this is, it's on her. If Avendondo had anything to do with it, the senator's house would be spotless and we'd never know this woman had been around. The mob doesn't work this far to the west. Not anymore. This is something else entirely. A love affair gone wrong, most likely. Sheppard was a well-known ladies' man. Who else would he let walk right into his house at night but a beautiful woman?"

Lincoln didn't bother to answer. Most crooks he knew preferred to work at night, not in broad daylight. Unfortunately, he was fresh out of Quantico, and his partner considered anything he said as useless. The fact that he'd investigated homicides for three years in Atlanta meant nothing.

This was Sacramento, and he was still a Probationary Agent.

"Be careful where you're stepping, sir. Those are blood drops next to your foot." Lincoln couldn't help himself. Darrell Byrne might be a Special Agent with seventeen years of experience, but he was still an ignorant ass when it came to crime scenes. And most everything else.

Byrne glared his direction. "I see them."

Then why did you step on two of them?

There was no point in having rules if you weren't going to follow them. It threw any conclusion into doubt.

"Let's get out of here. Sacramento PD has already taken

blood samples and photos. Nothing here's going to help us. She's in the wind, involved up to her neck. How else could she afford a ritzy place like this on a state clerk's salary? Probably wants us to think she's dead so we'll stop searching."

Byrne was half right. Unfortunately, it was the wrong half. Lincoln would bet his Space Cadet badge she was alive and hiding. But from Avendondo, not the FBI. Scared out of her skin to come forward. "I'd like to ask our Crime Scene techs to come take a look. There's blood in several different places. I'm not sure SPD did a thorough job. If she is involved, it's federal, and we're the ones who'll have to take it to court. Plus, I'd like to see what I can learn about her."

"Go ahead. Waste your time. I'll head back to the office. If you're so sure this is Avendondo's work, I'll try to sweet-talk some federal judge into issuing papers allowing us to search his compound for the missing Miss Duncan. I'm warning you, if I get lucky, it'll be my name on the warrant, not yours."

Byrne's threat left Lincoln cold. He didn't care about the glory, and the chances of Byrne succeeding where so many had failed were laughable. His boss was only doing busywork to make it look like they were actually investigating.

However, Lincoln did care about finding Duncan before the mob boss did.

The mob might not be as powerful as it once was, but the senator's disappearance and the papers scattered on his floor proved to him that Avendondo's reach wasn't confined to the East Coast.

This whole thing looked like a setup to Lincoln. He just wasn't sure if it was a setup by the killer to make her look guilty, or by her so she would look innocent. Sheppard was listed as six feet tall, 235 pounds. His body was missing, and someone had cleaned up enough of the blood to make it difficult to determine if he was dead or alive—although everyone concerned was betting on dead.

Jacqueline Duncan's driver's license listed her as twenty-four years old, five feet two, 137 pounds, but everyone lied about their weight on their driver's license. Any way you looked at it, she couldn't have disposed of his body. Not alone.

Sometimes he longed for the good old days when he was less skeptical of people and their motives.

That had all ended in one wild, six-week period when he was twenty. He still thought of her as *The Tornado* because she swept into his life, caused massive destruction, and was gone without a trace. The only good part . . . she hadn't lasted long enough to ruin his grade point average and keep him out of law school.

After she ditched him to run off with her old boyfriend, his father managed to get the marriage annulled. No harm. No foul. Like it never happened.

Yeah. Right. Tell that to his fear of failure.

Probably why solving this case and protecting someone he suspected was being framed felt so crucial.

Byrne gave Lincoln his most condescending smile. "Don't

worry, my boy. We'll find her, whatever she's up to. We always do."

They'd find her all right, but would she still be alive?

NICK PUNCHED THE disconnect button so hard, he almost knocked the phone out of his hand. No one had any idea where she'd gone, but silent eyes were searching for her all over the city. She was bound to show up somewhere.

An off-duty cop in Malibu was even watching her parents' home. The poor sap didn't know why, but he'd notify Mr. A if he sighted her.

Calling his boss had been tough. Not calling him would have been a disaster. Mr. A might be old. He might even be sick. That didn't mean he let anything slip past him. That he wasn't in complete control.

One call from the old man, and wheels were set in motion all over California.

Everything that could be done was being done, yet here he sat, waiting.

His orders from the top were clear—don't come home until you find her. If it took five days or five years, he wasn't allowed to set foot in New Jersey.

He needed to find that woman. His mom's health was going downhill fast. She wasn't able to travel. If he wanted to see her, he had to go there. And now he couldn't.

He was fourteen when Mr. Avendondo sent his father to oversee California operations. His sister, Nelia, was seventeen. By the time they were called back to New Jersey, Nelia was married and didn't come with them. After his father died and Mr. A sent him to earn his bones in Sacramento, he was ready. He was familiar with the place and had family nearby.

Now, five years later, he wanted to go home. He hadn't had a decent cannoli since he could remember. And even the best restaurant lasagna couldn't touch his mom's, though she didn't cook much anymore.

Sitting here stewing wasn't doing him any good. He started the car and pulled out of the darkened parking lot.

There was one thing he could still take care of.

Someone would call him the moment she reappeared. Until then, the senator's body wasn't getting any fresher, and he knew a building where the cement slab was due to be poured first thing in the morning.

CHAPTER THREE

Jax wasn't sure if it was the crick in her neck or the sun in her eyes that woke her. She was stiff, sore, hungry, and every bit as tired as she'd been when she pulled her car into the hotel parking lot and fell asleep.

More than anything else, she felt dirty. Her own body odor filled the car. One glance at the blood caked under her fingernails sent a bolt of panic zigzagging through her body. Had the quick wash and rinse at her apartment sink failed to remove all the blood from her face? Could that be why the clerk had sneered at her when she tried to check in?

No, that was caused by her look of dismay when he quoted the nightly rate.

She had exactly $120.67. A twenty she always kept in the console of her car for trips to the drive-thru, plus two quarters, one dime, and seven pennies from the cup holder. Then there was the hundred-dollar bill emergency fuck-you money still in the purse she had grabbed from her closet to stuff with a quick change of clothes, what was left of her jewelry, and the one thing she would never leave behind—the only photo she owned of her sister, Krista. Taken back in the days when Krista was a happy pre-teen.

The hotel was $274 a night, plus tax. How many times had she paid that much or more without a second thought? Plus, they wanted an ID and a plate number. She could lie about the plate number, but without an ID of some kind, she was screwed.

That was it. She had to go to the police. Sure, Ponytail claimed they were all in Mr. Avendondo's pocket, but in the light of day, that seemed preposterous.

If only she weren't so grubby. There would probably be reporters taking photos. All her friends would see her at her worst.

A sudden pain shot through her as her leg cramped from being in the same position all night. She stumbled out of the car and stretched until it eased. The faint sound of laughter and splashing came from around the back of the building.

She'd never stayed at this hotel, but at others of the chain. She knew the layout. Pool in the back, workout room, showers inside. You needed a pass key to get in through the front, but once in the spa area, you could go anywhere.

Her workout bag was in the trunk, and in it, an old bikini.

She climbed into the back seat and changed, keeping an eye out for passersby.

When she reached the pool, the kids had gone inside. Probably too cold for them. She tossed her bag over the fence, then placed one foot on an air conditioning unit and the other on the scroll design of the wrought iron fence. The next part was the hardest, but she muscled herself over.

The hot tub was heaven. She soaked until she felt human again. Inside were showers, shampoo, conditioner, lotions, and thick, soft towels. If she hadn't been so hungry, she'd have stayed all day.

When she finger-combed her hair, she realized she was still wearing her diamond earrings. The clothes she had grabbed off her closet floor may have been wrinkled and messy, but with her hair tucked behind her ears, she looked like she belonged.

The aroma of hot coffee filled the hallway, and she fell in behind a family of four as they headed toward the free breakfast bar.

Shoving thoughts of calories to the back of her mind— she'd missed supper, and the way her heart had been racing, her metabolism must be in high gear—she went straight for a sugar fix. After piling her plate high with waffles, muffins, and one decadent, chocolate donut, she located a seat in the back corner. When the TV switched to the news story of Senator Sheppard's disappearance, a businessman turned up the volume.

Her hand froze halfway to her mouth. If Ponytail had gone

back into the senator's house, removed the body, and cleaned up the evidence, where did that leave her—in more trouble or less? Even if she wasn't on the police radar, she certainly was on Ponytail's. And now proof of his culpability was probably destroyed.

She strained to hear the rest of the newscast over the din of diners eating, talking, and corralling rowdy kids.

The blonde anchor had on her *serious news* face. "When questioned about mob connections or rumors of corruption, the Chief of Police declined to comment."

Well, of course he did. There'd been stories of the chief's links to organized crime floating around the capital for years, but nobody *believed* them.

Oh God. If the stories were true, she definitely couldn't go to the police.

Not in Sacramento.

Maybe in L.A. or San Diego.

Certainly not Palm Springs. All the hoods from Vegas went there to play golf. Unless that was only a rumor, something gleaned from old-time movies.

The anchor's voice held a slight note of glee. "Chief Fulmer did say they were looking for Jacqueline Duncan, a woman known to have fled the scene. We have unconfirmed reports she was romantically involved with the senator."

A photo from her college graduation flashed on the screen.

"What?" People turned to look at her.

Shit. Did she say that out loud?

Jax lowered her head and kept eating as if nothing had happened. All she'd wanted was two or three days for the police to solve this thing before her name came up. Too late for that now.

"The FBI is said to be looking into the case. We'll have more on *News at Eleven.* Meanwhile, another witness scheduled to testify in the Benedetto Avendondo case has disappeared while in the Witness Protection Program."

Witness Protection. She'd read about that. They were part of the FBI.

She was so screwed.

The clerk who laughed at her last night started walking in her direction. "Miss?"

She grabbed a blueberry muffin, still in its cellophane wrap, stuffed it in her purse, and slid a granola bar into her back pocket.

"Just leaving. Thanks."

All she had to do was find a safe place to hole up for a few days until. . . .

Until what?

Nick Ross slammed his hand against his steering wheel. Where was that slippery bitch? He'd been all over town searching for her.

If whatever syndicate she worked for had whisked her

away and disposed of her body, that would solve Mr. A's problems, but without knowing for sure, he might never be able to go home.

So far, only one person he'd found had any idea where she might have gone. And he'd discovered that person himself, without the boss's help. Maybe he should have kept this screwup to himself a little longer.

He rounded a corner and stomped on the brakes. Her nice, clean car parked in front of the seedy motel stood out like a fly in the potato salad.

An amateur move if he'd ever seen one. She couldn't have been there long or some local lowlife would have lifted it.

Maybe she wasn't a professional after all.

Nah. An innocent bystander couldn't have gotten away from him so easily or hidden as completely.

He parked at the far end of the lot, away from her room, and entered the office. The sound of canned gunfire filled the lobby, accompanied by the smell of *Cheetos* and beer. The desk clerk flicked his eyes toward Nick and back to his video game.

Nick put his hand on the counter, a hundred-dollar bill folded so that only the amount showed. "I'm looking for my wife. We had a little spat, and she ran out of the house. That's her car parked in front of 107. If you could give me a copy of the key, I'd be extremely grateful. I want to apologize for being an inconsiderate oaf, but I'm afraid she won't open the door."

The clerk glanced at the bill and continued his game. "Not worth it if I have to pay the maid extra to clean up a mess in the room."

Nick peeled off another C-note. "There won't be any mess."

LINCOLN MONTGOMERY EASED around the corner onto the dingy street, driving a sedate fifteen miles per hour in order to check around every corner and down every alley. Not the area of town where you'd want to linger on a dark night, but this was late afternoon and his shiny, black SUV might as well have FBI emblazoned on the door panel.

All these mopes recognized who he represented with one glance.

One thing he knew in his bones—this was where he would find Jacqueline Duncan because she didn't have any money.

He knew it by the video of her face when she tried to rent a hotel room.

He knew it by the way she slipped in a back door to grab a shower and a free meal.

And he knew it by the way her friends and family talked about her.

All her girlfriends—and one guy he wanted to punch in the throat—said the same thing, if in different ways. Basically, she was a stingy socialite. A stuck-up brat who suddenly stopped buying rounds of drinks after work when everybody knew she could afford it because her daddy was rolling in dough and gave her anything she wanted.

Her parents were a piece of work. Her mother sat on the gold-trimmed sofa in subdued silence, worrying with the hem of her blouse until it began to unravel and letting her husband answer all the questions.

Her stepfather wore an Armani suit, half glasses, and a fake tan. He glared at Lincoln as if he'd disturbed their dinner. "We have no idea where she is. We haven't spoken to her since Christmas when she stormed out after demanding I buy her a new car. If she calls, we'll inform you immediately. I can't imagine why she would do something like this, but she was always wild. Ran with the wrong crowd. Lied. She had a problem with drinking and drugs. And now she's brought shame on the whole family and damaged my reputation."

Neither mentioned her older sister, Krista, until he brought up her name. Then they insisted the girls were never close, and since Krista died while they were both in high school, she wouldn't have been able to add anything about Jax's recent actions.

His request to see the girls' rooms brought on a frosty glare. Both rooms had been completely redecorated. Nothing personal remained, and neither had ever kept a diary.

Lincoln had scribbled something useless in his notepad before insisting he check out their rooms anyway. The Duncans were right. Nothing personal remained. No posters of rock stars, no ribbons from a spelling bee, no yearbooks with inscriptions.

Krista's room had been turned into a workout room

and Jax's smelled of fresh paint, but how fresh he didn't know. It could have been repainted after their falling out at Christmas—supposedly over their refusal to buy her a new car—or when they learned she might be involved with the senator's disappearance. There was no way to tell, and pressing the question would likely send them scurrying to their lawyer.

He'd check out the sister's death, but her parents were right. The odds of Krista having known anything that would relate to Jax's current activities were miniscule, and learning something useful from a yearbook inscription even smaller.

To Lincoln, the scene at the Duncan's home felt surreal. He could have committed cold-blooded murder on national television and his parents would stand by him, insisting there had been some mistake.

He couldn't begin to imagine how it would feel to lose a sibling, then have every trace of her existence erased. What effect it had on Jax, and how it contributed to this case, he couldn't fathom.

The whole episode had left him feeling dirty and more than ready to jump back on a plane to return to Sacramento and a real investigation.

Whatever else she was, Jacqueline Duncan was new to hiding. She'd sold her diamond earrings for a fraction of what they were worth and asked the pawn shop owner where to find a cheap motel that took cash and didn't ask questions.

If she'd had help from Avendondo or any of his pals, she'd be on the other side of the country by now.

Instead, she was somewhere in this three-block area.

He turned another corner and there it was. Her charcoal-gray Audi. In the parking lot of a rundown motel, square in front of what he'd bet his left nut was her room.

She really was an amateur.

He ought to call for backup, but his partner was busy trying to draft a warrant out of thin air, and the local cops would come in, guns blazing, after someone they suspected of killing a state senator.

Even if the body had never been found, everyone knew he hadn't simply gone fishing. Not with his car in the driveway, blood on the floor, and incriminating paperwork scattered around.

This woman might be mixed up in something bigger than she could handle, but she obviously wasn't a professional criminal. It was time to bring her in, get her to turn state's evidence, and tell all she knew about Avendondo and what happened to Sheppard.

Although, it wouldn't hurt his career any to be the one who brought down the last of the old-school mob dons.

A drunk stumbled out of the office, got in his car, and peeled away, leaving a half-inch layer of rubber on the road. He ought to arrest the guy, but he didn't have time.

What made her think she was safe in a place like this? He needed to bring her in before the wrong people found her.

He knocked on the door and held his badge up to the peephole. "FBI. I know you're in there. Open the door."

The sound of a security chain being removed came through the door. When nothing else happened, he tried the knob.

Unlocked.

The room was dark, but a muted light from the open doorway spilled across a shadowy form on the bed. There had been a lot of blood in her apartment. Sheppard might not have been the only one injured in whatever altercation took place. "Miss Duncan, are you okay?"

He took one step inside when his head snapped forward and pain exploded in his brain. Dirty, brown carpet rose to meet his face at warp speed.

Then the world went black.

NICK ROSS TRIED to act casual, but the sound of his tires squealed through the air as he pealed out of the parking lot. Damn, he needed to be more careful not to call attention to himself.

He'd have nailed the SUV as FBI even if he hadn't recognized the driver as the same guy who'd been all over town asking questions about Jacqueline Duncan. The same one who'd stood in the back row, looking uncomfortable, during the televised news conference.

Good thing he'd scanned the area for witnesses when he stepped out of the office, or he'd have plowed right into the guy.

He'd paid the pawn shop owner a hundred dollars to learn the woman was somewhere in the neighborhood and another hundred not to tell the cops. Didn't matter if the guy had blabbed to the Fed before or after accepting his money. It was a double-cross, pure and simple, and needed to be addressed.

Add the money he'd slipped the desk clerk for a key to her room and he was out four hundred dollars, only to have the agent step inside her door two seconds before he could.

He wouldn't have minded taking out the Fed along with the woman, but not without Mr. A's permission. Removing law enforcement was tricky. Sometimes it stirred too much interest. Plus, he couldn't keep track of who actually worked for the Family and who didn't.

Remaining anywhere close to the motel was too risky. He needed to ditch this car and find a new, untraceable one. He'd located her once. He could again. She was always reachable, whether in custody or in the wind.

His only problem was figuring out who she worked for. That made a difference in how he handled her. He'd make some calls. Somebody out there knew where she came from. Talent like hers didn't appear out of nowhere.

For now, he was heading to the pawn shop. Get his money back, one way or another.

A lesson needed to be taught. If the guy double-crossed him and walked away unharmed, Mr. A would consider him weak. And that was far worse for his future than screwing up the hit in the first place.

Didn't matter if he was tired of playing the heavy. He couldn't let that happen.

Sometimes, reputation was all you had.

THE FAMILIAR DRAG of his car ignition soaked into Lincoln's muddled mind. He tried to open his eyes, but the world around him was a solid white. Was he dead? He remembered soft hands touching him, promising him everything was okay. His own guardian angel?

This couldn't be heaven because his head hurt like hell.

He lifted his hand, and his fingers connected with something warm, sticky, and wet. A cloth covered his eyes, and he ripped it away as twin daggers of light stabbed into his brain. Another try and he managed to pry open his eyes in time to watch his SUV pull out of the parking lot.

What the hell?

She'd caught him off guard, bashed him in the head, and stolen his car. Shit! Where was his badge, his gun? If he lost those two things while still on probation, his career as an agent was toast.

He rolled to his knees and his badge, on a lanyard around his neck, swung forward. Thank goodness she hadn't taken it. Now he needed to find his weapon.

As he adjusted to the shadowy light, he saw his Glock on

the floor next to a broken toilet tank lid beside the half-open door.

So that's what she'd hit him with. No wonder his head was swimming.

He holstered his weapon before stumbling to the bathroom to splash water on his face. He reached for a towel when something sparkly winked at him from the floor. A rhinestone key fob. Probably fell off when she grabbed the tank lid.

Maybe, just maybe, he could catch her. He'd still be in trouble, but not as deep.

He scooped up the keys to her Audi and took off in the direction he'd seen her disappear. He reached the main street and paused. Right would be faster because she wouldn't have to turn across traffic.

He'd gone three blocks when he noticed the *low gas* light flashing. Damn. No wonder she'd taken his car. How much farther could he go?

Three more blocks, and he saw his SUV parked beside a dentist's office.

She was gone.

She'd either hitched a ride or stolen a car because a search of the nearest stores turned up nothing. He might as well go back to the motel and face the consequences.

He parked her car, wiped off his fingerprints, and drove his SUV back to the motel. Getting knocked out by a suspect wouldn't look good, but not as bad as losing his gun, his badge, and his car would have been.

Wherever she was, he'd never give up searching for her. And when he found her, she wouldn't get away.

He'd never underestimate her again.

CHAPTER FOUR

West Monroe, Texas
Four years later

The volume on the TV was muted, but even if it wasn't, Jax Duncan couldn't have heard the newscast over the commotion of the busy diner. And she didn't need sound to recognize her own face.

Or what used to be her face.

The twelve pounds she'd shed while on the run had revealed prominent cheekbones apparently hidden under layers of what her mother always called baby fat. No need to diet when you're on your feet all day.

These days, she wore her previously shoulder-length hair in a pixie cut she trimmed herself. The frosted highlights were a thing of the past, leaving only a nondescript mop somewhere between light brown and dirty blonde.

Had she really worn that much makeup? Talk about

raccoon eyes.

Now she was lucky to manage a swipe of lipstick before her shift started. If she did sneak in a five-minute break, she used the time to go to the bathroom or wolf down whatever meal someone had sent back, not to freshen her non-existent makeup.

She did miss perfume, though. And scented soaps. And shampoos. And rich, creamy lotions.

She glanced at her hands. Red. Raw. Chipped nails. A healing burn from the fryer.

The real difference was in the eyes. Not just the lack of mascara, but the dark circles that had taken up permanent residence. Losing her contacts was a godsend. She'd never have given them up voluntarily. Without the tinted lenses, her eyes were still blue, just not the striking, Hollywood-heartthrob shade.

How she'd hated the thick-rimmed, plastic glasses. Now they were part of her, like a second skin.

The noise level in the diner didn't dim as her photo filled the seventeen-inch screen at the far end of the counter. Maybe she had changed enough.

Or maybe she was invisible.

She straightened the *Hi, I'm Sandy* name tag on her mustard-yellow uniform and poured more coffee for the old farts' table. Grumpy old men thought a 10 percent tip entitled them to take up the biggest table for half the morning.

Not that it mattered much how late they stayed. By nine

o'clock, the farmers would be heading out for more fertilizer or to get gas for their combines. The ranchers would be headed to the feed store. And the truckers would be headed for Houston. Or Amarillo. Or St. Louis.

How she'd love to catch a ride with one back to California, but seeing her own face on the news meant that dream was as dead as Cory Sheppard and as unlikely to be resurrected.

She tried to sneak a quick peek toward the TV as she leaned over the table to refill Tom Jenkins' empty cup.

"Watch it, darlin'. If I gotta send these pants to the cleaners, I'll have to take it out of your tip."

The old man was kidding. She knew that. He actually thought seventy-five cents was generous, and he'd never sent a pair of jeans to the cleaners in his life.

"Don't get on my bad side, Tom. What's left of this pot might end up in your lap. Then what would your wife say?"

The rest of the table had a good laugh at Tom's expense and never glanced at the TV, which had moved on to the weather.

There had to be some way to find out what was going on. Learn why she was on the news. Just when she thought they'd forgotten her. That was the kind of mistake that could get you killed.

No one had forgotten her.

Not the police. Not the mob. Not the FBI. There was no statute of limitations on murder, and some computer jockey had measured the stains on Cory Sheppard's floor and declared he'd lost too blood much to live. Now every agency in the country was admitting the senator was dead and had decided she was involved. Some thought she was a scorned lover, while others said she was acting on behalf of the mob.

The cops didn't care which. They wanted to clear their books, find her, charge her, and sort out the details later.

Ponytail and the mob, on the other hand, wanted her dead before she talked. It didn't matter if she was in jail or Witness Protection. They could reach her. Benedetto Avendondo had proven that already.

But she didn't plan to get caught. As soon as she figured out what sparked the hunt this time, and how much they knew, she could decide if it was time to run again.

She was better prepared now. She kept her cash in her back pocket and a go-bag ready at all times. That was a trick she'd learned the hard way.

But she'd been here a year, longer than anywhere else, and it almost felt like home.

Roy wasn't the worst boss she'd had over the last four years. He didn't actually pay her a salary—that would have involved taxes for both of them—but he let her stay for free in the broken-down trailer that had once belonged to his mom and fed her one meal a day.

All she had to do in return was work in his diner from six to ten and his bar from seven to midnight seven days a week, and she got to keep her tips. Well, the bar was closed on Sundays, so she worked in the diner till after the church crowd left.

For now, her shift ended in half an hour. She'd change out of her uniform, wash the smell of bacon off her face, walk the fifteen minutes into town before the March sun had time to heat the humid air, and ask to use the computer at the library. See if she could figure out why her face had suddenly appeared on the news.

THE WEST MONROE Library smelled of ink and paper and dust and old-lady perfume and, judging by Mrs. Reynolds' beehive hairdo, two gallons of Aqua Net.

It was the ink and paper that called to Jax, although Hazel Reynolds had become the closest thing to a friend she'd had in years. Long before she went on the run, based on the comments her so-called gal pals made to the media in search of their fifteen minutes of fame.

"She definitely had a crush on Senator Sheppard. She rolled her eyes and fanned herself whenever his name came up."

That lie was a doozy, straight from Missy's pouty, red lips.

"We could never figure out where she got money to buy those Jimmy Choo shoes and the flat-screen TV. It was very suspicious."

Just not suspicious enough to stop them from letting her pay for drinks or spring for everyone's cover charge.

"Something changed about three months ago. She started avoiding us. Got very secretive."

She hadn't avoided anyone. They dropped her like sour milk at a picnic when she stopped paying for things. She sat next to Amy every day, and her supposed friend never once asked if anything was wrong. But she certainly rattled on about all her own troubles.

Her friends from high school were even worse. Going on and on about how she drank and did drugs. Apparently, not enough to affect her GPA or keep her out of Stanford. Where she graduated with a 3.8, thank you very much!

Jax took a deep breath and pushed back the anger. No point stewing over that now. File it away with *things-that-are-no-longer-important.*

Mrs. Reynolds' face lit up. "I didn't expect to see you before tomorrow. This isn't Sunday, is it?"

"Nope. Still Saturday. I can't stay long if I want to catch a nap before work tonight. I heard somebody mention a book today, but I'm not sure about the name so I wanted to look it up."

"Somebody in this town mentioned a book? It must be *Horse and Rider* or *Farming for Dummies.* Unless it was one of the kids. In that case, try *Cooking Meth for Fun and Profit.*"

"No, it was a trucker, passing through. Something to do with climate change and how it's responsible for the increase in autism." That didn't even make sense. Why hadn't she planned an excuse beforehand? She was slipping, and that could be dangerous.

That stupid news report had shaken her more than she

realized.

Mrs. Reynolds' eyes widened. "Sounds interesting. Let me know if you find the book and I'll order it. Alma June's little boy was just diagnosed as being on the autism spectrum. She took him to a doctor over in Houston. He's going to need specialized attention."

Damn. Alma June was slower than a herd of turtles, but she loved that little boy. She worked at the Dollar Store, another one of Roy's businesses. How often would he let her off for the two-hour trip to Houston?

Now she wished there *was* a book about climate change and autism.

"I'm going to pop over and use the computer for a few minutes. Is that okay?"

"You know our thirty-minute time limit on the computer?" Mrs. Reynolds glanced around the almost-empty library and winked. "I think we can waive it for today."

Jax scooted across the room, weaving between desks, colored posters, shelves of books, and reading displays. She chose the computer in the farthest corner, away from prying eyes, and took out her earbuds. This should be safe. No one could see or hear anything she pulled up.

Fifteen minutes later, she'd watched the newscast out of Houston four times and learned nothing. There didn't seem to be any particular reason to rehash the crime.

Still three weeks until the anniversary of Senator Sheppard's death, when news agencies sometimes revived the story. The announcer didn't mention any new leads or witnesses.

So why bring it up now? And on a local station, not the national news.

She needed to move on, but how fast? Things were easier if she had time to make plans.

If she could work the bar tonight—Saturday night was a big tip night—and then the diner Sunday morning, she wouldn't be missed until Monday.

By which time she could be three states away.

CHAPTER FIVE

The Sunday lunch crowd dawdled and laughed and visited until Jax thought she'd scream. Finally, one family at a time, they drifted out.

All except the Tuckers.

Penny pushed the food around on her plate, while her parents demanded she eat a few vegetables. Good luck with that. She'd never seen the girl eat anything but chicken fingers and fries. A few more years and she'd look just like her mother.

Mr. Tucker ignored the check on the corner of the table and threatened his daughter with loss of TV privileges if she didn't eat her green beans.

Penny made a big show of putting one bean in her mouth, but spit it into her napkin when her father's back was turned.

Come on, come on, come on. My ride won't wait forever. His load of frozen vegetables is due in Dallas by five o'clock.

The bell over the door jangled, and Jax turned to see a man slip into the front booth, his back to her.

No way was she waiting on the guy. Her shift was over.

"Pssst." Jax looked behind the counter and tried to catch Danny's eye as he ignored her. The lazy bum.

Outside, an eighteen-wheeler idled in the parking lot. Her ride, giving her a last warning.

Jax grabbed her backpack and dropped a menu on the faded Formica of the first booth. "Sorry. I'm leaving. You'll have to let Danny know when you're ready to order."

A strong hand circled her wrist. "I don't really need a menu, Jax. And you're not going anywhere."

Jax.

The name sounded foreign to her ears. She hadn't heard it in four years. The TV always called her Jacqueline.

She yanked on her hand, but the man's grip held.

Something had happened to her lungs. Hard as she tried, no air slipped through the blockage. Her heart couldn't decide if it wanted to gallop or freeze, so it simply vibrated in place, sending shock waves to her brain.

She should have left yesterday while she had the chance, but she was low on money. She'd bought a new pair of shoes. Not the Jimmy Choos or Louboutins she used to love, but some good quality, sturdy work shoes with a thick sole. Shoes had always been her downfall.

She forced herself to look at the man's face.

Not Ponytail with a better haircut.

The years had been good to the young FBI agent. He no longer looked like a kid playing cops and robbers. He'd matured into a handsome man. The type that commanded respect.

Of course, not having blood pooling around his unconscious head helped.

"Agent Montgomery?"

"It's Special Agent now, no thanks to you."

Well, they hadn't fired him. That was good . . . for him.

"Don't you have better things to do than chase me around the country?"

"Actually, no. Turn around and put your hands behind your back."

"Please don't handcuff me here, in front of my friends." Friends? Danny and the Tuckers? Sure, it was a ploy in hopes she could escape, but somehow she meant it. She didn't want Roy and Mrs. Reynolds and Alma June and a dozen other people she saw almost every day to think less of her. To wonder how many times she'd lied to them.

"I promise I won't try to pull anything." She honestly didn't know if that was the truth or a lie.

"And I should trust you? After the last time we met?"

He slid out of the booth, his grip on her wrist almost cutting off the circulation, but he didn't cuff her.

A shiny, black SUV waited in the parking lot, too new to be the same one from years before. How many of those things did the FBI have, because she'd stolen his last one.

He opened the driver's side door and motioned with his head. "Climb over and put your seat belt on. I want to hear it click. And keep your hands where I can see them." He grabbed her backpack and tossed it over the seat.

"Where are you taking me?"

He didn't answer, simply keyed in his radio. "Special Agent Lincoln Montgomery reporting. I have the suspect in custody. We are leaving the diner and returning to our previous location."

"What *previous location*? Are we going back to Sacramento?"

He actually rolled his eyes at her. As if she was some kind of idiot. What a jerk.

"Your place. I need to get my partner. We split up in case I missed you at the diner."

She tried to stall, but he glared at her and didn't back out until her seat belt was fastened. Tires ground against the gravel parking lot as her ride to Dallas pulled onto the highway and left without her.

The truck blocked her view of the diner until they were on the highway, heading the opposite direction. In the side-view mirror, she watched a silver sedan with out-of-state plates and a ponytailed driver pull into the diner parking lot.

Normally, the sight of anyone, male or female, with a ponytail sent her heart racing, but she had too many other problems to worry about that now.

Funny how her priorities had changed.

She had about five minutes to get away, while there was only one person to deal with. A quick glance around the SUV showed nothing she could use. She let her hand drop to her side, next to the seat belt buckle.

Near her trailer was a densely wooded area. If she threw herself out of the car, maybe she could hide in there until dark. No backpack or clothes, and wearing a waitress uniform, but her money was in her pocket.

She'd figure something out.

"Put your hands on the dashboard, or I'm going to cuff you. Guess I know what your promises are worth."

"I wasn't planning anything." Now she felt like a piece of shit, plus worrying about jail, or worse, getting killed.

They pulled in front of her trailer, and she saw it through his eyes—dingy, sagging at one end, windows covered with newspaper. For some reason, she hated him to see how far she'd fallen.

The rust-covered door hung half open. It never had shut right.

Special Agent Montgomery sat in the car and watched it, chewing on his lower lip. Finally, he shrugged and turned toward her. "Don't even think about running. I'd shoot you in the back and sleep like a baby. Keep your hands on the dash. Don't move until I come around and let you out."

Her door swung open, and before she could blink, he'd slapped one end of a handcuff on her wrist and the other to the grab handle over the door.

"Stay here and don't make a sound. Keep your head down until I get back."

With that he was gone, approaching the trailer from the side. A large, silver gun magically appeared in his hand.

Oh no. She wasn't sitting here with a target on her head. If Mr. Special Agent with the good hair and two last names thought they were in danger, all bets were off.

Jax tugged on the handcuffs with no result except a sore wrist. She twisted in her seat, grabbed the oh-shit bar with both hands, and tried to pull it free. Nope.

She reached into her pocket for her lip balm and slathered it around her wrist. Slowly, painfully, her wrist began to slide free.

Grabbing her backpack with one hand, she crawled across the center console to the driver's-side door.

Locked.

What the hell? She fumbled with the buttons on the driver's-side door. Nothing. No answering click or pop of the door lock, no window lowered. Even the sunroof stayed securely closed.

There had to be a way out. Breaking a window might alert Montgomery or his partner. The lock stuck up half an inch. If only she could get her fingers around it.

She was still trying to pry it up when Montgomery yanked the door open.

"Move! Out of the way," he shouted as he reached for the radio.

"What happened? What's the matter?" Something was wrong. She could feel it.

"Someone broke in and shot my partner. I have to report this and get help right away."

"No. Wait. Stop." She tried to grab his hand as he lifted the mic. "You can't call this in. Not yet. Not while we're here. Not while Ponytail can circle back and kill us both."

LINCOLN MONTGOMERY SWATTED Jax's hand away. She might look innocent, but she was trouble. He should have learned that the first time he tried to arrest her.

And look what that mistake had cost his partner.

"Enough, Jax," he snapped. "Get out of my way. I have to report this. *Now.*"

"I'm not saying don't call it in. Of course, call him an ambulance. Just don't tell them where you and I are. Let's get somewhere safe first. We can't save him if we're dead."

"It's too late. He's gone."

The weight of all the regret she'd fought to overcome the last four years crashed down on her heart, making each beat a struggle. "Nooooo. I never thought someone else might get hurt."

"That's what happens when you run. You have unintended consequences. If you'd turned yourself in back in California,

Hawkins would still be alive."

"And I wouldn't be."

Lincoln keyed in the mic. He didn't need her permission to do what he'd been trained to do. "Agent down at Jacqueline Duncan's trailer one mile off the West Monroe Highway."

Two minutes later, when he'd relayed all the needed information, Jax interrupted his thoughts. "You've done everything possible for him. Can we leave now? Even if you don't believe me about Ponytail, you know *someone* killed your partner while trying to get to me. Take me someplace safe while you figure it out."

"He's my partner, and I won't leave him lying there like that. Not for one minute. I'm an FBI agent with a gun. You're safe here with me." But he had left Hawkins alone to come sit out here with Jax because he couldn't trust her to stay put.

"Your partner was a trained agent, too. Wasn't he?"

He sagged back in his seat and looked in her direction. "Did you have anything to do with this?"

Her eyes snapped toward him, and the fire in them dried any tears he'd seen a hint of seconds ago. "How would I have managed that? I wasn't here when you drove off and left him, and I was at the diner when you got there. I'm on foot and you have a car. Even if you got lost and drove around the town three times, I couldn't have made it to the diner before you."

She was right. She couldn't have done it personally. Not without help. But who, the mob? Living in this town, protecting her? If they wanted to protect her, they'd have set her up better than this. That trailer needed to be condemned.

So if she was hiding from the mob, did that mean she wasn't working for them? Or had double-crossed them? Could it actually have been a love affair gone bad?

Those questions had tormented him for the last four years. And he still didn't have an answer.

He keyed the mic in again. "As soon as the ambulance gets here, I'm taking Miss Duncan to our safe house. I'll check in with you later."

Jax's eyes doubled in size. "I can't go to your safe house. He'll find me there."

"Of course you can. That's why it's called a *safe house*." The woman had him so aggravated, he spit the words out.

Or maybe it was Hawkins' death. The sight of his partner's empty eyes had shaken him to the core.

How much of that fell on his shoulders? He'd left the guy there alone and raced off to the diner. Hawkins was a trained FBI agent with twelve years' experience. He'd made the decision to split up and had chosen to stay at the trailer.

Somehow that didn't make him feel any better.

Sirens sounded in the distance. There was a place he knew outside of Houston, on Lake Conroe, that doubled as a vacation rental. That way, the neighbors were used to strangers coming and going.

All he had to do was call for the key.

NICK WAS RAISED in New Jersey and California. He wasn't an outdoors kind of guy. Yet, here he was, wearing his good shoes, traipsing through the woods toward the back of Jacqueline Duncan's trailer.

Stickers in his hair. Snags in his pants. And God knows what he'd stepped in.

Spiders were bad enough. If he saw a snake, the hell with stealth. He was blowing that sucker's head clean off.

He should have gone to the diner first. Now he was one step behind. The chances of a clear shot through the tinted windows of the black SUV were iffy. Not the way she kept scooting down in her seat.

Over the last two days, anything that could go wrong had gone wrong.

He was happily working out at his gym, contemplating a good dinner at his sister's house, when he received the call.

Go to Las Vegas. A guy there had fallen behind in his loan payments. Put the fear of God into him.

Fine. He liked Vegas. Mr. A didn't pay his expenses, but if a fool and his money were soon parted, there were plenty of drunken fools in Vegas and plenty of money to relieve them of. He'd get the boss his payment with enough left over for himself.

He jumped in the shower, grabbed the go-bag he kept in

the back of his car, and was in Vegas before dark.

Things started out okay. Of course, the guy claimed not to have the cash. Nick pointed a gun at his wife, and she handed over her diamond wedding ring. "This will barely cover the vig. I'll be back tomorrow for the rest. Until then, I'll need a hostage. Just to make sure you take this seriously."

Immediately, the woman started crying and hid behind her husband, who called out, "No, no, no. Don't hurt my wife."

Ha! If only they knew how far off they were. One slap and women were useless. They were such weak creatures.

He nodded toward a kid, maybe eight or nine, who was peeking around a door. That's when the parents went ballistic. Sometimes he got tired of people acting like he was an animal. "Bring me that dog, kid. You'll get it back tomorrow. If your dad pays up."

"You can't take Lucy. She my son's diabetic alert dog."

"Then you better keep a close eye on him tonight. I'll be here at noon. Have the money, or I'll shoot the dog in front of the kid."

The dog was kind of nice. No trouble. Friendly. When he took it for a walk, someone gave him the evil eye for not poop scooping, but that wasn't happening.

An hour looking up service animal websites showed those trained dogs were worth a shit ton of money. Now *that* was a pleasant surprise.

With the long wait period they described, there had to be desperate people needing a trained dog and a black market he could exploit.

Then he received the second call. Jacqueline Duncan had been spotted in Podunkville, Texas.

He returned the dog, but not the ring—the guy had to pay *some* price for his inconvenience—with a warning that this was only a twenty-four-hour reprieve. Have the cash ready when he got back.

With that, he hopped on the next plane to Texas. Only to miss Duncan at the diner by five minutes.

He nearly skidded off the road, trying to hide behind that semi, when he saw the shiny, black SUV pull away with Duncan inside.

Mr. A had said, *Take out the old agent if necessary. Leave the new one. He's my guy.*

Nick would have thought the young, good-looking agent was the one who should go, not the middle-aged slob, but that wasn't his decision.

Mr. A had his reasons, and questioning the boss was never wise. If the younger agent worked for the Family, it was a good thing he hadn't taken him out back in Sacramento.

He'd found the old guy sitting in Duncan's trailer, playing *Words with Friends*. Guess he'd never have a chance to figure out that last letter.

This shot, however, was more difficult. Take her out, but don't hit the guy sitting next to her. The one who'd been dogging his footsteps for the last four years.

He was concentrating so hard, he almost didn't hear the

sirens. In a second, the air filled with the *whoop, whoop, whoop* of trouble. Time for him to disappear while he still could.

He'd find the girl again. He always had.

CHAPTER SIX

Jax kept her mouth shut on the forty-five-minute ride, but she kept her eyes open for any suspicious car following them. She was getting a crick in her neck from trying to watch through the side-view mirror.

"You don't have to do that, you know." Mr. Special Agent man's voice was softer than she'd ever hear it. But really, she hadn't ever actually *talked* to him before.

"Do what?"

"Watch for someone tailing us. I've been trained for that. I know what I'm doing."

Yeah, and how well did that work out for you in the past?

Some things were best left unsaid, so she watched vacationers enjoying the lake instead. This was a beautiful area with lots of little restaurants that might need extra help, especially in the summer.

But she could never live here.

It was much too close to West Monroe, and she had a once-a-state rule. Although, with the size of Texas, she could try someplace down in the valley or out in the panhandle. But not this year. Or next. Or the year after.

She was so tired of running. Would she ever be able to find a place to stay and just . . . live?

Not unless she got away from this Bozo.

He had to sleep sometime. As soon as they settled into his *safe house*, she was out of there.

Speaking of which, she should have slept on the drive out here. Then she'd be ready for tonight. She leaned her head back and tried to relax.

Her eyes snapped open when he reached for his radio.

"What are you doing?"

"I have to pick up the key."

She bolted up straight, any thoughts of sleeping gone. "You can't use the radio."

"How am I supposed to let them know we're here?"

If he rolled his eyes at her again, she might have to hit him.

"You're not. That's the point. Every time you find me, they do, too."

"Who? Your imaginary friend, Ponytail?"

She was going to hit him all right. He wouldn't even have to roll his eyes at her. "Yes. The guy I saw kill Senator Sheppard, and in my old apartment, and again at that motel, and in Albuquerque, and Little Rock, and maybe at the diner today. He works for Benedetto Avendondo."

"How come this is the first time I'm hearing about some strange man with a ponytail?"

"Because we're such good buddies and we dish all the time?"

They had stopped in front of a small frame house painted white with red trim. A sign above the door read *Target Realty, Vacation Rentals.*

Montgomery got out of the car and came around to her side. "Come on, or would you rather I handcuff you again? Before you say anything, I'd make them much tighter this time."

She didn't answer. What was the point? Inside, a woman with hair the color of an orange traffic cone and twice as high sat behind a polished desk. She had a brass nameplate squared perfectly on the edge that read *Fran Clark.*

Either Lincoln knew her or he was a fast reader because he said, "Good afternoon, Mrs. Clark. How are you today?"

She offered a smile that cracked her pancake makeup. "Very well, thank you. How may I help you?"

He grabbed Jax's hand. "My wife and I are here to pick up the keys for the house at 127 Lake View Drive. Did my office notify you we were coming?"

"Why, yes they did. About twenty minutes ago. I didn't have time to send anyone to air it out. It's clean, but it hasn't been used in a couple of weeks."

"Don't worry." His laugh sounded as fake as his smile looked. "We'll open a few windows and be fine."

The woman's face contorted, and she emitted a strange, gurgling sound. She seemed to find Lincoln's statement either amusing or horrifying. Jax wasn't sure which.

Her unwanted guardian must have been there before because he knew the way. They stopped in front of the ugliest house Jax had ever seen. All the other houses on the block were sprawling, ranch styles, painted in pastel colors.

Theirs was a muddy-brown stucco reaching up two stories without a window in sight. Like a medieval fortress not seen since the crusades.

The inside wasn't much different. The furnishings were cold and sterile. Like something straight from an assemble-it-yourself store, but without any colored throw pillows or charming knickknacks to give it personality.

One small, heavily tinted window was covered by dark drapes. Who would build a house on a lake with no view of the lake?

No wonder it wasn't rented often.

"Where am I supposed to stay, Special Agent Montgomery?"

"Pick any room upstairs, and maybe you better start calling me Lincoln now that we're married."

She stared up at the ceiling and saw a couple of windows too small to crawl through.

As if reading her mind and getting the wrong message,

he tried for a soothing tone. "Don't worry. We should be safe here until they catch whoever shot Hawkins." He dropped her backpack at the foot of the stairs and flipped on the alarm system.

As guilty as she felt about Hawkins' death, that wasn't her biggest worry right now. With few windows and the alarm set, how was she going to break out of this place?

THAT WOMAN WAS actively trying to figure out how to escape. She'd be the death of both of them if she didn't settle down and trust him.

Hawkins' death should have been a warning.

Lincoln still couldn't believe it. He'd been in The Bureau five years now, and this was the first time anyone he worked with had been killed.

The man had been sent down yesterday from the Dallas office with the information that Jax might be living two hours away using the name Sandy Hoffberg. All he'd learned on the drive to West Monroe was that the guy's name was Stu, he was married, a Cowboys fan, and expected to return to Dallas as soon as Jax was in custody, taking her with him.

It was obvious whoever killed Stu wouldn't hesitate to kill a Fed. Which meant he and Jax had barely escaped the same fate. Now he had to keep an eye on her while watching their surroundings.

At least he'd be spared the job of notifying Hawkins' family. That unpleasant task would fall to his old boss, now Special Agent in Charge at the Dallas office.

When this was all over, he'd drive up to Dallas and visit with Hawkins' widow. He'd tell her what a great guy Stu had been and how much he enjoyed his company.

He didn't understand why, but that seemed to make people feel better.

Jax grabbed her backpack and headed up the stairs without speaking to him again. If she thought she'd find a way out up there, she was sorely mistaken.

He took the extra key the woman at the real estate agency had slipped him and unlocked a door next to the pantry. It opened into a room lined with computer screens. Each screen came alive, flooding the room with light as he flipped the switches.

Within moments, he had a view of the perimeter of the house, all the downstairs, and the upstairs hallway. He synced his phone to the videos. Now they really were safe.

He watched Jax head toward a bedroom, but lost her once she stepped inside. Damn legal weasels wouldn't let them put cameras in the bedrooms or bathrooms.

This wouldn't work. He needed her where he could keep an eye on her. "What do you want for dinner?" he called up the stairs. "This freezer is stocked better than most restaurants."

"I'm not hungry," her voice floated down.

"Come on. We didn't have any lunch. I'm starving. How

about I stick a pork roast in the oven?"

"If you want to. There's a shower in here bigger than my trailer. I plan to stand in it until I've emptied the water heater."

He could hear the water running but he couldn't see her, and that made him nervous. Every screen showed no movement, and there was really no way she could get out except past him.

Which he knew all too well wouldn't stop her.

JAX PUSHED HER plate back and smiled. The first genuine one Lincoln had ever seen from her. Well, maybe when she'd come down from the thirty-minute shower that had left him chewing his nails with worry.

She had strolled into the kitchen in worn jeans, a loose-fitting, black T-shirt, tennis shoes, wet hair, and a scrubbed-clean face.

In every photo he'd ever seen of her, she looked plastic with her designer clothes and heavy makeup. Tonight, she seemed more like a real person than at any time since he started working the case.

She bit back a small burp and laughed. "Apparently, I was hungry. That was absolutely as wonderful as it smelled coming down the stairs. Thank you."

"You're welcome." Lincoln picked up their plates and carried them to the sink.

Jax pushed her chair back and stood. "You cooked. I'll do the dishes. If there's any hot water left."

Okay, so the woman did have some manners. That didn't mean she wasn't a murderer. "Sit down a minute. I want to talk about this mysterious, *ponytailed* guy I never heard of whom you said killed the senator."

"Are you sure you want to go there? The story doesn't turn out so good for you, and I don't mean only personally. For the FBI in general."

No, it didn't, but he still needed to know the truth . . . or her version of it. "Hit me with it. I'm strong. I can take it."

He winced and put a hand to his head. That might have been a poor choice of words.

The table was circular, and Jax squared her chair so she was facing him. "To start with, I never had any kind of affair with the senator. I only met him once before the day he died. He winked at me, so it became sort of an office joke and I played it up for laughs."

He had always found the story of an affair too convenient and unlikely. But she had offered to go to the man's house, unasked and after hours. "Then why did you suggest driving out of your way to take him something that could have waited until Monday?"

"He *did* want the papers that night. He called to see if someone could bring them. Didn't Missy tell you?"

He'd read over all the notes and interviews on this case a dozen times, and no, Missy DeLuca hadn't mentioned that.

She claimed Jax saw the papers and offered to take them.

"His house wasn't *that* far out of the way. I got to leave the office ten minutes early, and there was an In-N-Out Burger that direction and not one by my apartment."

He'd have to check on that. It had seemed to him when he lived in California they were everywhere.

"He was semi-famous, and I wanted to see how he lived. Really, my life was boring, and it was something different to do. Also,"—she sighed, as if embarrassed—"I thought I might be able to use him as a reference for a better job." Her shoulders drooped, as if the events of the day, not to mention the last four years, had finally caught up with her.

This might be his last chance to talk to her alone. Tomorrow, someone from the Marshals Service would likely take her away. If he wanted to hear her story, it had to be tonight.

Lincoln scanned through the videos on his phone. All clear. "Why don't I make us some coffee and we sit out on the deck to finish your story?"

Her shoulders straightened and her head snapped up. "There's a deck on this house?"

CHAPTER SEVEN

Jax held the coffee cups and tried to watch as Lincoln punched in the alarm code. The jerk hid it with his body. She could almost swear the first number was a five with a two next to last, but there were seven numbers instead of the usual four, so getting them all would be tough.

Plus, he kept the keys fastened to a carabiner hooked on to his belt. Not as easy as lifting them from his pocket.

Oh, the things she'd learned these last years. Not stuff they taught in life skills class, but much more useful.

The deck stretched almost to the water. One end was an outdoor kitchen with a grill that was bigger and better equipped than the one at Roy's Diner. Near it was a rectangular, wrought iron table that would seat six. Eight if you scooted closer.

The other end was more of a living area with a porch swing,

comfortable, rattan chairs and sofa, a large, square coffee table, and a fireplace.

A night-blooming jasmine grew somewhere nearby. Its aroma filled the air.

Maybe you didn't need windows if you could sit out here.

There was no way she could escape from that house without him knowing. She'd have to go over him. But if she could get onto the deck. . . .

Meanwhile, there wasn't any harm in getting her side of the story on the record. If law enforcement stopped chasing her, she'd only have to worry about the mob.

Only.

She followed him to the living area and placed the coffee cups on the table before settling into a comfortable chair with flowered cushions.

"You were telling me about your trip to Senator Sheppard's house."

Oh yeah. That.

Lincoln leaned back in his chair and sipped his coffee, as if talking about a murder was no different that describing a shopping trip for new shoes.

"The evening was getting dark by the time I got there. The front porch was in the shadows and I couldn't see a doorbell, so I knocked. I guess the door wasn't shut tight because it swung open. I was about to call his name when I heard angry voices—his and a guy with a New Jersey accent."

"How did you know it was the senator, or a person from

New Jersey for that matter?"

Now it was her turn to roll her eyes. "I had met the senator, remember? Plus, he was on TV every chance he got. I don't know if the other guy was from New Jersey, but that's what he sounded like to me. When he mentioned working for Mr. Avendondo, I just assumed."

Lincoln sat up, nearly spilling his coffee. "Whoa, wait a minute. He actually said he worked for Benedetto Avendondo?"

"He said Mr. A had given him orders."

"So you don't know if he was referring to Avendondo?"

"Do you want me to tell the story or not?"

"Go ahead." He sat his coffee on the table and held his hands up in surrender.

"The two men were arguing. The senator told Ponytail— and yes, I saw him later and he had a ponytail—to go back and tell Mr. Avendondo he wanted more money or he wouldn't sign the papers. Then Ponytail said Mr. A had given him orders on what to do if that happened."

A boat went by, only its lights visible in the darkness, and laughter floated across the air. She had forgotten the joy of being out at night on the water when everything was still and calm.

Lincoln was no longer relaxed . . . if he ever had been. He never took his eyes off the boat until it was almost out of sight. "This wasn't a good idea. We should go back inside."

"Not yet, please." If he didn't believe her, and she couldn't get away, this could be the last time she ever sat outside and listened to waves ripple against the shoreline or crickets call to each other in the night.

Lincoln used an app on his phone to turn off the outside lights and plunge them into darkness. A slight glow indicated he was checking his phone again.

What the hell was so interesting on his phone?

"Are you finished? Do you want me to go on?" She shouldn't be such a jerk. He was doing his best to keep her safe.

He glanced up. "Sure. You were telling me about Sheppard's and Ponytail's argument."

He didn't sound at all convinced. She was probably wasting her breath. "That's when Ponytail killed the senator."

"You saw this?"

"No, I heard the gunshot."

"Only one shot?"

It was years ago, and she'd been so shocked and scared. She couldn't remember. Amazing that she could forget something that important. "One or two. No more than that."

"How did you know the senator was dead? His body has never been found. There was a lot of blood at the scene, but head wounds do that." He rubbed a spot on the back of his scalp.

"About a year after I'd been on the run, I heard on the TV that he'd been declared legally dead. Some kind of expert was supposed to have reexamined the scene and decided he'd lost too much blood to survive. Isn't that right?"

"Yeah. Turns out Sheppard was on blood thinners for a

heart condition and maybe he bled out easily. The Bureau brought in a forensics blood specialist who sprayed the house with so much luminol, I had to wear a gas mask. Then she strung a row of ultraviolet lights. The place lit up like fireworks on New Year's Eve. She got down on her hands and knees and measured every drop, put it in her computer, and *voila!* He was dead."

"Are you saying you don't believe her?"

"I'm not saying I don't believe her. I'm saying I trust my own eyes. I knew he was dead the minute I walked into that house. Still, we always prefer to have a body. When a dead guy turns up in Mexico running a surf shop, the agency's reputation is damaged. Is that report all you're going on, or did you actually see something?"

"I saw him fall. He was in the back room, out of sight, then . . . *bamm*." She placed her elbow on the side of the chair and let her arm drop. "Straight back. Like a tree that's been hacked down. His body was in one room, out of sight, and his head and shoulders were in the hall with a big pool of blood spreading around. Then his head disappeared, and Ponytail stepped into the hall with the senator over his shoulder, bouncing with each step. I screamed and he came after me."

In a way, she had died along with the senator. The old Jax was gone forever. She'd never be the same.

"And you're sure the senator was dead."

"He had a hole in his forehead and eyes that didn't reflect light." Was he going to question every word she said?

She had adjusted to the darkness and could make out Lincoln, leaning forward in his chair, his phone pointed her direction. "Why did you destroy your apartment and disappear? Why not call the police?"

Shoot. She hadn't realized he was recording her. It was too late now. She might as well finish the story.

"I didn't tear it up. Ponytail did. I saw him from the elevator, trashing my TV and breaking things."

"He beat you home? How did he know where you lived?"

"From when I dropped my purse. So he had my name and address." She wasn't telling this right. He kept confusing her. "When they were arguing, Ponytail said how Mr. A owned the police and FBI." She probably shouldn't have said that, but at this point, did it matter if she offended him?

"The next morning, I saw the news report calling me the main suspect in his disappearance. Which, considering all the blood stains, didn't bode well for me, especially since I knew he was dead and expected his body to turn up at any time. Then the reporter started talking about the death of another mob informant. I thought if I hid out for a couple of days, I could stay safe while you found the right guy. But every day that went by, I looked more and more guilty."

There. She'd told the story and hoped never to have to again.

Lincoln picked up his phone. "It's getting late. Let's go back inside and start over. I have some questions."

Lincoln poured them both fresh coffee and placed his phone on the kitchen table between them. He had turned on the room's recording device, but the phone copy was for him alone.

The chairs in the den were more comfortable, but the kitchen had a warmer, more relaxed feel.

And he wanted Jax relaxed.

Until he was ready to ask the tough questions.

Like why was her blood at the crime scene and Senator Sheppard's blood at her house? And why did the surveillance photos from the hotel show a woman who looked like she'd been in a fight?

"So you got to the senator's house and the door was open—"

"I told you this once already." She gazed into her coffee cup as if it were a crystal ball, holding all the answers.

"I know, but people leave out things . . . forget. Decide something isn't important. Humor me. Start at the beginning."

Twenty minutes later, she had repeated her story with a few new tidbits, but not the ones he wanted. He'd have to phrase his questions carefully so as not to lead her to the answers he wanted.

"How did you lose your purse? Was it when you were running from Ponytail?" No purse had been at the scene, but a woman's lipstick was found under a hall table. He wasn't sure he believed in Ponytail—except perhaps as her accomplice—but no point in letting her know that.

"I dropped it earlier. When I fell."

Fell? That was something new.

"When I first stepped into the senator's house, I stopped for a second. I wanted to see what it looked like. That's when I heard them yelling and talking about payoffs and Mr. Avendondo. So I decided to back out, close the door, and ring the bell. But my foot caught on the doorsill and I fell, hard, on my rear and bit my lip." She touched her lip as if remembering.

That explained her swollen lip . . . maybe.

"Everything flew up in the air—all the papers, my purse—everything."

Papers had been found, strewed about, but none of them were complete. As if someone had gathered up the closest ones in a hurry. "And that's when you screamed?"

"No, wait. I have it wrong. At first, they were only yelling, so I wasn't scared, but it would have been embarrassing for the senator to know I overheard them, so I tried to scoop up the papers. That's when I heard the shot and saw the senator fall. When his head started moving backward, I wanted to scream, but I didn't. Just got up, ready to run."

Now they were getting somewhere. Slight changes in the story didn't bother him. Otherwise, it felt too perfect, rehearsed. But then she'd had four years to practice.

"When I saw Ponytail come out of the office with the

senator over his shoulder, his head bouncing with every step, *that's* when I screamed. He was on me before I could turn around. He grabbed my wrist. He was so strong." She shivered and sloshed coffee on the table.

"How did you get away?" This should be good. Supposedly, she had outsmarted a mob enforcer.

"Blood."

"What?"

"Blood. Everywhere. Dripping off the senator's head. Up and down the guy's arms. On his shirt. I can still smell it. If I see any blood now, even a little cut, I get sick to my stomach. Ponytail had it on his hands when he grabbed me. It was warm and slick. My wrist was covered in it. I yanked my hand out and ran."

She gave a slight chuckle. He hadn't expected that.

"Five years of gymnastics. I vaulted over the porch rail and hid in a neighbor's backyard until I felt safe to head home. Who am I kidding? I haven't felt safe for one minute since that night."

"And you never considered calling the police?"

"That day? I lost my phone, remember? I had it in my purse. After seeing Ponytail in my apartment and realizing he knew who I was and remembering what he said. . . ."

"What about later?"

"At first, I kept thinking someone would solve the case and I could go home. Yes, I know. I was very naïve to believe it would all go away, but at the time, it seemed logical. After a year passed, then two, and no one seemed interested in anyone but me, I just kept moving around. It became my life."

"Did you ever think about contacting your parents?" Sometimes his family drove him crazy, but in case of an emergency, they were the first ones he'd call.

"Have you tried calling anyone when you lose your phone? How many numbers do you have memorized? Besides, my mother changes hers every couple of months, sure somebody's out to get her."

"Did you try calling your stepfather's office? He could have helped you."

"Yeah, right."

He knew it. There was something about her family she was hiding. And he'd find out what.

He took a breath, ready to confront her, when the alarm on his phone beeped out a warning.

CHAPTER EIGHT

Jax searched wildly around the kitchen for the cause of the blaring alarm. Was something burning? Had Lincoln left the oven on?

He shoved his chair with such force, it tumbled backward onto the floor.

She followed as he sprinted across the room. She didn't plan to be left behind in a fire.

Lincoln stopped in front of a door painted to be inconspicuous—no doorframe, no knob, only a small, octagon-shaped keyhole—and fumbled with the carabiner attached to his belt. He produced an oddly shaped key, inserted it into the hole, and flung the door open.

Inside, a bank of computer screens filled one wall.

The screens ranged from outside scenes that were almost

black, to ones a dingy gray in the ambient glow of the security lights.

Making a shocking contrast was the brightness of the indoor scenes, showing the stairs, hallway, and every room. Jax could see Lincoln's upturned chair in the kitchen, the deck they had just been sitting on, and the door to her bedroom, which she had left open on her way down to dinner.

"Were you spying on me?" Her voice edged up as her throat closed. "Did you get your jollies watching me shower and change clothes?" The pervert. And she had almost trusted him.

Almost.

Lincoln's back and shoulders were hunched over a keyboard as he zoomed in and out and moved camera angles. He paused as her words broke through his concentration.

"What? No. Can't you see? There aren't any cameras in the bedrooms."

He might have whispered *thank goodness* under his breath, but she couldn't swear to it.

"You can move some of the cameras around. What about those inside the house?"

"Doesn't matter how much I can move them around. There aren't any cameras in the bedrooms!" He was shouting by the last words. "Now I have something more important to worry about. What set off the alarm?"

She placed her hand on his shoulder and leaned forward to get a closer look at the screens as he adjusted each picture.

"Hey, look there." She tapped a view of the side of the house. "Is that a cat?"

The landscaping in the safe house yard was flat and bare, but Lincoln zoomed to a tree on the neighbor's property. "Or maybe a possum."

"It's really ugly."

"Then it's definitely a possum."

He moved the video back fifteen minutes. The cat/possum turned its head and stared at them with glassy eyes. "I'm not sure that could have set off the alarm."

He rewound each screen to before the alarm first sounded, but didn't find anything else. The area closer to the neighbor's house was in deep shadow. He should never have turned off the outside lights. "I don't know what to think. Could have been a bird or a branch moving, but it's not supposed to be that sensitive."

"Well, *that* makes me feel safe."

"We're safe, alarm or no alarm. This place is a fortress. No one can get in, and no one knows we're here."

"You reported to your office where we are, didn't you?"

"That's protocol. I had to." He swung his chair to face her.

"And the lady from the rental place knows we're here."

"Yeah, but she had to pass a background check."

He didn't seem to be getting her point. "And this is a regular safe house that you and others have used before, right?"

"Okay." The look on Lincoln's face wasn't reassuring.

"Then lots of people know we're here."

"Only FBI, not the mob."

"Like I said, I *really* feel safe now." She should have realized . . . he was FBI. He'd never understand the terror she'd lived with for the last four years. The daily struggle to survive.

"Why don't you go up to bed? I'll stay here and watch for anything unusual."

Could she sleep, trusting her life to someone else? She hadn't depended on anyone but herself since the day her stepfather stuck his tongue down her throat and grabbed her ass.

"Without any sleep, you won't be on top of your game if anything happens."

"How about this. You stay here and watch the screens while I grab some rest. Call me at midnight and I'll take over. The hours between two and four are the most dangerous."

She'd be by herself for three hours to attempt an escape. She couldn't have planned it better if she tried.

Lincoln switched off the lights in the living room and stretched out on the sofa.

That wasn't going to work. "Don't you want to go up to your room?"

He glanced at her and grinned. "I may be tired, but I'm not stupid."

LINCOLN'S BREATHING WAS deep, slow, and steady, but he

wasn't asleep.

He'd fooled Jax once when she slipped into the living room an hour earlier. He'd turned his head in her direction and she'd screeched to a halt.

"I needed some water," she had mumbled as she pivoted toward the kitchen.

He should have kept her handcuffed, but that was no guarantee of anything except encouraging her to cause trouble. Convincing her to stop trying to escape would work much better. If he could manage it.

The time was now twenty minutes before midnight according to the blue numerals glowing on the key lock pad. An important distinction because that was the alarm code— the time plus the agent's initials, in reverse order. That way, the code changed constantly, and a record was kept of who unlocked the door.

She'd probably come out of the room any second now. This was her last chance, and she couldn't afford to wait much longer. He let out a practiced snore. That should do the trick.

And here she came, right on time.

One step into the living room, and Lincoln's eyes fell on her.

She said exactly what he expected. "I need to go to the bathroom."

"If you come out with a toilet tank lid, I'll shoot you on the spot."

"What?" If that was her best look of surprise, she should

never go into acting.

He swung his feet around and sat up. "Oh, come on now. Don't think you can attack an FBI agent and steal his car without facing the consequences."

"I'm sure I don't know what you're talking about. Did you see me do it?"

Had he? No, not really. Just the impression of a feminine form.

"Maybe it was Ponytail. He might have been hanging around." She slumped into the chair across from him.

"And he was the one who wrapped a towel around my head and left my badge and gun? Not exactly what you expect from a hired assassin." And one of the reasons he could never get his mind completely around the idea that she'd killed Sheppard.

Although, there had been a guy who took off the minute he spotted the black SUV. Probably a coincidence.

He remembered something else. "Then he stole the three hundred dollars from my wallet that I was saving for a new guitar, leaving me with only seventy-five dollars for lunch all week?"

"I didn't know you played the guitar."

"I don't. I never got around to buying one."

"But if you had bought the guitar, you'd still have had seventy-five dollars, right? Any idea how long I could eat on seventy-five dollars?"

The conversation was spiraling out of control. "Let's get back to the night at the No Tell Motel. Why didn't you mention

Ponytail hanging around before this?"

"How could I? I didn't know it happened."

Still with the denials. This was getting old. All he wanted was to solve this case and be rid of her. "But you did see Ponytail in the vicinity of the motel?"

"Hypothetically."

He was getting a headache, and it was at least twelve hours before he could turn her over to the Marshals Service. "Go upstairs to bed. I'll take it from here."

She shook her head. "I could never—"

"Lock your door. Pull the dresser in front of it if that'll make you feel safer. No one can get in here without setting off the alarm. Actually, no one can get in here, period."

She shot him the finger and trounced up the stairs without another word.

He waited fifteen minutes and followed. On her closed bedroom door, he attached an alarm that would sound with any movement.

No matter how careful she was, she couldn't open it without him knowing.

Now he could get some actual sleep.

CHAPTER NINE

Jax's arm shot out from under the covers, searching for the alarm clock. All she managed to do was knock over her glass of water.

Where was her nifty, Dollar Store, wind-up clock? Without it, she'd be late for work.

The bed was warm and comfortable. The pillow was soft. Even the sheets felt smooth, like floating on a cushion of air. She didn't want to get up.

Was she back home, in her own bedroom, with her mother down the hall, trying to get her up for school?

A tear formed in the corner of one eye. No, that was the dream she'd been yanked out of.

She lifted her head and stared bleary-eyed at the unfamiliar room. Why wouldn't that noise stop? She couldn't think with that alarm blaring in her ears.

Alarm.

No. Not the alarm.

She threw back the covers and jammed her feet into her shoes, the only thing she'd removed last night.

The noise stopped, but another, softer, started chiming outside her door as she tried to yank it open. The door hung on the chest she'd pushed in front of it.

She was trapped with who knew what outside.

One. Two. Three. Shove. And the chest moved. She shoved again, and the chest slid away from the door. She threw it open and ran into Lincoln, hiding something behind his back.

"What is it, what's going on, did they find me?" The words ran together in an incoherent rush.

He put a hand on her shoulder. "It's nothing. The guy next door, working in his yard."

"Are you sure? How do you know?"

Lincoln held out his phone, showing the image of a man pruning trees near where the cat/possum set off the alarm last night.

Okay. Maybe.

"I want to see on the big screen."

Jax grabbed her backpack and followed Lincoln down the stairs, trying to figure out what he had slipped into his pocket. In the video room, he pulled out the chair and let her study each screen while moving the camera angles.

She paused on the image of a man working in the yard,

wielding a large pair of pruning shears. "Something's wrong. Have you met this man before?"

"Not personally. I know a retired couple live there, and they passed a background check."

"He doesn't look old enough to retire, plus he's pruning a Pink Dogwood."

"What?"

"A Pink or Japanese Dogwood. There was one near my trailer in West Monroe. So spectacular, it almost made living there bearable. I took a sprig to the library and looked it up." *And made friends with Hazel Reynolds.* "The flowers start out pink and get darker, so it can have all shades of flowers at the same time. That one is just starting to bloom. Why would he prune it now?"

"Maybe he doesn't know what he's doing. My father used to trim things back whenever he decided they were too big. Drove my mother crazy. Why don't I go outside and talk to him. I'll lock the door so you'll be safe."

"Then I'll be trapped."

"Okay, come outside with me."

And face Ponytail? A wave of panic paralyzed Jax. She couldn't. She really couldn't. No way.

That would be her every nightmare come true.

She scrubbed at her wrist where his slimy fist had grabbed her, and the remembered smell of blood and gunpowder made her gag. "I'll wait here. Only don't lock the door."

Lincoln's eyes may have held a hint of pity, but that didn't change anything. "I don't think so. In or out. Make up your mind."

Jax tried to swallow, but the lump in her throat didn't budge. Her knees shook so badly she had to place her hand on Lincoln's shoulder for support.

Her legs didn't want to cooperate. She slid first one foot, then the other forward and stepped outside.

"Hello there, neighbor."

The man next door stopped pruning and looked up at the sound of Lincoln's voice.

Jax strained to get a good look at him, but a faded Astros cap shaded his face.

"Well, howdy." He dropped the pruning shears and took a step forward, his hand on his back as he tried to straighten up under the low-hanging branches.

"We were wondering if you could recommend a nice place to eat. This is my wife's birthday, and I wanted to take her someplace fancy."

Jax managed the world's most unconvincing smile while holding on to the edge of the open door like a security blanket.

"Well, let me think on that. There's a couple of places in town." He mumbled like he was talking through a mouth full of marbles. Maybe he'd had a stroke. That would explain retiring at a young age.

The man took another step closer, and his ball cap caught on a branch. Long, brown hair in a ponytail tumbled out.

Jax's heart threw itself around in her chest like a pinball machine. Her mind screamed *run*, but her knees locked and her feet felt nailed to the wooden flooring. Her mouth opened to yell a warning, but only a high-pitched *eeeee* escaped.

The breeze created by the passing bullet touched her cheek before her brain registered the sound of the gunshot.

A second shot hit the doorframe as Lincoln fumbled for the gun hidden at the small of his back, under his shirt.

She sucked in as much air as her frozen lungs allowed, yanked Lincoln's arm, and bolted for the back door, ripping the dangling keychain from his hand as she ran.

Her backpack sat at the foot of the stairs, and she scooped it up, along with his go-bag, without breaking stride as she ran for the garage.

Which key? Which key? Her fingers were thick and uncooperative. There were several to choose from. The third one she tried slid in and the door opened, setting off a beeping alarm.

She jumped into the black SUV and searched for the ignition. She stabbed the key at the steering column but couldn't find the slot. On the dashboard was a button the size of a silver dollar. She pushed it and the engine roared to life.

What else had changed since she'd last driven a car?

Lincoln had backed the car into the garage, so she faced a closed garage door. Shit! She jumped out and hit a switch on the wall. The door began an agonizingly slow ascent.

She could see half the living room, but there was no sign of Lincoln. Why hadn't he followed her?

The reverberation of gunshots sounded over the whine of the motor and the shriek of the alarm. She tried the horn.

Still no Lincoln.

She didn't plan to wait long.

Daylight flooded into the garage as the door inched upward. She floored the accelerator and scraped the top of the SUV on the still-rising door. Over her shoulder, she glanced into the living room.

No sign of Lincoln. That man would be the death of her yet.

She pulled forward and turned left. The sound of gunfire came from behind her, louder now that she was outside. She leaned on the horn. A flash of white moving toward the street caught her eye.

Lincoln's white dress shirt.

She slammed on the brakes as he threw himself into the back seat and sped forward before his door was closed. She rounded the corner on two wheels, the odor of burning rubber filling the car.

He lifted onto one elbow. "You almost got me killed!"

"Me? You were the one who insisted on going outside."

"You pulled me off balance while a man was shooting at us, then locked me out of the house."

"I did not!"

"You swung the door closed when you ran inside. It locks automatically."

"How was I supposed to know that?"

"If you had stayed still, I could have gotten him."

"I felt the bullet whiz by my face, and I was supposed to stand still and hope you had better aim than him? Did you hit him?"

Lincoln struggled to a sitting position behind her. "He didn't hit us. That's what matters."

Not completely. For years, she'd only wanted this over so she could resume a normal life. Now she wanted Ponytail dead.

"Pull into that parking lot on the left and I'll take over." He leaned forward, his breath warm on her ear.

"We can't stop yet. We don't know if he's following us." If Lincoln had any idea she hadn't been behind the wheel of a car in four years, he'd never agree.

THE ROYAL-BLUE 1998 Cadillac wasn't exactly inconspicuous, and while the bench seat was as comfortable as an old sofa and the engine had been well cared for, its acceleration left a lot to be desired.

Didn't matter.

Jax or the Fed might have spotted the silver sedan Nick had been driving when he passed them at the diner. He had to change cars, and the Caddy was the only one the old couple had. The fact that the keys were in the kitchen hanging on a pegboard marked *Keys* made it all the easier.

Killing them hadn't been his first choice, but what was he supposed to do when the old man came after him with his cane? Stand there and let the old coot bash him over the head until his arm got tired? After he'd dispatched the man, he had no choice but to take out the old woman also. Even if she did remind him of his grandmother.

She sure didn't cook like his grandmother. The only food in the house was TV dinners and canned soup.

If things had gone as planned, he'd be on his way to New Jersey and his mother's homemade spaghetti bolognese by now.

Except, things hadn't gone as planned.

The deadbeat from Las Vegas had called. He had a good run at the poker table and caught up on his debt. There went any plans for selling the dog. At least for now. The guy was an addict. He'd be back in the hole eventually.

The old people didn't have but sixty dollars cash between them and nothing worth selling. The place was full of fancy figurines that ought to be worth something. He slipped one shaped like a little dog into his pocket. If he had the time and energy, he'd take it to a pawn shop. If not, he'd give it to his niece. Her birthday was coming up.

He was going broke chasing Bonnie and Clyde, and the only jewelry the old lady had was a cross around her neck that held a few tiny diamonds.

He couldn't take that. He wasn't a barbarian.

He wasn't having much luck finishing off his nemesis and her boyfriend, either.

He'd tried to ambush them last night while they sat on the deck, only to have a boat come by and put the agent on guard.

Then he'd tried again an hour later and set off some kind of alarm. Good thing the outdoor lights had been turned off.

His last chance had been this morning, but the damn bushes had knocked his cap off before he was ready. Then his shirt hung on a branch, and he couldn't get his gun out fast enough. He got off one shot at Jax and missed before she ducked inside and he'd lost his chance at her.

Then the Fed started shooting at him, and it all went to hell.

Trying to take her out without harming the Fed was bullshit. When somebody shot at him, all bets were off.

He still couldn't figure out how Jax had gotten the car around fast enough to save the guy.

She had to be a professional. That move to pick him up was like something out of a James Bond movie. But maybe she'd saved his butt, also. He could use the excuse of protecting the Fed when Mr. A asked how he could have missed.

By the time he ran back to the house and maneuvered the tugboat-size car out of the garage, he'd lost them.

He bit back a curse. This wasn't over yet. He had a good idea where they were headed.

CHAPTER
TEN

Lincoln needed two tries to climb over the center console and into the front seat. If Jax didn't stop making like a NASCAR driver, he'd break his neck.

Once settled, he fumbled for the phone in his back pocket. The quicker he contacted his office the better. The ponytailed guy—whoever he was—would be in the wind within minutes.

He pulled out his cell when Jax reached over and snatched it away.

Driving with her left hand, she thumbed in 911. With a voice all breathy and shaky, she yelled, "I heard gunshots over on Lake View Drive. Either that big, ugly, brown house or the one next door. One twenty something. I think someone is hurt. Hurry."

She disconnected, buzzed down her window, and tried to

toss the phone into the street. He grabbed her wrist just in time.

"What are you doing? That's my phone."

"Trying to save your life, for the second time in five minutes."

The woman was literally crazy. "How do you figure that?"

"Ponytail is getting his information from somewhere. He's never more than two steps behind you. Usually one step ahead. Every place you've turned up, so has he."

"That's what you keep saying, but when I had an agent check the diner yesterday afternoon, no one had seen him."

"You called your office from the safe house? Why didn't you just post a sign in the front yard that said *come and get us*?"

"You do realize The Bureau knew where we were going when I radioed from in front of your trailer. That's when I asked them to send someone to check out the diner, before you told me your story and long before he started shooting at us. My office is, literally, the FBI. You know, an entire agency devoted to keeping citizens safe. They're pros at asking questions. My boss assured me no one saw a guy with a ponytail after we left."

"Ponytail's not stupid, you know. The Tuckers were finished eating when we left. Even if they weren't, Ralph and Doris had their backs to the door and Danny was watching a basketball game on TV. Ponytail wouldn't even have needed to go inside. He could have looked through the window. Or seen us drive off and followed."

"I told you. I'm a pro at spotting a tail. That's one of the things they teach us."

"Were you worried about being followed when we left the diner, or not until your partner got shot?"

He decided not to answer. He hadn't been that careful when he first left her place for the diner. He'd been in a hurry after Stu took so long searching every room of the trailer. Driving back, he'd been worried about keeping her in the car. He'd started watching closely when they were on the road to the safe house, and he would gladly swear in court no one had followed them.

So where had Ponytail—if that's who shot Stu—been hiding, and where had he picked up their trail? Unless he'd found them through the rental agency like Jax suggested.

No way. That would mean a leak in the FBI and that was inconceivable.

Her sigh filled the car, and her jaw turned white as she clenched her teeth. *She* was exasperated at *him*? He'd spent years chasing her, and she'd slipped out of his hands every time he got close. Sometimes with minutes to spare. Now she'd tried to escape again, almost leaving him in a precarious position. Okay, so she'd stopped and let him in. That didn't make up for four years of frustration.

She took a deep breath, as if settling her nerves. "You know someone killed your partner. And you know a man with a ponytail tried to shoot both of us while we were at your so-called safe house, long after I had warned you someone of that description had been hunting me. If you don't believe a word I've told you over the last two days, you know those are facts."

"I know he was trying to kill me. I don't know if he was trying to kill you or rescue you. But I do know if you don't pull over and let me drive, I'm going to handcuff you and drop you off at the nearest jail."

"Fine. I'll pull over. I don't have a driver's license anyway."

Like that was the main thing on his mind.

She slowed and put on her blinker. "How much money do you have?"

What the heck? "About forty-five dollars. Somewhere along the line, I've learned not to carry too much cash. Why? Are you planning to rob me again?"

"Hypothetically robbed you. And if I had, I would have tried to pay you back. Did you get a Valentine card last year with ten dollars in it, and a similar Christmas card?"

Damn. He thought those were from his grandmother. Maybe Nanna wasn't getting senile after all.

"It's hard to disappear without cash. Since everybody and their dog knows where we are now, maybe you could get us a little running money before we move on."

Lincoln glanced up to discover they were parked in front of an ATM. "Hand me the keys and move over. I'm driving from here."

It was tough, but Lincoln managed to keep one eye on Jax and one eye on the ATM as she moved to the passenger seat and he withdrew some cash.

"How much did you get?" Jax asked, buckling her seat belt.

"Two hundred dollars."

"That's all? We can't last long on that."

He didn't plan to last long on this crazy escapade. He intended to call his office as soon as he was sure they'd lost Ponytail. "That's all the machine would dispense at one time." Not completely true, he could ask for more, but it was all he was willing to risk, knowing the FBI would never reimburse him.

For now, he was glad Jax hadn't tried to run while his back was turned. She was probably waiting until she could relieve him of his entire two hundred forty-five dollars.

"Where are we going?" They had wandered through some backroads at first, in case Ponytail was trying to follow, but Jax recognized exactly where they were headed. Interstate 45 ran directly into Houston, which offered plenty of hiding places. But if he was planning to take her to FBI Headquarters, she was a goner.

She'd do better to take her chances and jump out at the first opportunity.

She glanced at the speedometer. Lincoln was driving at a careful 68 mph. Traffic zoomed past them like they were standing still.

"To headquarters. I'm tired of playing games. You'll be

safe there."

A semi blew by, causing the SUV to shudder. She'd have to wait until they were off the freeway.

"Can't you at least buy me dinner first?"

Lincoln blinked in astonishment. "This isn't a date."

"We never ate any breakfast. I haven't had even a sip of water since I went to bed last night. It's already almost three o'clock. By the time we get to your office, they question me, and take me to jail"—which would probably get her killed—"it'll be too late for supper. I'd really like something to eat first. It doesn't have to be fancy. I'm feeling kind of light-headed."

That last sentence might have been overkill.

Concern flashed across Lincoln's face. "I'm sorry. I didn't think about that. I was up before you and had a big breakfast. I've got a bottle of water right here and a power bar in the glove compartment. Help yourself."

Damn him.

"The FBI is perfectly capable of feeding their *guests*. What kind of sandwich would you prefer, tuna or chicken salad?"

Double damn him.

"What I'd like is some Tex-Mex. Beef fajitas with refried beans and rice. I won't even ask for a margarita."

"What's a rich California girl like you doing eating Tex-Mex and drinking margaritas? I thought you'd be into chateaubriand and white wine."

"I haven't been rich for a long time, and you should never drink white wine with chateaubriand. A good cut of meat like that deserves a full-bodied cabernet." Where were her manners? She didn't have to get pissy with him just because he was taking her to her death. Her mother would be so ashamed.

"How much longer till we get there?"

"About an hour."

"I don't think I can wait that long."

There he went with that eye roll thing again. "What is it this time?"

"I really have to pee. It's been hours." The minute she said it, she realized it was true.

Lincoln didn't answer, but five minutes later, he pulled off the freeway, wound back a couple of blocks, and stopped in front of a service station. "Can I trust you, or do I need to get out the handcuffs?"

She turned her back and reached for the door handle. It didn't budge. He must have the childproof lock engaged. She twisted to face him, but he didn't move. "Okay, I promise."

He came around and opened the door for her instead of switching off the lock.

Fingers interlocked like long-lost lovers, they strolled into the store, past racks of chips and peanuts and jerky and snack cakes and batteries and week-old hot dogs rotating on a spindle.

Lincoln glanced at the hot dogs. "I'll spring for one of those and an orange slush if you don't give me any trouble."

Her stomach roiled at the thought. "Not unless you want me to lose it all over your nice, clean seat covers."

As they neared the beer cooler, a customer opened the door and chilled air spilled out. What were the odds he'd buy her one last longneck for the road? "Now one of those I could go for."

"And have you tell your lawyer I plied you with alcohol? Not a snowball's chance."

He opened the door to the women's restroom and peered inside. No back exit. No window. Nothing but concrete walls. He made a sweeping motion with his hand, like ushering her into a golden chariot. "Go ahead."

She counted to sixty and opened the door a crack. He was standing in front of it.

"Sorry. I was making sure it was locked."

"Uh-huh. You about finished?"

"Give me a couple of minutes." She might as well use the facilities while she was in there.

He was still waiting when she came out. He swiveled to face her and she saw the phone in his hand. "Haven't you learned anything? You can't use that. They'll be able to track us."

"That's kind of the point. I need to check in and let my boss know when to expect us."

She might as well eat the hot dog. They'd probably both be dead before she had time to get sick.

CHAPTER
ELEVEN

Lincoln fastened his seat belt and waited until he heard the click of Jax's belt before starting the engine.

He avoided the freeway and took the back way to the FBI building. The drive didn't take any longer and lessened the threat of traffic jams as rush hour approached.

But that wasn't why he chose the less direct route.

Conversation was easier without the constant roar of diesels and semis racing past, and over the last two days, he'd begun to enjoy her company. Bantering back and forth with her was fun and kept him on his toes.

The criminals he usually dealt with were talented and cagey, but that's as far as it went. Even his boss, while an expert at playing politics, was unable to carry on a conversation without trying to find a way to use it to his advantage.

He hadn't had a regular partner for several months and, after what had happened to Stu, didn't want one. He'd carry the guilt over his death for the rest of his life. He only hoped someone had already taken care of the official notification. He didn't want to think of his wife waiting, wondering why he hadn't called.

The years he'd spent chasing Jax, while frustrating, had given him an appreciation of her ability to adapt so quickly from a life of privilege to one on the run. Not that it made any difference. He didn't plan to let his admiration cloud his judgment.

He'd always harbored a nugget of doubt about her guilt, but for now, she was a fugitive and he was taking her in. Once she was safely in jail, he could start examining her explanations.

After that, the lawyers could battle it out.

He glanced to the side when he realized she hadn't spoken for several minutes. She had reclined her seat and leaned back with her eyes closed.

Let her rest. The next few hours would be hard on her.

This was his favorite part of the drive, and he hated she was missing it. No one seemed to know about this part of his shortcut. It was surprisingly agrarian even for Harris County, which boasted dozens of hidden pockets of undeveloped wooded areas. The narrow road curved and dipped like a country lane, leaving him feeling as if he'd stepped away from the city, if only for a few minutes.

In his rearview mirror, he noticed a blue car gaining on

him. Let the yahoo have the road. He didn't plan to argue with someone who thought speed limits were for other people.

The car came closer, its wheels straddling the center lane. There was no shoulder, and the car was as big as a blimp. He glanced at Jax to make sure she still had her seat belt fastened.

Should he put on his siren, let the fool know who he was approaching?

The speed limit was fifty-five, but Lincoln sped up to sixty, then sixty-five. The car continued to draw closer. He had reached seventy when the road curved to the left.

The big, blue car clipped his left rear fender and disappeared around the corner unharmed, while the weight of it caused Lincoln and Jax to sail straight off the road and into the woods. Lincoln gripped the steering wheel and madly tried to gain control as he maneuvered through the brush and between trees.

A drainage ditch appeared directly in front of them, its steep sides covered in concrete. He spun the wheel to the left, scraping his door against a tree to stop their forward momentum.

Jax's scream was the last thing he heard as his head snapped back and then forward into the steering wheel.

"LINCOLN. LINCOLN. PLEASE. You have to wake up."

Why? He was happy where he was.

Lincoln opened his eyes and saw a woman straight out of a Picasso painting, her face distorted and swimming before his eyes.

"You need to get up before he comes back."

The woman's face stopped swirling and settled into one he recognized. "Jax?"

"Yes."

"What happened?"

"Ponytail ran us off the road. We have to get out of here before he returns to finish the job."

He tried to stand, but something yanked him back. Everything hurt.

Jax reached across him and unfastened his seat belt. Her hair brushed against his face. Soft. Like a feather. He closed his eyes again and thought of a bird. Doves. He always liked doves. Their call in the evening air, so calm, so soothing.

"No. Don't go to sleep. Get out of the car."

He took one step on the uneven ground, and pain shot up his leg. All thoughts of birds or feathers or anything pleasant were gone. He stumbled and grabbed the edge of the door. "My ankle. I can't walk anywhere. I'll call for a wrecker." He touched a hand to his head and it came away bloody. "And maybe an ambulance."

"We can't sit here and wait. He could be back any minute."

"I remember a blue car, but I never saw who was driving. Are you sure it was him?" It wasn't possible. He was positive no one had followed them, and while his boss knew Lincoln was bringing her in, he didn't know the route. This road wasn't even on most maps. He couldn't figure any way Ponytail could have found them, unless Jax had sent him some signal. And he'd watched her closely.

Except when she was in the bathroom.

She didn't have a phone—he'd made sure of that. So that left what, a note written in lipstick on the bathroom mirror? Get real.

He couldn't concentrate. His stomach churned, and his head felt like it did the day his big brother talked him into sitting in an old truck tire while he rolled it down a hill.

That hadn't ended well, either.

Jax's voice cut through the ringing in his ears. "Are you willing to risk your life on it—and mine? Because I'm not and I'm not waiting. Let me help you into the back seat, and I'll see if this car still runs."

He didn't have the strength to argue, and there was always the possibility she was right. *Someone* had run them off the road, whether Ponytail, one of his minions staked out at every intersection, or a local yokel with a death wish. He braced himself against the SUV and hopped to the back seat. His head protested when he lie down, so he propped himself in the corner while she tried the engine.

It drug and sputtered and finally caught. She shifted into reverse and didn't do the rear of the SUV any good as she backed out between trees. A sledgehammer tried to pound its way through his skull with every bump and jolt.

She paused at the street and looked both directions. "How do I get back to civilization?"

The inside of his mouth felt like he'd been chewing kitty litter, every word a separate agony. "Turn left and go back the way we came. There are some businesses not that far away."

They limped along like a shopping cart with one bad wheel, and the smell of burning oil filled Lincoln's nose, but fifteen minutes later, they stopped in front of a run-down motel. She left the motor running while she ran inside.

He had drifted off to sleep when she came out with a key and drove around to the back of the motel.

"Let's get you comfortable," she said as she maneuvered him inside.

The next time he woke up it was dark, his foot was propped up on a pillow, a melting bag of ice was on his ankle, and she was nowhere to be seen.

He was so screwed. Maybe he could get a job at his father's used car lot.

NICK WAITED AT a Whataburger five miles from the crash scene. He backed in next to a dumpster so the dented fender didn't show. If there had been sirens, he should have been able to hear them.

So they hadn't called the cops. Did that mean they were dead or unconscious? Mr. A would want to know for certain.

And giving the wrong answer wasn't an option.

The rancid odor from the dumpster took his appetite away, but he finished his milkshake. He needed to leave before the damaged Cadillac attracted notice.

As soon as he made his decision, a state trooper pulled up to the drive-thru. Yep. Time to move.

He drove the legal limit of fifty-five toward the curve where the SUV had left the road. The guardrail was bent and hanging loose. Skid marks stretched across the roadway. Bushes were flattened. Several trees had bright-yellow scars against their dark wood. He could smell the resin from inside his car.

But no black SUV sat mangled among dense underbrush.

They had been airborne when he watched through his rearview mirror. The SUV was big and heavy. Maybe it had traveled through the brush and down the culvert on the other side.

No traffic was in sight, so he took a chance. He parked beside the road and got out. Scrambling across the ditch and through the woods, he followed the vehicle's path.

It ended abruptly. As if by magic. *Poof.* Gone.

He picked his way deeper until he reached the cement culvert. He needed to know for certain if the Duncan woman had survived. Holding on to a tree for support, he leaned as far over the rim as possible.

No SUV.

No tire marks.

No sign of a wrecker.

No Jacqueline Duncan. No FBI agent.

He'd done his best to avoid hitting the agent during the shootout at the lake because Mr. A wanted him alive. That ended here and now.

He was going to kill that blonde bitch and her dark-haired friend no matter what the boss ordered.

LINCOLN HEARD A voice echoing up from the bottom of a deep well.

"You need to get up now."

His eyes cracked open a slit, slammed shut against the glare of the overhead light, and opened again.

Jax sat on the edge of his bed.

"You came back. I thought you'd left."

"I know. I've woken you every two hours all night, and you've said that each time."

"I got up once and you were gone."

"I walked to the nearest drug store and bought you some crutches." She held up a pair of shiny, aluminum crutches. "Let's see if you can stand, walk around a little."

He sat up and swung his legs over the side of the bed. His eyes swam for a minute but then focused. The pounding in his head became a dull ache. "What time is it?"

"Four a.m. Try to stand. We need to get moving."

"Where to?" Sure, The Bureau office was staffed around

the clock, but only by a skeleton crew. If they waited till six or eight, everyone would be there. Plus, he could sleep a while longer and be more alert to answer questions.

"Away from here. I've been thinking. This place is too dangerous. If I found it, so can Ponytail. Besides, they might have me on camera at the drug store. I kept my head down, but they'll spot it eventually and I need to be somewhere else by then."

Thinking made his head hurt. He lifted the crutches from Jax's hand and stood. The room only swayed a little. His wrists were swollen and sore as he maneuvered his way into the bathroom, turned on the tap, and splashed cold water on his face. The water in the sink turned pink.

He glanced up in the mirror and almost fell backward. The face staring back at him was almost unrecognizable. Dried blood from his nose still coated his upper lip like a disgusting, red Hitler moustache. His eyes were bloodshot. A purple bruise was forming on his forehead, and his hair fanned out in seven different directions.

He wet his hand and tried to smooth it down.

"No one cares about your hair, Romeo. Wash the blood off your face and let's go." Jax's reflection stared back at him from the mirror.

He could learn to hate that woman.

Five minutes later, he hobbled out to find Jax standing by the open door with their bags, a pillow, and a blanket.

Good, he could sleep in the car while she drove to

headquarters.

He made it to his SUV and waited for her to unlock the door.

"Forget it. That rolling advertisement for the FBI has breathed its last. That's part of the reason we need to hurry and leave. I tried to start it so I could hide it on the next block, but it wouldn't even turn over. Just coughed out a little black smoke and died."

He gazed around the dark parking lot. Three of the rooms had junky-looking cars parked in front. Surely she wasn't planning to steal one. He was an officer of the law. He couldn't allow that.

"We don't need to go far. If you can drag yourself across this parking lot and down that alley, there's a small park. You can stretch out on a picnic bench till daylight."

Sleep on a park bench? Not likely. You could get arrested for that. He jerked back toward their motel room and juggled the knob. Locked.

Jax shook her head. "You'll thank me for this later. You can make it. I have faith in you."

By the time he reached the alley, the thought of lying on a cement bench sounded like heaven. When they got to the park, he was drenched in sweat. Jax spread out the blanket and pillow and he lie down.

Fifteen minutes. That's all he needed. Then he'd feel strong enough to argue with her.

When he opened his eyes, the sun was creating pink streaks on the horizon and sirens filled the air. Jax came bursting through the bushes.

He threw back the blanket. "What is it? What's happened?" His body ached like he'd flown through the air, hit a tree, smashed his face on a steering wheel, sprained both wrists, and twisted his ankle, but his mind was clear for the first time in hours.

"I'm not sure, but it's bad. I heard gunshots in that direction not long after we left. Now police are everywhere, and the door to our motel room has been kicked in."

"If the police are here, we'll be safe. Let me call 911 and get us some help."

"You know I'll never be safe in jail as long as Ponytail and his boss want me dead. You can stay here and wait for the cops to find you—you haven't done anything wrong—but I have to disappear. Give me time. I'll hitch a ride and be long gone before they start looking for me. Tell them you got knocked out and don't know what happened. Promise me you won't call anyone for an hour. I understand you can't bring yourself to believe the cops and your precious FBI are in on it, and they can't all be, but we don't know which ones we can trust."

He'd spent four years hunting her. In the forty-eight hours since he found her, someone had killed his partner and tried to kill them twice. He wasn't letting her go, but it was his responsibility to keep her safe.

"I know someone I can trust." He patted his pocket for his phone. It was gone. Damn. She'd stolen it while he was sleeping.

CHAPTER TWELVE

Jax paced in front of the picnic bench. The wail of sirens grew stronger every minute. Soon the police would start searching the park for anyone suspicious.

She and Lincoln were about as suspicious as you could get. They needed to get away far and fast. She tugged on his hand.

"If we cut through those bushes, we'll come out on the next street over. There's a Valero station with the entrance to the bathrooms on the outside. We can hide in there and lock the door behind us until things die down. Then I'll hitch us a ride." She never had trouble finding someone willing to give her a lift. Truckers liked her. Especially if she didn't fasten her top button.

Although, explaining Lincoln on crutches might be a problem. She'd say he was her brother. Yeah, because they looked so much alike. What was he, a foot taller? Black hair to her blonde. Her wearing heavy glasses.

Even beat up, he looked like the movie-star version of an FBI agent. She looked like the real-life version of an escaped con.

She grabbed their bags, and he followed her across the park.

"How do you know so much about this neighborhood? Have you been here before?"

"Running for Your Life 101. Learn the area and all possible escape routes. I scoped it out while you were asleep."

"Did you get any rest?"

"I slept a few minutes in the car. When I woke up, we were flying through the air. Good thing I had my seat reclined, or I'd be in as bad a shape as you are." She was stiff and sore, and had a seat belt bruise across her shoulder, but basically unharmed.

Lincoln looked like shit, but he must be feeling better. He had mastered the crutches and was keeping up with her sprint across the park.

The service station bathroom was a cement cell with only one way in or out. Once inside, they were trapped. The place gave her the willies. She preferred multiple exits, but traveling with Lincoln slowed her down.

Why was she dragging him along, anyway? She could have left him behind at any time since the crash. The memory of last night's gunfire caused her stomach to knot.

Ponytail had seen Lincoln. She'd put him in as much

danger as she was.

The room was cramped and foul smelling. With two people, her backpack, Lincoln's crutches, and his go-bag, she barely had room to turn around.

"Wait here. I'll get us a ride. When I whistle, you come out. Not before." She dug in her backpack and found a lipstick. She slapped it on, fluffed her hair, unbuttoned the top of her blouse, and stepped outside.

Five minutes later, she was flirting with a middle-aged man gassing up a pickup loaded with building materials. "Where ya heading?"

"Taking 59 down to Mexico. I can make a good profit across the border on leftovers I pick up at building sites."

"Wow. That's smart. I wouldn't have thought of that. Do the builders mind?" She smiled so big her jaws hurt.

The man ran his tongue under his lower lip. "I don't exactly ask them. You know, trash is fair game."

"Like I said, smart." She drew the smile even bigger.

"Hey, I smashed up my car last night." She eased down the shoulder of her blouse, showing the seat belt bruises. "Do you think you could give me a ride as far as Sugarland? My mom could pick me up from there. She's old and can't drive on freeways. Believe me, nobody wants to see that."

The guy's eyes narrowed, and the corners of his mouth turned up. "I guess that could be arranged. You sure you don't want to come all the way to Mexico with me? We could drink some tequila. Listen to music. Have a grand old time." He slipped the hand with the wedding ring behind his back.

"That sounds fun. How often do you go?"

"Whenever I find enough stuff to make the trip worthwhile. Once every week or two."

Jax forced herself to look up into his eyes. "I'm supposed to work tonight, so I can't go this time. If you give me a day's notice, maybe I can make the next trip with you. I haven't been to Mexico since spring break two years ago."

The guy finished gassing up his truck and opened the door for her.

She put one foot on the running board and twisted back toward the gas station. "Let me get my brother so we can be on our way." She placed two fingers between her lips and blew out a piercing whistle.

Lincoln limped over and climbed in beside her.

The guy was no longer smiling.

The inside of the pickup smelled about like she expected from a truck carrying stolen material to Mexico. Not any better than the bathroom, just different. Cement dust and sweat instead of gas fumes and motor oil.

"This is my brother, Billy Ray. I'm Jolene. What's your name?"

"Dwayne," the guy mumbled as he stretched the seat belt over his protruding stomach.

"I tell you what, Dwayne. You stop at the Denny's on Main Street in Sugarland on your way home tomorrow, and I'll give you a free appetizer . . . and my phone number." She winked.

The ride took forty-five minutes through downtown while she tried to keep Dwayne entertained with made-up stories of waitressing at Denny's.

They weren't completely made up. Many of them had happened to her over the years.

She let her hand linger on his knee as she pointed to a service station on the right. "You can let us off here. Our mom knows this place. I'll look forward to seeing you tomorrow, Dwayne."

They piled out, and she headed for the bathroom. Lincoln followed. "What is it with you and gas station bathrooms?"

"If they open to the outside, the people who see you go in are different from the ones who see you come out. You lose your tail. You can head off again and it doesn't seem strange. Let's wait thirty minutes and pick up another ride. We're safe for the next twenty-four hours. Dwayne is headed for Mexico. He won't know anyone is looking for us."

"And where do you plan to be in twenty-four hours?"

"I don't know." *If it wasn't for you, I'd be in Mexico.* "I saw a motel half a block back the way we came." Maybe it was time to ditch him and take out on her own. Let Lincoln take care of himself.

"This is ridiculous. I'm an officer of the law. I shouldn't look the other way while someone smuggles stolen property into another country, and I can't keep hiding a fugitive from the authorities. We need help and a sensible plan, and I know who can supply us with both."

She swung around to argue with him. When she did, she found Lincoln pulling his phone out of her backpack. Shit. She should have destroyed that thing when she had the chance.

She had to make him see the danger in calling for help. "Just because some guy is a friend of yours doesn't mean he can keep us safe."

Lincoln glanced up. "He's not my friend. I'm not even sure I like him. I know for certain he doesn't like me."

Detective Noah Daugherty waited on his back stoop while his five-pound Yorkie, Sweet Pea, made a circuit of his backyard, searching for intruders. Almost two years since his late wife passed, and the dog still watched him as if she were afraid he might disappear also.

Satisfied no cat, squirrel, or unknown human had visited during the night, the Yorkie ran inside, hunting for her breakfast.

Noah groaned when his cell played the opening notes of *Clair de Lune.* He had the day off and planned to spend it sprucing up his neglected flower beds.

He groaned even louder when he saw the name that popped up on the screen.

Lincoln Montgomery.

What could the two-last-named FBI agent want with him? Nothing good.

His finger moved toward the disconnect button.

Naw. He owed the guy. Although, a case could be made that the guy owed him.

The agent had given him information that helped him put away a nasty gang of Norwegian murderers, but when they discovered the gang was also into money laundering, blackmail, and other federal crimes, it didn't hurt Montgomery's career to help close the case.

That made them even. He didn't have to deal with the guy again.

He had to get over feeling like the Feds were the enemy. Especially since his partner—former partner—Conner Crawford had quit the Houston Police Department to join the FBI.

In the end, Noah couldn't help himself. Lincoln wouldn't call to pass the time of day. It had to be important.

"Daugherty."

"I need help." The agent's voice was weak and barely above a whisper.

Lincoln was the most self-assured person he'd ever met. He wouldn't ask for help unless it was serious. "What'd you need?"

"We're in the women's restroom of a Valero station. Can you pick us up?"

"What's the address?"

"I'll text it to you."

When the text came in, Noah stared in disbelief. Lincoln

was within twenty miles of the FBI Headquarters, yet hadn't called his buddies in The Bureau for help. Then there was his use of the term *we* and waiting in the women's restroom. Something was seriously screwed up.

He texted back. *Thirty minutes.*

His day just got a lot more interesting than planting petunias.

WHERE THE HELL had they gone? Nick paced the parking lot, his hands in fists, his teeth clamped tight. People didn't disappear into thin air. Especially not if they were injured and the blood in the Fed's wrecked car said they didn't come out of that accident unharmed.

Finding it parked in front of the motel had been a stroke of luck. Blood on the dashboard confirmed the driver—and he'd seen the Fed behind the wheel—was injured. The next piece of luck was the insurance certificate with the Fed's name and address.

He could have gotten the information from one of Mr. A's contacts, but this was faster, easier, and the boss didn't have to know he was hunting the guy. That way, he could insist the Fed's death was unavoidable.

He immediately headed for the guy's apartment. What a joke. His own was nicer, and rent in Sacramento was twice what it was in Houston.

It did give a few insights to the guy, however, and that always helped in a hunt. The place was so neat and organized, it could have passed for unoccupied if not for food in the fridge.

Sure, his own apartment back in California was a bit on the messy side. He liked it that way. It felt like home. Besides, he'd been called away at the last minute.

Photos of people who could only be family members caught his eye. Finally, something he could use. He pulled out his phone and snapped a few pictures. There'd been times when knowing who a mark cared about had come in handy.

The agent's socks, boxers, and T-shirts were folded precisely enough for a store display. His suits, all gray or black, were on one side of the closet, shirts, blue or white, on the other.

How did a prick like this throw away all caution and run off with a suspect? Why wasn't the Duncan woman in jail where he could arrange for her to have an "accident"?

He backed out of the apartment, placing a mark on the underside of the knob that would tell him in an instant if anyone had come through that door.

He'd check it from time to time, but if he had his way, the guy wouldn't be coming back at all.

JAX DIDN'T PLAN on trusting Lincoln's mysterious *friend* for one minute. Even if the guy himself was honest, once in the system, she was dead meat.

She could use the guy, however.

Leaving Lincoln on crutches and with a probable concussion while Ponytail was loose in the area was too risky. In the last two days, the thug had found them in West Monroe, at the FBI safe house, on the road, and at last night's motel.

Not to mention Sacramento, Albuquerque, and Little Rock. The last time she'd seen him was in Philly, and it was pure luck she'd escaped in time.

Whether he was after her or both of them now, she wasn't sure. If Lincoln trusted his friend to keep him safe, that was his choice. She hadn't counted on anyone but herself for four years and she was still alive.

The sudden wail of sirens convinced her hitching a ride would be too dangerous. If Lincoln's friend could get them well away from the area, she'd ditch them both and set out on her own.

She could get a lot farther if she had Lincoln's two hundred dollars.

No, then she'd owe him five hundred dollars. Make that four hundred eighty dollars. She'd keep her backpack close and disappear first chance she got.

The bathroom door was thick, but the sound of a car stopping close by filtered through.

Lincoln's phone chirped with a text. "He's here," he said.

She cracked the door to peer out.

A black pickup with an extended cab idled in front. The

windows were tinted, and other than a large man in the driver's seat, she didn't see anyone.

Jax opened the door wider and glanced around. When she didn't spot anything suspicious, she stepped out and held it open for Lincoln. He hobbled out and into the back of the pickup.

She took a deep breath—even gas-station fumes smelled like a day at the seashore after half an hour in that putrid bathroom—and followed, pushing Lincoln into a prone position on the seat. "Keep down before someone sees us."

"Ready?" asked the driver.

"Yes, hurry. But not too fast. Don't call attention to yourself." She was babbling. She felt it but couldn't stop.

"I know how to drive," the guy grumbled. "I'll get you out of here, but then you two have some 'splaining to do. I *am* a cop."

THE NOISE AND traffic of town died away, and shade trees took over as Lincoln's friend coasted to a stop. "Everybody out."

Jax jumped out, but Lincoln needed help getting down. The guy came around and offered his arm for support, and Jax got her first good look at him. He was at least six feet two—a hair or so taller than Lincoln and heavier, bulkier. As if he lifted weights while Lincoln jogged.

His hair and eyes were dark, like Lincoln's, but managed

to give him a tougher look. Like someone you didn't want to cross.

They followed the man through a double gate into what seemed to be a dog park. Dogs of all breeds and sizes ran, sniffed, and chased balls while their owners played with them or sat on benches or visited with other dog owners.

She watched, but no one paid any attention as the three people with no dog made their way to a secluded corner and an empty bench. Overhead, trees rustled in a slight breeze. A German Shepherd barked and took off running as his owner threw a Frisbee and yelled, "Go get it, boy." A long-haired dachshund yipped incessantly while trying to catch up with his friend.

Jax had to admit, with all the noise and activity, this was a great spot to talk without being overheard.

"Okay. I'm ready. What's going on?" He didn't cross his arms over his chest, but his body language wasn't warm and welcoming.

Lincoln swiveled toward her. "Jax, this is Noah Daugherty. He's a detective with the Houston Police Department. We've worked on a couple of cases together. Noah, this is Jax. I'm trusting you on this. You might know her as Jacqueline Duncan."

"I recognized her the minute she stepped out of that bathroom."

He didn't take me straight to jail. That's a good sign.

"Then you know the story. Jax is suspected of killing a

California state senator by the name of Cory Sheppard. She fled the jurisdiction, and the FBI has been looking for her for four years."

"Yet, you have her, sitting next to you like a best friend."

A friendly mutt ran up for a head scratch, and none of them spoke until she returned to the melee.

Lincoln waited until he was sure the mutt's owner wasn't coming their way. "Jax was definitely there the night Sheppard was murdered, but she says she saw a man with a ponytail kill the senator and he claimed to be working for Benedetto Avendondo. I don't know if she was the killer, involved somehow, or an innocent bystander—"

"Hey. Wait a minute." Heat bubbled up inside Jax's throat. After all this time, he still doubted her?

Lincoln held up his hand in a stop motion. "But a lot of things have happened since I found her, none of them good. My partner was killed while Jax was with me, so I know she didn't do it. A man with a ponytail shot at us while we were at the FBI safe house on Lake Conroe. Jax pulled the car around for me, or I'd be toast right now."

At least he didn't mention I locked him out first.

"On our way to Houston so I could turn Jax in, someone—I didn't have time to see who—deliberately forced us off the road and nearly killed me. Then last night, someone shot up the motel room where we'd been resting only an hour before."

"I heard about the agent who was killed on Sunday. He was supposed to be on a case, but he was found in a woman's trailer so there's been a lot of speculation."

"That was my trailer." She yanked off her glasses and rubbed her eyes. Everywhere she went, she caused heartache. "I'd hate for the man's wife to think he was up to something hinky."

Noah glanced her direction, but his eyes didn't look as wary. "There's something else you might not know if you haven't been watching TV. An old couple was found dead in their Lake Conroe home. They're calling it a murder/suicide. Add to that, a woman from a real estate agency has gone missing. Local police don't want to do anything because she's an adult and it hasn't been that long, but her husband is retired FBI and he's making a stink."

A red-hot knife plunged into Jax's chest. She couldn't breathe, the pain was so intense. A low moan escaped from her lips. "Oh, no. That's four people dead because of me. Maybe I should go ahead and turn myself in. Take my chances." She spun to face Lincoln. "I'd do that in a second if it would stop the killing. But he'd still come after you. You saw his face."

CHAPTER THIRTEEN

Noah watched as Jax had a mini-meltdown over the deaths that had followed them across Southeast Texas.

He didn't know if her tears were real or fake.

She spun a good story, but she'd had four years to practice.

Noah turned toward Jax. "I gotta ask. Why didn't you go to the police the instant you saw Senator Sheppard die?"

"You think I haven't asked myself that question every day for four years? I guess I was in shock. I had just seen Ponytail murder the senator, then grab and threaten me, wreck my apartment, and kill my cat. I was afraid. I knew what Avendondo had done to previous witnesses. In my fogged-up brain, it made sense to hide out for a few days. It would all blow over by then, right? It never occurred to me I might become a suspect."

"The way I heard it, your dad had more money than God. Or at least he did in those days. He could have gotten you an expensive lawyer. You'd have walked away a hero, not a suspect."

He watched as her eyes widened in surprise. So she hadn't known about the guy's fall from grace. Interesting. That meant she hadn't contacted or received help from her family in all the time she'd been missing.

"At the time, my *stepfather* and I weren't speaking. He wouldn't have spent a penny on me unless he could make a profit out of it. Still, after a night's sleep and a chance to wash all the blood off, I had decided to contact the police. That's when another prosecution witness turned up dead. I didn't have a choice. I had shot to the top of Avendondo's to-do list."

A tennis ball, covered in disgusting slobber, landed at their feet. Noah glanced up to see a pit bull charging full out toward them. Jax picked up the ball and strolled to the far edge of the path. The pit bull's owner raced across the park, yelling, "I'm sorry. Bad throw. He won't hurt you. He's completely harmless."

Jax threw the ball as the pit bull screeched to a halt in front of her. The owner came up to her, still apologizing.

Most women Noah had met wouldn't have picked up the soggy ball, much less faced down the dog without hesitation. His opinion of her edged up a quarter of a notch. On the other hand, maybe that was a sign she wasn't another spoiled dilettante. Maybe she was tough enough to take out a guy like the senator.

He half-whispered to Lincoln while she was busy talking to the dog's owner. "Why didn't you take her straight to lockup so you could investigate this thing unencumbered?"

"That was the plan. After Stu, my partner, got shot, I didn't know where the killer might be hiding, so we went to a safe house and waited for the Marshals Service to pick her up. When the guy ambushed us there, I headed for FBI Headquarters and he found us again. For now, it's my job to keep her safe, and until I figure out how this guy is tracking us, I'm not letting her out of my sight."

Jax had thrown the ball again and was coming back to the bench. Noah lowered his head and spoke out of the side of his mouth. "I don't know if I believe a word she says, but she's right about one thing. You saw his face. You're not safe, either."

Lincoln was in bad shape. He'd obviously had a blow to the head. The knot on his forehead looked like something that should land a person in the hospital, not to mention bruised, swollen wrists and an ankle that had to hurt like the devil.

The guy wasn't in any condition to be making critical decisions. The death of his partner alone was cause to yank him off the case.

Would he have handled things any differently if his partner was the one shot? Hell, no. If Conner had been killed, he'd never have stopped hunting for the culprit. On his own time, if necessary.

"I know a place where you can stay for a couple of days.

After that, she waits in jail, whether you've found the guy or not."

LINCOLN NEEDED TO stretch out his leg across the back seat, so Jax sat in the front with Noah. Almost twenty-four hours had passed since some psycho ran them off the road. The swelling in his ankle hadn't subsided, but the pain had dulled into an annoying throb.

If he could stay off it, keep it elevated, instead of racing down alleys and through parks, he might be able to stand on it by tomorrow. He flexed his foot, and a jolt of hot lava shot up his leg.

Maybe not.

Noah spoke over his shoulder. "My girlfriend is planning to put her townhouse up for sale, but she's been busy moving in with me and studying for her broker's license. For now, the place is empty."

He hoped it was the same woman a serial killer had abducted last fall. If so, he approved. She was one sharp lady, leaving clues as he and Noah chased them through the streets of Houston.

Maybe that explained the widowed detective's *somewhat* better disposition.

They stopped in front of a convenience store, and Jax reached across the seat and held out her hand, palm up. He fumbled for the wallet in his back pocket and handed her a twenty. She glared at him, unmoving. He slipped her another twenty, and she slid out of the truck.

"Do you want me to go in and keep an eye on her?" Noah spoke over his shoulder to Lincoln.

"The whole front is glass. I think it's okay. If she's out of sight for more than a minute, go in."

Noah unbuckled his seat belt.

Fifteen minutes later she returned, loaded down with plastic bags. He could see bread and milk and cereal but wasn't sure what else she got.

She didn't offer him any change.

He stared at the loaf of bread peeking out from one bag, and his mouth watered like Pavlov's dog. He hadn't eaten anything since yesterday morning. Jax had skipped breakfast yesterday but eaten a nasty hot dog when they stopped to use the restroom. She must have a cast-iron stomach to have digested that thing.

Noah backed out, and they drove in silence until they reached a quiet, tree-shaded street lined with townhomes. He helped Lincoln out of the truck, unlocked the front door, turned off the alarm, and flipped on the air conditioner.

Lincoln headed for the sofa and let Jax unload the groceries while Noah brought in Lincoln's go-bag. Jax hadn't let go of her backpack.

"You two look beat. I'll leave you here for tonight and come back in the morning. Laurel took her computer but left an old laptop in the closet. The Wi-Fi is off, but if you sit at the kitchen table, you can hook into the free Internet for the restaurant around the corner. If you need to call me, use the landline, not your cell."

Lincoln glanced at Jax. She raised one eyebrow. Yeah, he should have listened to her earlier. He'd used his cell to call Noah from the gas station.

Probably a big mistake.

NICK SAT IN the car he'd stolen and watched the morning turn into afternoon. He'd driven well away from the motel, left the old couple's dented Caddy at an apartment complex, walked a block over to an office building, and jacked a nondescript, three-year-old Toyota—black, no scrapes or dented fenders, no bumper stickers. He should be in the clear until five o'clock, unless the owner went out for lunch.

The temperature in the car edged up along with the sun. There ought to be a law against having a black car in Texas. He should have picked the white one two rows over, but it had a baby seat in the back.

He turned the air conditioner to high and directed the blower toward his face. In New Jersey, spring was making its first appearance. According to his weather app, the high would be in the mid-fifties. Houston, on the other hand, was expecting a high of eighty-seven. And it wasn't even April for two more days.

Three hours, and no word from his source. Surely the Fed had used his phone to call for help by now. Or had before he'd kicked in their door and sprayed shots across an empty room.

Another near miss. The woman must be psychic. She always managed to slip away every time he thought he had her. For years, he'd had nightmares of watching her hand in slow motion sliding out of his grip. Then her circus-worthy leap over Sheppard's banister.

She was a witch. That was the only explanation. She had put a curse on him, and his life had gone steadily downhill since that day.

His stomach rumbled and he considered his options. Find a drive-thru and be prepared to move on a moment's notice, or relax for a sit-down meal and see what passed for Italian food in the South.

His taste buds rebelled against the thought of more fast food, and he drove in circles until he found something called *Buono*. If he had a restaurant, he'd call it *Bellisimo*—wonderful. Not *Buono*—good. Who the hell named a restaurant Good? Didn't they have any pride?

Inside, the air was cool and carried the aroma of garlic. He considered ordering *Parmigiana di melanzane*, but one look at the waiter, who was closer to Irish than Italian, and he simply mumbled, "Eggplant Parmigiana." No point in being remembered.

His dish, when it came, definitely lived up to the name

good, but didn't quite make it to *wonderful*. Fake Italians seemed to think adding more garlic would cover any defect.

His mother had a light touch, using spices to bring out the natural taste, not cover it up.

He pushed his plate aside, and the redheaded waiter appeared like magic. "Dessert?"

Why not? His phone hadn't rung yet. "I'll have the cannoli."

He took one bite and shook his head. He'd like to take the redhead out to dinner and teach him what real Italian food tasted like.

It was time for him to get back home. If he could ever get out of this mess, he had his life all planned out.

His sister was established in California, but as the oldest son, he'd been expected to follow in his father's footsteps. And he'd been happy to—at the time.

After Pop's death, he sat down with his little brother, Robby, and helped him pick a career of no use to the mob. Lawyer and accountant were out, so were doctor and even vet. Pharmacist, ha. No way. They settled on electrical engineer.

Robby may have gotten the brains, but he got the street smarts and knew how to protect those he loved.

Now Robby was out of school and working. He could take care of Ma.

With rumors of Benedetto Avendondo on his deathbed, the Family was falling apart. It was his chance to get out.

Every time he went to a new city hunting the Duncan woman, he checked out the nearest cooking school. He had even picked one—Dexter University in Philly. He could get a B.S. in Culinary Arts and specialize in Baking and Pastry.

He'd be far enough from New Jersey that he was unlikely to run into any members of the Family but close enough he could visit his mother. After graduation, if the old fart hadn't died yet and he still needed to lie low, he'd get a job on a cruise ship for a couple of years and save enough money to start his own bakery.

Where the cannoli would be made with real ricotta, not some type of fake custard.

But first, he had to get rid of that blasted woman . . . and the Fed. That guy had seen his face.

The phone in his pocket vibrated. He slapped a twenty on the table next to his uneaten cannoli and left.

He had work to do.

JAX BOLTED THE front and back doors and propped a kitchen chair under the knob for good measure. She double-checked that every window, upstairs and down, was locked and pulled every curtain tight.

She dug around in the almost-empty pantry and found a gallon plastic bag, filled it with ice, and took it to Lincoln for his ankle. "How does a grilled cheese sandwich and a bowl of chicken noodle soup sound?"

"Like heaven, but I thought it was supposed to be tomato

soup with grilled cheese."

"You want tomato soup, you hobble your raggedy ass into the store next time."

"Chicken noodle sounds great, thanks. Can I help?"

"I've got it. You keep the ice on your ankle. I don't care how safe Noah thinks this place is, we might have to run again at any time and I'm not waiting on you from now on."

That was a lie. She'd probably wait for him, but he didn't need to know that.

She glanced at Lincoln, and he didn't meet her eye. *He's thinking about that phone call he made from the gas station and knows it was a mistake. Couldn't be helped. Trying to hitch a ride from a stranger was too dangerous.*

A thought hit her, and she spun back toward him. "Do you still have your gun? You didn't lose it along the way, did you?"

"No, I've got it." He sat up and pulled a huge, silver pistol from a holster at the small of his back. He set his weapon on the coffee table beside him and lie back against the cushions.

Looked like a Glock to her. She'd carried one for a few years as a just-in-case precaution. It got left behind once when she had to run and she never replaced it. Having it hadn't really made her feel safer. Only more on edge.

But he was a cop, and that was different. "Good. Keep it close and loaded."

"I always do."

"You any good with it?"

"Want to see my medals?" He gave an almost smile. The

first she'd seen since . . . ever.

"You missed Ponytail." If he'd only killed the guy, this nightmare would be over. No, it wouldn't. Avendondo would still be after her, and there was no guarantee the cops would believe her.

"I was busy chasing you and I didn't miss. I grazed his arm."

That was news to her. "Are you sure? It didn't seem to slow him down much."

"I'm sure. Unfortunately, I hit his right shoulder and he's left-handed."

She tried to picture the scene at Senator Sheppard's house as she grilled the sandwiches. Ponytail had Sheppard over his left shoulder and had grabbed her with his right hand. Was that why she was able to pull away?

"Ready?" she asked as she set the plates on the coffee table. Her glasses fogged from the steam floating off the soup.

She sat cross-legged on the floor, facing him. She could almost see the color returning to Lincoln's face as he downed the food.

They watched the evening news in silent companionship. The story of the old couple at Lake Conroe was being played up as a murder/suicide. Even the anchors didn't look convinced.

Jax bit back a yawn. Lesson number two, right after check all exits—never show any weakness. "There are three bedrooms upstairs. I'm taking the one on the left." She'd already checked. The window opened over the garage for an easy escape, and she'd watched Noah punch in the alarm code.

Lincoln eyed the stairs. "If you'll toss me a pillow and blanket, I think I'll stay right here. That way I can hear if anyone tries anything."

Somehow, that actually made her feel safer. Maybe she *could* trust him. Maybe he *could* protect her. Maybe she could go to bed tonight without worrying about being killed in her sleep.

She yawned again and didn't hide it. "You don't have to sleep on the sofa on my account. I'm not going anywhere."

Maybe she even meant it.

CHAPTER FOURTEEN

Lincoln searched in the cabinets until he found a jar of instant coffee. It smelled wonderful. Unfortunately, the grounds were hard as cement.

A tap at the back door caused him to drop the jar, and the coffee spilled out in one solid lump. His ankle was almost normal, and he'd left one crutch and his Glock next to the sofa. Too far to reach quickly.

Noah's voice called from the other side of the door. "You guys up yet?"

"Coming." Lincoln hobbled to the door and unlocked it.

"I have a key but was afraid I might get shot if I barged in without warning."

Not if I don't quit leaving my gun in the other room.

Noah entered, carrying a tray with three containers of

coffee and a white paper bag.

"Whatcha got there?"

Noah opened the bag, and a familiar aroma wafted out. "Bacon, egg, and cheese croissants. Thought we could eat while we talked. Where's Jax?"

Lincoln's heart froze for an instant. He hadn't seen or heard her this morning. What if she'd slipped out during the night? "She's not up yet. Let me go get her."

"I can do it. You shouldn't be climbing stairs."

"I'm fine. Swelling is way down. I'll be right back. Don't eat my share."

He rushed up the stairs, doing his best not to limp. Her door was closed and he knocked softly. "Jax, are you awake?" He tried not to panic when she didn't answer. He called out again as he turned the knob and peeked inside.

The light was on and the bed unmade, but no sign of Jax. The sound of running water came from the bathroom, and he let out a sigh of relief. She was taking a shower.

Unless she wasn't. What if this was a ruse to fool him?

His knock on the bathroom door was hard enough to be heard over the shower. "Jax? Noah's here with breakfast." He held his breath and waited, his mouth so dry he couldn't call out again.

A muffled voice came back. "I'll be right down. I'm washing my hair."

He leaned his forehead against the door and willed his heart to slow down.

Noah had uncapped his coffee and was taking a sip when Lincoln eased into the chair across from him. "What is it with women and washing their hair? Although I can't blame her. We've been shot at, crashed in the woods, and spent an hour hiding in a putrid bathroom. I kinda want to wash mine, too." He reached up and pulled a twig from the back of his hair.

"I don't mind a few minutes to talk alone. What do you make of her story? Do you believe her?"

"That's the question I've been wrestling with for the last seventy-two hours."

"And have you come up with an answer?"

"No. And it's driving me crazy. Everything I think I know could have several explanations."

Noah took a croissant and passed one to Lincoln. "Like what?"

"She couldn't have moved the senator's body by herself, so does that mean she didn't do it or she had help?"

"Wasn't her apartment broken into?"

"Yes. Unless she trashed it herself to make it look like she was in danger, too. Or her partner could have turned on her."

"I see what you mean. Every story could have multiple interpretations. Are you sure she saved your life, or was she covering her ass?"

Lincoln ran a hand through his hair. It was dirty and matted. As soon as Jax finished, it would be his turn for a long shower and a hair wash. "The first time, during the shoot-out on Lake Conroe, is a did-she-or-didn't-she situation.

She yanked me off balance, then shut me out of the house. She claims she didn't realize the door locked automatically. However, she stopped to pick me up as I chased after her through the woods. The other two times, when we were run off the road and at the motel, she got me out of a dangerous situation when I couldn't have done it myself."

"So does that make her completely innocent, involved in the bribery and money laundering but not the murder, or a killer with a conscience?"

"I don't know, but there's one other problem. I kind of like her."

Noah raised one eyebrow.

"No. Not that way. I've just grown to like her as a person. Now I'm worried I'm being too hard on her so I won't be too soft on her."

Footsteps on the stairs said Jax was on her way down.

Noah's eyes bored into Lincoln's. "When you figure that one out, let me know."

FROM THE GUILTY looks between Noah and Lincoln, Jax figured she was the subject of their conversation.

She was exhausted from trying to do everything alone. Like juggling seven balls at a time, and you could never put them down. Never let your guard down. Never forget who you were.

If only she could pass this mess off to someone else. Let them take over for a while.

Somehow the term *dead tired* managed to have dual meanings, and she wasn't ready to give in.

Not yet.

"Anything left for me?" She ran her fingers through her damp hair. She'd towel-dried it and hit it one blast with a hairdryer she found in a drawer, but that only got it to the point where it didn't drip down her back.

"Coffee and a croissant. I think both are still hot." Noah slid them in her direction.

She took a sip. Not exactly hot, but close enough. The caffeine hit her and finished the wake-up job the hot water had started.

Lincoln pushed back from the table. "I'm finished, and the idea of a shower, shampoo, and shave sound like heaven. I think I have clean clothes in my go-bag. See you in fifteen minutes."

Jax watched him gimp his way up the stairs. His clothes looked like he'd crashed in the woods and slept in them two nights. He didn't smell like a spring rain, either.

She couldn't fail to notice that he hadn't been willing to leave her alone long enough to clean up until there was someone to keep a watch on her.

This shit was getting old.

"You going to eat that?" Noah eyed her breakfast.

"Absolutely. Thanks for bringing it." She took a bite and

savored the hickory-smoked bacon.

"So Jax. What's up with your family? Think I caught a little tension when I mentioned them yesterday."

Four years had passed. Did any of it matter now? "We were dirt poor when Mom married Gavin Duncan. I was six, my sister nine. I thought I had died and gone to Heaven. Plenty of food, a nice house, a pool even. We took vacations. He bought me anything I wanted. Pretty soon, I forgot how hard we struggled. Never enough food. Kicked out of places when we couldn't pay the rent. Mom couldn't hold down a job. I realize now she was clinically depressed."

"Yet Gavin married her. How did that happen?"

How indeed? "Mom was completely sober—had been for a couple of months—and things were looking up. She had a job at a jewelry store. Gavin came in to buy something for his latest floozy and Mom waited on him. He immediately recognized her lack of self-confidence, her basic insecurities. His kind always does. Within three weeks they were married, although I'd bet my next paycheck—if I had one—he had her sign some type of prenup. I can remember her crying and saying she couldn't divorce him. I didn't understand why at the time."

"Was he abusive toward her?"

What was this, Interrogation 101?

"You have to realize, I'm seeing things now through adult eyes that I saw as a child, and everything is topsy-turvy to what I thought I knew. Gavin ran hot and cold. They would go out, party, drink, maybe do drugs, I don't know, and she would sparkle she was so happy. Then he started disappearing. Working late. Taking business trips. Finding fault with everything she did and she would deflate. Take to her bedroom for days, weeks at a time. She didn't bathe or dress, and I blamed her for running him off. And the cycle would start over again."

Noah drained his cup and nodded. "He had girlfriends."

"Bingo. Right on the first guess." She nibbled on a corner of her croissant. Her mouth was so dry, it might as well have been cardboard. This was the hard part. There wasn't any reason she had to tell him all her family's dirty secrets. It wouldn't help catch Ponytail. Time to change the subject. She hadn't talked about herself this much in years, a habit that had served her well. If she had to run again, she didn't want to slip up.

"Your turn. Are you sure your girlfriend doesn't mind us staying at her place? I wouldn't want to put her in any danger."

"She's helped me out before. She can handle it."

Lincoln came down the stairs like a new man. There wasn't exactly a spring in his step, but he wasn't dragging, either. He sat next to Jax and smelled of shampoo and soap. He'd ditched the suit and wore casual clothes—jeans and a blue polo shirt. "So, either of you have any idea how to catch the bastard who keeps shooting at us?"

Jax wasn't sure, but she might have smiled. Finally, someone was taking this seriously.

Noah glanced uneasily from Jax to Lincoln. "The first thing we need to do is figure out how the guy with a ponytail is finding you." *Unless Jax is sending him signals. She hasn't been hurt in any of these confrontations.* "I'm coming to this thing late. You say he's shown up several different times. How do you think he did that?"

"The first time was easy. I dropped my purse in the senator's house. It had my address and credit cards." She glanced at Lincoln. "I'm guessing he found me the same way you did the other times. How was that?"

"Good old-fashioned police work. The owner of the pawn shop where you hocked your earrings gave me the same directions he gave you. After that, it was a matter of driving around until I found your car. Parking in front of your motel room door wasn't a great idea."

"I was heading out to move it when I saw Ponytail going into the office. I ran back inside to see if I could squeeze through the bathroom window when you knocked on the door. I thought it was him. I grabbed the only thing I could find—the toilet tank lid. Sorry about what happened to you. Hypothetically."

Noah watched Lincoln touch a spot on the back of his head like it still hurt. That was a story he'd love to hear sometime. It wasn't often someone got the drop on an FBI agent, and he wouldn't mind having something to hold over Lincoln's head.

"How'd you get out of Sacramento?" Noah was getting curious now.

"Helped an old lady get on a Greyhound bus. They thought I was her daughter. Rode all the way to Elko, Nevada. Saw a diner with a help wanted sign. Those first few shifts nearly killed me. Would have quit if the TV hadn't shown a documentary on Avendondo and the people he'd killed. From there, I went to a little town in Arizona where I cleaned motel rooms for a place to stay and a little cash. When I saw a guy with a ponytail, I had a panic attack. It wasn't our guy, but I moved on anyway."

"We followed you as far as Elko, but you'd been gone a week by the time we got there. How'd you get to Albuquerque?"

"A trucker. I was learning to hitch by then. I always carried a knife, just in case."

Noah didn't blame her. He outweighed her by more than a hundred pounds, and he wouldn't get in a truck with a stranger without his gun loaded and ready.

Jax gave a quick now-you-see-it-now-you-don't smile. "I have a good idea what happened in Albuquerque. It was the forger, wasn't it?"

"Yep." Lincoln nodded.

"I had figured out by that time I had to have some form of identification. One of the other maids in New Mexico was illegal. She told me about a guy in Albuquerque who could get me some paper. I saw on the news when he was arrested. I knew it wouldn't take you long to find me. I was staying in that old rooming house on Third Street. I stuffed a few things in my backpack and was getting on a city bus when I saw Ponytail go in the front door."

"He was there that fast? I didn't get there until the next day. The landlady didn't mention anyone else looking for you. She only said you disappeared without paying your last week's rent."

"That damn liar. I only owed for one day, and I left the money on my dresser. I'll bet she pocketed the cash and told the owner she never got it. The old witch."

"Wait a minute. Wait a minute." Noah held up one hand. "I remember hearing about that on the news. He'd made fake IDs for half the criminals on the West Coast. How do you suppose Mr. Ponytail got there before you?"

Lincoln shrugged. "He learned about the guy's arrest the same way we all did—from the news report. The only difference was I was in D.C. at the time. My orders came from my boss, who got them from his boss at The Bureau. Ponytail worked out of Sacramento and didn't have to wait on a chain of command."

Noah started shaking his head before Lincoln stopped talking. "That doesn't explain how he got hold of the list."

"I hate to admit it, but there are freelance hackers out there who put the FBI to shame. If he's working for Avendondo, money's no object. They wouldn't even need to have been searching for Jax. Just scanning the list in case any of their people were in danger."

Maybe. But it was all a little too coincidental for his taste. How many times had he and Conner been working a case when his ex-partner had a fit over the *no such thing as a coincidence* rule? "Jax, how long was it from the time you heard about the arrest till you got on that bus?"

"I didn't actually hear the newscast, only some customers talking about it. I cashed out, pocketed my tips, caught the bus home, grabbed my bag, and left. Not more than forty-five minutes. Since that time, I've always carried a backpack with the few things I couldn't stand to lose."

"So if the news came on that morning. . . ."

"Probably. It wasn't any later than eleven. The lunch crowd hadn't started."

"Then Ponytail couldn't have driven from Sacramento. He would have to have flown. We can check rent-a-car records for that morning. It's a place to start." He was going to have to learn the guy's name. He refused to keep calling him Ponytail.

"I agree. Can you check that through HPD? If I call anyone at The Bureau, a red flag will go up."

"Yeah. I have a guy named Earl. Used to be a cop till he got conked on the head. Now he's a part-time civilian employee. He won't mention it to anyone if I ask him not to."

Jax pushed her cold coffee aside. "We're missing something here. Even if Ponytail got up in time for the five o'clock news, he'd still need to contact the hacker and pour over the names of at least a hundred clients."

"More like several hundred clients. Although, some could be the same client with multiple identities," Lincoln added.

Noah agreed. It didn't add up. "Doesn't make sense, timewise. Every hacker in the country would have been working overtime with clients calling in. Time-consuming work that needed to be started the night before the news hit the TV. Somebody, somewhere, let the information out early."

Jax rubbed her temples. "So who let the cat out of the bag?"

"We may not be able to answer that, for now at least. Let's concentrate on questions we can answer."

Noah glanced over to see that Lincoln had started a list.

"So far, we can check car rentals on the morning you left Albuquerque." He pointed to the one line on his notepad.

"Okay, what's next?" Jax leaned toward Lincoln, waiting, drumming her fingers on the table.

"Little Rock. I hate to tell you this, Jax, but someone dropped a dime on you."

"My boss. I was working in a bookstore, under the table, for cash. She was in trouble with the IRS. Barely making ends meet. One day, she started acting weird. Wouldn't look at me. Nervous as hell. The hairs on the back of my neck didn't just stand up, they were dancing all over the place. She got a call, offered to pick us up something for lunch—she'd never done anything like that before—and almost ran out the door."

"Wasn't me. I certainly didn't call and warn her. Risk an operation like that? No way." Lincoln was starting to look upset. Noah had never seen him anything but calm and collected, even when he was hobbling around on crutches.

"The minute the door closed, I raced into the storeroom, grabbed my go-bag, and slipped out the back door, down the alley, and around the corner. I almost ran into the back of Ponytail as he started for the shop. Scared me so bad, I nearly wet my pants. That's when I knew for certain. I could never go home."

This was too much for Noah. Her story was getting hard to believe. "How do you know it was your Ponytail? There's more than one guy in the world with long hair."

"A tattoo." Jax stroked the side of her neck. "Right here."

"How come you haven't mentioned a tattoo before?" Noah didn't like it when he didn't get all the information at the same time. Made him suspicious.

"Not sure you ever asked me to describe him. He's a big guy, tall, heavyset, brown hair, wavy. I hate it when guys have better hair than I do." She glanced at Lincoln as he ran a hand through his still-damp locks. "Scary green eyes. The one tattoo on his neck and another on his right wrist. There could have been others. He had on a long-sleeved shirt."

"Anything to add to that, Lincoln?"

"A bit over six feet four, probably two hundred eighty pounds, most of it muscle, but not all. Definitely left-handed. Jax claims he has a New Jersey accent. That's about it."

"What's the tattoo of?"

Jax screwed up her face. "I don't know. Not a woman's face or a cross."

Lincoln leaned back in his chair and stretched out his sore leg. "I couldn't see it all, but I think it was a half moon and stars. The one on his wrist was an infinity symbol. You know, like a sideways figure eight."

"What happened when you got to the bookstore?"

"My partner and I split up. He went in the front. I went in the back. The door was wide open, and I knew we were too late. I wanted to search the neighborhood, but the owner lady was a mess, crying, disheveled, a bloody nose. We called an ambulance for her. She said Jax became violent when she realized she'd been set up. Threw a book at her face, destroyed a valuable first edition, emptied the cash drawer, and took off."

"What is it with these women?" Jax shoved her chair back and stomped across the room. "I never touched her, and I certainly didn't steal anything. She still owes me my last paycheck. And that book? She'd been trying to sell it since before I got there, but it was in poor condition. I'll bet insurance paid her top dollar for it. Can I sue her? Please tell me I can sue the Birkenstocks off her."

Noah lowered his face into his hands. "I'm not a lawyer, but why don't we worry about keeping you alive first?"

Lincoln glanced at Jax. The first time he'd looked square at her since he got back from his shower. "By the time we got around to searching the neighborhood, you were long gone."

"Guy was dropping off a load of bread to a shop down the street. He took me to the far side of town, and I caught a ride with a college student heading home for the summer. Told him I went to OU. Said my ride home got fresh, and I ditched him when he stopped for gas. By the time you started looking for me, I was already in Tennessee. Took me a couple of days to get there, but I spent the summer in Maine, selling lobster rolls before heading down to Philly by way of Albany. Nice city, but I have a thing against state government. You ever get to Maine, I can tell you where to find the best lobster rolls."

Noah didn't say anything for several seconds. Her ability to lie, make up a story on the spur of the moment, worried him. But the constant time lags between discovering her location and swooping in worried him more. The Feds didn't have the manpower of big-city PDs, but they had the toys, the technology, and the tools to get there and get it done.

"I'm sorry, Pal, but something about this smells." Noah turned to face Lincoln. "The FBI isn't looking so great."

Lincoln dropped his head back and stared at the ceiling. "Wait till you hear about Philly."

CHAPTER FIFTEEN

Nick had finished swapping license plates with another black Toyota when the phone in his back pocket vibrated. Nine o'clock and edging up over eighty degrees. He could learn to hate Texas.

He climbed back into the car and kicked the air conditioning on high before he answered. "What'd you find out?"

"Addresses cost more than phone numbers."

Nick knew the voice, how to make contact, and where to send the money for services rendered. He just didn't know the guy's name. That was fine with him. The guy didn't know his name, either. "I paid you for the requested information, not half the information. Don't try to jack me up for more money. It won't go well for your future."

"The guy's a cop."

Shit. That complicated matters. He'd already checked out the Fed's place again. No one had been back there. They had to be hiding somewhere and he needed that address. "Do you have it or not?"

"Soon. I'm working on it."

"Work harder. If you get it by noon, I'll throw in an extra hundred." With an ounce of luck, he could be out of the state by suppertime. He'd already spotted a place where he could ditch the car with the windows down and key in the ignition. It would be chopped into pieces by the time he walked the two blocks to the bus stop.

The only question now was, should he fly back to California and collect his gear or head straight home to Jersey? Hell, he'd call his sister. She could have anything she wanted and toss the rest.

No. There were photos and phone numbers on his computer he couldn't risk having the Family see. Neither the Rossini nor the Avendondo branch.

He'd come back later, clean it up, and grab the cash and jewelry from his safety deposit boxes.

He adjusted the vent and let the cool air blow on his face. The heat had caused the cut on his arm to burn. He'd cleaned and bandaged it last night, but if it got infected, that Fed would pay.

He hated to sweat. Made him look like a fat slob. Which he wasn't.

The only thing he liked about Texas was the ease of finding clothes for big men. He didn't even stand out around here. If he'd come in the winter, he might feel differently about the place.

But this was the first of April, and he sure didn't want to still be here in August.

He'd checked out of his motel—another expense that would never be reimbursed. Rush-hour traffic had died down, but this was Houston. It never went away entirely. He drove aimlessly for half an hour, trying to get a feel for the layout of the city. Not knowing which direction he'd need to go when he learned their location.

He couldn't keep this up all day. He needed someplace to lie low while he waited for the asshole to call.

Too early for a movie, his favorite hideout. Before they got all fancy and had reserved seating, he'd slip from one theater to the next and back again.

He'd spent many an afternoon sitting in the dark, eating popcorn and laughing while some make-believe tough guy pulled off an impossible stunt.

Hollywood wusses. They'd probably cry if they got a splinter in real life. He'd like to see one of them stand behind a tree for two hours without moving, or carry a couple of hundred pounds of dead weight through the woods to a muddy sinkhole.

How many of them knew exactly where to punch a guy so he pissed blood for a week but could still go to work with no visible bruises? Women were easy. You didn't even have to touch them. Make a move like you were going to grab their crotch and they folded.

Movie stars with all their money and fame. Let one of those so-called heroes get shot for real and never slow down. He reached up and adjusted the bandage on his arm.

You could hate your job and still take pride in your work.

LINCOLN KNEW IT was coming, but he tried to put it off as long as he could. He tapped his list. "So far, all I have is check airport rental cars for Albuquerque and check phone calls for the bookstore lady in Little Rock. Anybody have anything else?"

Noah didn't look happy. "No. Why don't we head over to my house and pick up Laurel's car. You can use it while she's in Austin. On the way, you tell me about Philly. After that, we can discuss what happened in Houston."

Lincoln wasn't thrilled about discussing either of those things.

He and Noah picked up the trash in the kitchen, while Jax put her shoes on and grabbed her backpack. He'd feel more confident she wasn't planning to escape if she left it behind.

He followed Noah out to his truck, pausing to enjoy the spring morning. The heat of the sun felt good on his poor, aching muscles, and the sky was a deep blue with puffy clouds, reminding him of a Monet landscape he'd seen one time in Chicago.

His mood brightened as he stepped aside to let Jax in Noah's truck first. Instead of getting in the front, as he'd expected, she tossed her backpack in the back and climbed in after it. He got in the front, but would have to twist to keep an eye on her.

He could walk without crutches, but he couldn't run. If she jumped out and took off, he might not be able to catch her. And if he did, what then? Wrestle her to the ground and handcuff her?

Now he couldn't relax until they were back at Laurel's townhouse.

Maybe not even then.

Noah put his truck in reverse to back out of the driveway when it began to issue an insistent *ping, ping, ping.* "Seat belts on, everybody," he called over his shoulder.

Lincoln waited until he heard Jax's belt click before he fastened his own. Noah kept his face straight ahead but gave Lincoln the side-eye.

Yeah, they were on the same wavelength. She hadn't earned their trust yet. With someone to help keep tabs on her, all he had to worry about now was everything else.

Time was passing, and while he could use his concussion as an excuse for not contacting The Bureau on Monday, possibly Tuesday, this was Wednesday and he was running out of excuses. They would definitely be searching for him, and every hour that went by made him look worse.

Didn't matter how he looked. Trust her or not, he couldn't contact The Bureau until he was sure Jax would be safe. And so far, he wasn't. He hated to admit it, but Noah was right.

Things weren't looking so good for the FBI.

JAX SAW THE look that passed between Noah and Lincoln. They still didn't trust her. That was okay. She didn't trust them, either, but they were her only chance to get her life back.

And that was a risk worth taking.

Right now, three different groups were after her—the FBI, Ponytail, and Benedetto Avendondo. She'd *seen* Ponytail kill Sheppard, but she'd *heard* him implicate Avendondo. That meant they both had their reasons for wanting her dead.

If they caught Ponytail and convicted him, that took him and the FBI off her back, leaving only the mob. *Only* the mob. But how much longer could Avendondo live?

She'd hidden out for four years. She could last another four without those two chasing her.

She would stick with Lincoln and Noah long enough to see if they were actively hunting Ponytail. If they gave up, she'd be gone like mist in the morning.

Noah put on his blinker and eased into traffic. "I'm waiting to hear about Philly. I'm guessing it's a good story."

Lincoln glanced back at Jax. "I wasn't there until later.

Why don't you tell what happened?"

"I *liked* Philly. I had a good job at a doctor's office, getting paid cash under the table and not on my feet all day."

"Who did you work for?"

"I'm not telling you. You'd arrest the poor guy. He was doing a public service. Treating underprivileged people with no insurance."

Lincoln let that pass. She was right. He'd have to arrest the guy if he knew his name.

"Philly is a great city. Booming. Lots of arts and music. There was a bar I could walk to from my apartment that had live bands three nights a week. They served great three-dollar hamburgers and dollar fries. The beer was a dollar till nine o'clock. I could spend all evening for five dollars. Six if the band was decent and I stayed for two beers. I knew it was too good to be true, but I never expected to see Ponytail and Benedetto Avendondo walk in."

"What was the New Jersey mob doing in Philly? Money laundering?" Noah asked.

"Oh, yeah." Lincoln's laugh was painful to hear. "It wasn't my case, but the local office was keeping an eye on them. They got wind Avendondo had picked that spot for his fall meeting with some of his cronies and staked it out. This was what, almost two years ago? Before his last stroke. The rumor was he was expecting a fight, and both sides had doubled up on their muscle. Philly had one agent inside and microphones trained toward the windows, but couldn't make out much over the band."

Jax stared out the window. Streets, houses, trees, little stores with people going about their business. As foreign to her after the last four years as if she'd been living in Italy or Mars. "I didn't know about the guy inside. All I knew was I was sitting in the corner and wanted to leave because the band was too loud. When I looked in the mirror over the bar and saw Ponytail with another bodyguard type come in and scope out the place, I couldn't believe it. A minute later, a group straight out of *The Godfather* came in, Avendondo among them. I was too scared to move. When Ponytail left to check the back room, I threw some money on the table and slipped out. God it was hard to walk normal. I was never sure they knew I was there."

Remembering made it all come alive again. Like she was still at that table, watching Ponytail scan the room. Seeing Avendondo glad-hand people who'd wring her neck if he gave the nod. Her knees started to shake, and she gripped her backpack until the circulation in her hands turned her fingers to ice.

Noah drove onto a street with shady trees and cozy homes. "Did they? Know she was there?"

"Not at the time, though I heard they found out later. And yes, I know, that doesn't look good for The Bureau. The microphones didn't pick up anything incriminating, and no riot broke out, so they let everyone go undisturbed. Afterward, the locals swept in and took fingerprints of everything. That's how we found out Jax was there. They sent me in, but I never found a trace of you."

Noah started laughing. "You mean to tell me, Jax was sitting in a room that was full of Avendondo's men and surveilled by the FBI—both of whom were searching the country for her—and she casually got up and walked out with no one the wiser?"

By this time, Lincoln was laughing, too. "It didn't do me any good, and I wasn't even there! No telling what Avendondo did to Ponytail."

Jax couldn't help it. She felt a laugh bubbling up from deep inside. "Damn. I knew I should have wiped down that beer bottle, but I was afraid that would be too obvious. Plus, I only had a few seconds to get out while no one was watching."

"You're looking at it all wrong. This is our first break." Lincoln tried to look serious but only half-succeeded.

How could he say that? The Feds probably saw that as proof she was working for the mob.

"Ignoring the fact that your mother was thrilled to know you were alive, if I can manage to access those records without giving away our position, we can figure out who Ponytail is."

The only thing that registered in Jax's mind was that Lincoln had talked to her mother. Did her mother care? Did she care? Her step-father wouldn't have cared that she was alive…except for the trouble it might cause.

Noah pulled into the driveway of a neat, gray house with towering trees and flower beds lining the walk. He turned to face them and said one word. "Conner."

CHAPTER SIXTEEN

Nick stepped out of the public library and into the sunshine. Two hours of poring over cookbooks and baking tips had made him hungry. Halfway to his car, the phone in his back pocket vibrated.

The bastard had the info the whole time. He tried to hold me up for more money. Nobody cons Nick Ross and walks away clean. I'll deal with him when I get to Jersey.

He quickened his speed and reached into his back pocket when he realized the vibration came from his other pocket. The one with his personal phone, not his work phone.

This had to be bad news. His family never called him. They knew better. They waited for him to call them. But there was his brother's name, staring back at him.

He started the car and pulled out of his parking spot before thumbing the connect button. He refused to speak on the phone outside. You never knew who might be eavesdropping. Even Podunk PDs had fancy listening devices. No telling what Houston had.

He cranked the radio up a notch before speaking. "Robby? What's up?"

"Hey, bro. How are you?" His brother's voice was hesitant.

"Good. Working. Everything all right? Ma okay?"

"She's fine. Took her to the doctor last Friday. He increased her blood pressure pills and told her to lose twenty pounds. But we both know that's not going to happen. Other than that, she's great. Got home from the appointment and made lasagna to take up to the church potluck supper. How about you? Coming home anytime soon?"

They both knew what he meant by that, but even the best phone wasn't completely safe. Best to be careful and say little. "It could happen. Sooner than we expected. I've been craving some homemade lasagna. Was there something special you wanted?"

"I have some kind-of good news."

"What is it?" Only kinda good news and it rated a phone call?

"I have a girlfriend and we're getting pretty serious."

"The same one you brought home for Christmas?" He wasn't allowed to go home himself, but he'd seen the pictures. She looked okay. Pretty but not stunning. The best kind.

"Yeah. Her name's Emmy. We're thinking about moving

in together."

"That's great. What's holding you up? Ma? She won't like it, but she'll get over it." She would if she ever wanted any grandkids, and Robby was her only chance. His brother was lucky, finding someone he cared about.

He hadn't had anyone special in years, making do with an occasional hookup. Steady didn't work when you couldn't explain what you did for a living and why you sometimes flew out of town without warning. And couldn't take them home to meet your family.

"I haven't mentioned it to Ma yet. The thing is, I can't afford my own place."

What the . . . ? Robby still lived with Ma, but only to help her out. He had a good job. Made decent money. Maybe not all he was capable of with his genius level IQ, but steady, dependable. Safe. "What ya been spending it on? If this Emmy broad is costing you that much, she might not be such a good catch."

"I don't know if you knew. I didn't want to mention it in case it upset you, but Ma hasn't been getting her regular pension for the last two years. I've been covering some of her expenses. I can't keep doing that and get my own place, too. The cost of her medications is killing me. My only other choice is for Emmy to move in with me at Ma's, and that's not such a good idea. I was hoping maybe you could send Ma a little every month."

Fire danced in front of Nick's eyes, and he almost rear-ended a Subaru stopped at a red light. Robby knew better than to say it out loud, but her pension came directly from Mr. Avendondo and the Family. His dad had given his life for Mr. A. He owed Ma that money.

Two years. Ever since Philly. And no one had mentioned it to him.

"I'll take care of it. You start looking for apartments."

Lincoln followed Noah and Jax through the fence into Noah's backyard. He made a point of keeping Jax between them. But seriously, where could she run? They were in the middle of a suburban neighborhood with no taxis or busses and no friendly truck drivers ready to give her a lift.

Noah unlocked the door, and a pint-sized ball of fur tumbled out. It yapped and jumped and circled Noah, its tail wagging so hard its entire body shook.

It froze when it saw him and Jax, cocked its pink-bowed head to one side and began investigating Jax's jeans.

She took an involuntary step back and nearly fell. "Sorry, I'm not used to pets. Never had any of my own."

The hairs on the back of his neck tingled. "Didn't you have a cat in Sacramento?" There'd been a cat carrier on her bed and she had definitely accused Ponytail of killing it. Had she forgotten that part of her story?

"Cleo. She was a rescue from the pound. I'd only had her a

few days, and she hid whenever I was home. The only reason I knew she was still there was when her food bowl was empty and the litter box full."

Noah scooped up the little Yorkie in one hand and held the door open with the other. "Sounds like Laurel's cat. She named him Harvey after the invisible rabbit in that Jimmy Stewart movie. Took him a few weeks, but he came around."

"You have a cat and a dog? I thought they weren't supposed to get along." Jax looked puzzled as she pushed past Noah into the kitchen.

Noah chuckled. "That's just bad PR. They get along fine. Although, Harvey is twice the size of Sweet Pea, and Pea learned the first day not to give him any trouble. Sit down." He motioned to the kitchen table. "I've got something for you I forgot to bring over this morning."

He grabbed a plastic bag from the counter and emptied it onto the table. Three black flip phones fell out. "I think we need to start using these."

Lincoln reached for the nearest phone. He flipped it open and closed, turned it over, and set it back down. It represented everything wrong with this case. The running. The hiding. The lying. "So it's come to this. Burner phones. Have we turned into the criminals now?"

Jax reached over and placed her hand on top of his. "We have two choices. We can take you back to the area around the park, put you in a different motel, and tell the authorities you were still suffering from a concussion. I'll disappear and you won't know where I am. Or we can try to solve this case once and for all. Put Ponytail and Avendondo away for good. What we can't do is put Noah and Laurel in danger."

Noah held the plastic bag in one hand but didn't pick up a phone. "Laurel's in Austin for a couple of days taking the exam for her broker's license, and I can take care of myself. But you need to decide what you want to do."

Noah certainly looked like a guy who could take care of himself, and Lincoln knew Laurel wasn't exactly a fragile flower. She'd left cryptic clues for him and Noah to follow when a serial killer kidnapped her.

The one stupid call he'd made to Noah from the gas station bathroom concerned him, but what else could he have done? They couldn't hide in there forever.

The only thing he had to worry about now was his own moral code. "I've worked this case for the last four years. Forty-eight more hours won't matter. Then, whether we catch the guy or not, I've got to take this to The Bureau."

Jax glanced down and away. She wouldn't run for forty-seven of those hours. After that, he wasn't sure.

"Then let's get started." Noah pulled one of the burner phones closer and opened it. "I'll call Conner and see if we can find Ponytail's real name."

The hand Jax had placed on top of Lincoln's turned to ice. She looked like she might throw up any second. "Are you okay? You said you wanted to put these guys away."

"Yes. No. I don't know. I want them gone, but. . . . I've done all right the last four years. Learned how to take care of myself. Not depend on anyone. Faced some dangerous situations on my own. It's the only way I know how to live now. I'm not sure I can learn how to do it any other way. Now you want me to trust you, and then you bring in Noah, and he wants to add a guy I've never met named Earl, who isn't even a cop, plus his ex-partner, who's in the FBI. And I don't trust the FBI from here to that door. It's a lot to accept on faith."

Lincoln squeezed her hand. "I met Earl once last Christmas. He and Noah and another detective have a band called The Singing Detectives, or something like that. They play at the children's hospital on weekends and holidays. Noah invited me to come hear them last year. Earl seemed like a stand-up guy. I know Conner better. I've worked a case with him. He's as straight arrow a guy as I've ever come across."

Noah set the phone down. "I trust both those guys with my life. And have on several occasions. I won't tell Earl any more than I have to, and he'll go along because *he* trusts *me*. I'll try that with Conner, but it won't work. He'll see through me like a sheet of glass. Not even the frosted kind."

Lincoln faced her. "Say the word, and I'll drive you to Dallas or New Orleans or wherever you say, drop you at the bus station, and you take out any direction you want, but I've got to warn you . . . someday, somewhere, someone is going to catch up with you and it won't be pretty. Now, do you want

Noah to go ahead or not?"

Jax sucked in a deep breath, held it, and let it out in one big *whoosh*. "Do it."

CHAPTER
SEVENTEEN

Jax's breath came in quick gasps. It was possible she had just signed her own death warrant. No, Lincoln was right. He'd found her. Someone else would, too.

That didn't make her decision any easier to accept.

Noah picked up the flimsy flip phone and dialed. He put it on speaker so they all could hear. "Hey partner. How ya doing?"

"That's Agent Partner to you. Did you get a new phone, or did you go to Austin with Laurel to distract her so she won't pass her big test and make more money than you?" Conner's voice sounded tinny through the cheap phone.

"I'll have you know, I'd be thrilled if she made more money than me. I might even break down and ask her to marry me, but no, this is a temporary loaner."

"That's funny. I've heard of loaner cars, but never a loaner phone."

"If you're through razzing me, I'd like to ask a favor."

"On a loaner phone on your day off."

Noah glanced Jax's direction as if to say, *See? I warned you.*

"I realize you're only a Probationary Agent, but do you have access to the record of a raid," he glanced at Lincoln who mouthed *February*, "two years ago this February at a bar named . . ."

Jax grabbed a notepad and scribbled on it.

". . . *The Rusty Nail*, in Philly? You guys went in after a mob meeting and took a bunch of prints. I'm only interested in one person. He's a tall guy, bigger than me, brown hair worn in a ponytail, green eyes, a couple of tattoos, one on his neck and one on his wrist. Left-handed. Can you get me his name?"

"I guess you want me to call you back on your loaner phone?"

"If you don't mind."

Jax's leg jiggled under the table. She couldn't sit still. She got up and prowled the kitchen. It was what she considered *bachelor clean*. A couple of dirty dishes in the sink. Dregs of coffee in the coffeepot. A few crumbs next to the toaster.

A calendar on the wall featured a photo of two smiling girls holding Easter baskets. One was missing a front tooth. Must be the two nieces he'd mentioned. She peered closer and saw dates circled for *dentist* and *haircut* and *vet*.

That didn't mean anything. Even traitors had to get their

teeth cleaned and their hair cut. A bad guy could still love his relatives.

When the phone rang ten minutes later, they all jumped.

Noah set the cell in the middle of the table and punched the speaker button.

"You there, partner?" Conner's voice came through still tinny but barely above a whisper. "Tell me you're not stupid enough to get involved with that case."

"What do you mean?" Noah's innocent act didn't fool anyone, least of all Conner.

"I may still be in Virginia, but I know what's going on in Houston. I talk to my wife every day. That woman's photo is all over the news. You're going to get yourself killed. And that's after you get fired."

Jax couldn't stand it. She leaned over the phone. "I know you don't know me, but I swear to you I didn't do it. I saw that man with the ponytail shoot the senator and I ran. I've been running every day since. Without Lincoln and Noah's help, I'll be running for the rest of my life."

"Lincoln's there, too? I'm surprised he fell for it, but at least Noah has some backup. The guy's name is Dominic Rossini, AKA Nick Ross, and probably a bunch of other aliases also. He's a cleanup man for Benedetto Avendondo, but you already knew that. Not a regular member of the Family like a made man. More like the second cousin you give all the dirty work."

For years, Jax had longed to know his name. Now she did, and it didn't make her feel any better.

"The guy's bad news. He's suspected in a dozen murders and plenty of rough stuff. Jacqueline, if you're there, turn yourself in. Let the Feds handle this. We'll keep you safe."

She leaned over the phone again. "I promised Noah and Lincoln I'd do that if they haven't found him in forty-eight hours. But give us a chance first, please."

"Partner, I'll hold you to that. I expect to hear from you in forty-eight hours. On the dot. Meanwhile, I'll send you his photo. On your *loaner* phone."

NICK PULLED OFF the road near a small park. He stumbled out of the car and started down the jogging path at a fast walk, trying to shake off the anger that consumed him. A blinding rage against Mr. Avendondo was all he could think about.

He jammed his hands into his pockets to keep from hitting something—anything. A fluffy, black-and-white dog on a leash yipped at him. For a moment, he pictured kicking a soccer ball.

How dare the man cut off his mother's pension? And without even warning him.

If the boss was dissatisfied with his work, have the balls to tell him to his face. Not penalize his mother. His father had earned that pension. Had given his life protecting Mr. A when a rival Family tried to take over his territory.

Her pension shouldn't have anything to do with his own

performance.

Having the Duncan woman on the loose hadn't harmed his boss in the least. In fact, the longer she was on the run, the guiltier she looked.

Missing her at that bar hadn't been his fault. He'd been tasked with checking the right side of the room. Big Tommy's job was to check the left. That was the only thing that saved him because Mr. A wouldn't believe she wasn't there to kill him.

And Big Tommy had paid the price.

But apparently, so had his mother.

If he'd been in charge of the left side of the room, would he have recognized her? Sitting in the dark, sipping her beer. He liked to think so, but who knows. She slipped away before he had time to find out.

It wouldn't happen again. He never passed a person, male or female, without checking their face.

Now he was so close he could taste it. The FBI agent had to go, but that was just business. He'd seen his face. She was a different story. It was personal with her. She'd caused him too much grief.

He didn't plan to make it easy for her.

He circled the park once and climbed back in the car, his shirt soaked with sweat. The anger that had started to cool flared up again. He struck at the steering wheel with the heel of his hand, missed, and hit the horn. A mother in a minivan turned to look at him.

He needed to calm down. Hotheads made mistakes.

The phone in his back pocket vibrated. About time. The son-of-a-bitch was an hour late. He hit *accept* and waited.

"I've got the address," sputtered the nervous voice on the other end.

LINCOLN FOLLOWED JAX outside where she stood on the back porch. "Noah talked to Earl. It'll take him an hour or so to gather all the information we asked for. The guy didn't seem to question why Noah wanted to keep it confidential."

"That's good." Jax seemed distracted as she gazed around the yard. If she was planning to change her mind, it was too late. The wheels were already in motion. He needed to keep a close eye on her.

"I guess we're doing this," she said.

"I guess so." She didn't seem to realize running a covert operation outside The Bureau would impact his life as much as hers. Maybe not if she ended up dead.

"You promise it'll be okay?"

He wanted to say yes, but he couldn't lie to her. "I think so. I hope so. All I can promise is that Noah, Earl, and Conner are upstanding people. They won't rat you out to the mob. But we don't know where this guy is getting his information. We have to stay on our toes. You ready to come back inside?"

"I'd like to stay out here while we wait. If that's okay. There's every chance I could be in jail for the rest of my life by this weekend. I saw a flat of pansies over there. Maybe I could plant them for Noah. Make up for all his help."

"Do you know how to do that?"

"How hard can it be? You dig a hole and put them in."

He glanced up. Soft, white clouds floated in a sky so blue, the color defied description. No wonder she wanted to stay outside as long as possible. "Well, those are petunias, not pansies, so I had to ask. Why don't I help you? My mother grows the best tomatoes in Southeast Alabama, and that makes me something of an expert in hole digging."

He grabbed the petunias and was wrist deep in dirt within five minutes. The smell of clean soil and fresh plants took him home.

He felt more alive, more useful than he had in months.

CHAPTER
EIGHTEEN

Lincoln pressed the soil around the last petunia and brushed the dirt off his hands. He surveyed the flower bed with satisfaction. Nothing like working in the ground to bring you down to earth. "I'll mix up a batch of root stimulator to pour over these and they should do well. This spot will get just the right amount of sun."

Jax stood and admired their work. "Thanks for helping me. I would have clumped them too close together."

"No. They'll grow and spread. If he keeps them watered."

He wandered toward the garage to see what Noah had available while Jax turned on the hose to wash her hands.

Noah stepped outside with a pleased grin. "Earl sent me the first batch of documents. He'll send more shortly, but we can start with these."

Lincoln stopped at the garage door and spun around to face him. "That's great. Let us wash up and we'll be right there."

"I got a call from Laurel, also. She passed her exam. She's now a full-fledged Real Estate Broker. Her boss has promised to add her name to the business and let her start buying him out a little at a time."

"Wonderful." Jax's smile was almost as large as Noah's. "Those tests are hard work. Lots of studying. I know you're proud of her."

"I am. It hasn't been that long since her husband dumped her and left her completely broke. She pulled herself together, found a job, and worked her way up."

Lincoln joined the smile fest. "I knew she was a tough lady, but super smart, too."

Noah's grin turned sheepish. "The thing is, I'd sure like to go to Austin and take her out to dinner tonight. Come back in the morning. Do you think you guys could go over Earl's list by yourselves?"

"After all you've done for us? This is not your responsibility. You go to Austin. Tell Laurel how proud we are of her. Jax and I will go over the list. See what we can figure out."

"There's one little problem—Sweet Pea. My neighbor, Mrs. Powel, usually takes care of her if I go out of town, but she's in Portland visiting her sister. Do you think you could take her with you back to Laurel's townhouse?"

Jax's eyes got big, and Lincoln remembered she wasn't used to pets. She cleared her throat twice before managing an answer. "Sure, we'll take care of her. You go have fun on your day off."

Lincoln had a brother and a sister. He'd grown up in a house full of dogs, cats, hamsters, and birds. His sister once had a bunny and his brother a boa constrictor. He'd begged for a pet bat, but his mother put her foot down on that one. "What about Harvey? You want us to take the cat, too?"

"Nah. You'd never find him. I don't even know where he hides. I'll leave out some food and water, and he'll be fine for one night."

Noah mumbled feeding instructions to Jax, who looked like she'd been entrusted with a test tube of TNT, grabbed a duffel bag, and was gone so fast, Lincoln still had dirt under his fingernails.

THE GPS ON Nick's phone gave him easy-to-follow directions. He tucked his ponytail under a baseball cap he'd found on the front seat and cruised by the cop's house.

One story. No car in the drive. Quiet neighborhood.

He thought about that. It could mean a gunshot would be heard, or that everyone was at work or inside their house with the TV blaring. A pillow should muffle the shot enough to allay suspicion.

According to his source, the guy wasn't married. One less body to worry about.

He circled the block once more. A tree caused the driveway of the house next to the cop's to curve slightly. He pulled in past the bend, where his car was less noticeable, and walked across to the cop's front door, the gun in his hand hidden under a clipboard he'd bought at an office supply store.

With any luck, he'd be gone before the neighbors noticed a strange car in their drive.

He kept the gun hidden and tried the knob. Locked. Lifting the knob, he hit the door with his hip.

Nothing.

He tried again, adding the weight of his shoulder. The lock held, but the doorframe splintered. One more shove and he was inside.

Silence. The front part of the house was dark, and no sound came from the other rooms where lights were on. He hugged the wall and walked on cat's feet through the formal living room into the den. A large-screen TV was mounted on one wall, facing a comfy-looking sofa. A pair of women's sandals peeked out from under the coffee table.

Three bedrooms—one made into an office/workout room and one an unused guest room—all empty. He checked under the beds and in the closets to be sure.

A turquoise ring sat on a nightstand. His mother had loved turquoise ever since their drive through the desert to California, stopping at tourist-trap trading posts along the way.

A woman lived here. Who was it? Not the elusive Miss

Duncan. Too many clothes and bath products to be a visitor.

That made four people he had to watch out for—the cop, his girlfriend, the Fed, and Jacqueline Duncan. As long as he knew what he was dealing with, he could handle it.

He moved on to the last room in the house.

The kitchen had been used recently. Ice cubes melted in the sink.

Wherever they were, they'd be back soon. He'd wait next door. Although, that hadn't worked out well for the old couple on Lake Conroe.

JAX HELD SWEET Pea in her lap while Lincoln drove. The dog didn't look any happier about it than she did. It wasn't that she didn't like the dog, just that it made her uncomfortable.

If she held it too tight, she might break its tiny bones. If she held it too loose, it tried to wiggle away. Then it headed straight for Lincoln's lap. While he was driving.

They were a block from Laurel's townhouse when Jax spotted a Kroger. "We don't have much to eat at the house. Half a loaf of bread and some lunchmeat. I sure would love a steak."

Lincoln parked near the front. She could see the wheels turning in his mind. Should he go in and leave her with the dog, let her go in while he waited, or take the dog in with them?

This was a turning point because she was damn tired of

not being trusted.

Lincoln handed her three twenties. "We need coffee and something for breakfast, too. Maybe a bottle of wine. I shouldn't drink while on duty, but I shouldn't hide out with a suspect, either."

"How about with a witness?"

"Better, but not by a lot."

She was used to shopping on a budget, adding prices as she went so as not to go over her limited funds. She had a bottle of red wine—not great but decent—two baking potatoes, and salad. Now for the meat.

She picked up two cheap steaks, studied them, and put them back. Lincoln didn't look like the type to scrimp on food quality.

When she returned to the car, Lincoln was petting Sweet Pea and talking to her. A big man cuddling a dog the size of a can of Spam. Her only experience with men who had dogs was farm dogs that did a job and nothing else, or guard dogs that could tear your arm off.

This was new. Plus, he could cook . . . at least a little.

Add Noah, with his obvious love for his late wife and genuine feelings for his girlfriend, tending to his house and dog, and planting flowers. Perhaps cops and their ilk weren't all bad.

Okay, she was willing to trust Lincoln and Noah and maybe even their friends Earl and Conner.

That didn't mean *somebody* up the chain of command

wasn't spilling secrets.

Noah understood this, but Lincoln wasn't quite ready to admit it . . . yet.

NICK HAD PLACED his car in the empty garage, then disconnected the automatic door opener so the homeowner—whoever she was—wouldn't be able to surprise him.

He knew it was a woman, and an elderly one, because he had searched the house. Only women's clothes and orthopedic shoes. Add to that a somewhat *old lady* smell of camphor and menthol, and he could almost picture her. She reminded him of his mother, only a few years older.

He sure hoped he didn't have to kill her.

The one good point was the treasure trove of pain medication. Old bottles with two or three pills left. New bottles, almost full, of a different brand.

His favorite was the half bottle of cough medicine. The good kind . . . with codeine.

He took a swig to settle his nerves. He wasn't big on pills himself. They messed with your mind just when you needed to be sharp. But there were occasions when they could be a godsend. Any he didn't want would be easy to sell and could help with Ma's expenses.

He was tired of sitting in the dark. The kitchen clock read 10:07. If the old lady wasn't home by now, she wouldn't be here tonight. He'd skipped dinner when he learned the cop's address, so he checked the fridge and pulled out the ingredients for an omelet.

He'd barely finished when the work phone in his pocket vibrated. The caller ID read *Blocked Number*, but so did most of his business calls. That didn't mean he didn't have a good idea who it was.

He pushed back the plate of what was easily the best meal he'd had since he came to Texas and answered his phone. "Hello."

"The boss wants to see you." The voice had a heavy New Jersey accent, and Nick recognized it immediately. Mr. A's right-hand man.

"And I want to see him, but I have eyes on the house of the guy who's helping my targets." He didn't know if he'd helped the two fugitives or not, but they'd called him so that was the best place to start.

"Are they in there?"

"Not right now. But somebody has to come home sometime." Shit. That wasn't the best thing to say.

"Then maybe they'll be there when you get back. If you go back. There's a flight out at midnight and a ticket waiting for you at the counter. I'll text you the information. Our friend will be awake, waiting for you."

With that, the voice was gone, replaced by the hum of an empty line.

According to Nick's phone, the call had lasted thirty-seven

seconds. His gut told him those few seconds would impact the rest of his life.

JAX HAD OFFERED to cook and Lincoln agreed. That way, he could start going over the list Earl had sent of cars rented at the Albuquerque Airport on the morning Ponytail—he needed to start calling the guy by his real name, Dominic—came looking for Jax.

Jax put the potatoes in the oven to bake and left the steaks to marinate, then headed up the stairs to take a shower. The atmosphere between them had improved a thousand percent since he made the decision to trust her.

He still wasn't sure what part she played, but watching her every move exhausted both of them. If she wanted to run, she'd do it when he wasn't looking and he'd never be able to stop her.

Every minute she chose to stay put her farther on the right side of this case.

He was so deep into his research, he didn't hear her come down. A light touch on his shoulder, followed immediately by the combined aromas of grilled steak and shampoo, yanked his attention away from Lauren's computer.

"Dinner's ready. Can you take a break now?"

"Yeah, I think I've got it." He tapped a postage stamp-size photo on a driver's license. "Do you think that's him?"

Jax squinted and put on her glasses. "Can you make it any

bigger?"

"I tried. That makes it blurrier." He handed her a magnifying glass he'd found in the desk drawer. "See if this helps."

She leaned across his shoulder, and the smell of shampoo was all he could concentrate on.

"There's definitely something on the side of his neck that might be a tattoo. I can't tell if his hair's in a ponytail, but from the way it's pulled back, it sure looks like it is. It's the eyes, though. I'd swear to it. They're the same ones I see in my nightmares."

She'd never mentioned nightmares, but he wasn't surprised. He'd have nightmares, too, if someone that size grabbed him with a bloody hand and wouldn't let go. "This shows his eyes as green and his height as six feet four. I think it's our guy. His name is listed as Brandon Littlefield, at an address in Roseville. That's right outside of Sacramento."

"I know where Roseville is. I lived in Sacramento. Remember? Can we get someone to check it out?" Excitement tinged her voice.

"I thought you said it was too dangerous to contact anyone. Have you changed your mind?"

She deflated before his eyes. "I know. I know. And it is. But what can we do? We know his real name, his alias, and where he lives. Are we supposed to sit here and wait for him to come kill us?"

"First of all, we don't know where he lives. I doubt that

address is anything besides an empty lot or an office building. And if he has that alias, he has others. We'll get Earl to check on it, but we'll have to wait until tomorrow. According to Noah, Earl only works till three."

Still, he had to admit, they were making progress and it felt good.

CHAPTER NINETEEN

The sky was still dark, but a thin line of pink showed on the eastern horizon as Nick approached the Avendondo compound. Eight acres facing the sea with two swimming pools, a tennis court, and guesthouses for whichever of his children were in his good graces. The five-car garage sported upstairs living quarters so various maids and servants would always be close at hand.

Because, God knows, you might want something in the middle of the night, and you wouldn't want to have to get it yourself.

Nick shook his head, trying for an attitude adjustment that didn't come. He glided to a stop in front of a speaker and announced himself. No voice answered, but the mechanical gate swung open.

An ornate, bulletproof, glass door opened as if by magic as he climbed the curved brick stairs. A man in a black suit and tie stood inside, neither smiling nor not smiling. He gave a slight nod as Nick approached.

A butler? The late Mrs. Avendondo number three was well known for her admiration of all things English royalty and her desire—something she never accomplished—to fit into the top reaches of society.

But a butler was stretching things a bit.

"Good morning, sir. If you'll wait here, I'll ask if Mr. Avendondo is able to see you now." The guy may have been dressed as a butler, but the bulge under his arm told Nick he was carrying. Not that he'd have expected anything less.

Nick paced, willing the butler to hurry. Another flight left for Houston at eleven thirty. If he changed his ticket, he could visit his mother for almost an hour.

Five minutes later, alone but certainly not unwatched, Nick heard the echo of footsteps as the butler returned. "This way, please, sir. Mr. Avendondo is ready for you."

Nick attempted a deep breath. *Ready for me? What the hell does that mean?*

He should have called Ma from the car and warned her where he was headed. That way, if he disappeared, someone would know where to start searching.

No, he couldn't do that to his mother. If the boss wanted him gone, nothing his mother or anyone else did could stop him, and no amount of searching would produce his body.

The trick was to remember everything his father taught him. Be respectful but stand your ground. Show no fear.

Easy to say but tough to manage. Especially with Avendondo's notorious mood swings. What were the chances the guy had mellowed with age?

Nick followed the butler across the marble entry—his tennis shoes squeaking with every step—up a flight of stairs, down a thickly carpeted hall, to a door indistinguishable from a dozen others.

The butler tapped lightly, opened the door, and took one step inside. "Mr. Rossini to see you, sir."

Nick longed to roll his eyes. The guy was a New Jersey hood who'd made good. Not the Duke of Dirty Tricks.

"Dominic, my boy. It's been too long." An old man wearing a brocade dressing gown leaned forward in his lounge chair, his arms open wide as if in welcome. Nick wasn't fooled.

And whose fault is that, you old bastard?

Nick crossed the room, a fake smile plastered on his face. "Mr. Avendondo. You're looking well."

His first lie of the morning. No doubt there'd be more to follow.

The boss's hair had been white for years. Now it was thin and limp, with patches of scalp showing through. His face had shrunk almost beyond recognition, with hollow cheeks and prominent bones.

Maybe the rumors were correct. The old man looked like death warmed over and served with a side of fries. If so, he needed to hurry and get his mother's pension restored before the guy croaked.

"Come closer, my boy. You look more like your dad every day."

That might actually be true. It had been four years since he'd seen the picture of his father hanging in his mother's hallway, but the face he remembered now stared back at him from his mirror every morning.

"I loved your father like the son I never had."

What the fuck? The boss had two sons. Were they out of the loop now?

Avendondo gave a phlegmy cough. "He saved my life. I remember it like it was yesterday. The Koons Family came after me at my place in Boca Raton. Your father shoved me inside the car and drove like a madman to get me home, where I'd be safe. It wasn't until he got out to open my door that I realized he was shot. To this day, I regret I couldn't let your mother bury him. I don't forget loyalty like that."

Apparently you do, you son-of-a-bitch.

This was the tricky part, but he had to do it. Later today or tomorrow, he might need to go up against a cop, a Fed, and a woman who had possibly been trained by the Asian mob. If he died, what would happen to his mother?

Nick moved forward to stand on an expensive-looking, oriental rug. Mr. A could certainly afford to replace it if his blood ruined the weave, but there was a chance his late wife had bought the rug and it aroused sentimental feelings.

Or the old coot was too cheap to risk it.

"I know, sir. You're well known for your loyalty." *The fact that you don't have any.* "That's why I was so surprised to learn my mother's pension had been cut off."

The two men standing silently in opposite corners of the room placed their hands on the butt of the weapon on their hips.

He was unarmed. He'd left his weapons in his car parked at the Houston airport. He couldn't smuggle them onto the plane or into this house. If Avendondo wanted him dead, he had no protection.

Was he about to join his father somewhere deep in the Atlantic Ocean, his feet encased in cement so that no trace of him remained?

Avendondo waved a hand, and the men relaxed. "Was it? I didn't realize. Things got so confusing after the debacle in Philly. I can't think straight with so many worries hanging over my head."

"I totally understand, sir. I had the Duncan woman tracked to a house in Houston when I had to stop and wire my mother some money for groceries. It's difficult to concentrate on two things at once."

Eyes that had been a cold, watery blue seconds before suddenly turned to fire. Maybe the old guy wasn't as sick as he'd thought.

Five seconds passed. Ten. Nick straightened his back and didn't falter. *Don't show any weakness. Don't show any weakness.*

A barrel laugh escaped Avendondo's parched lips and he slapped his knee. "You're right, my boy. Loyalty isn't to be disputed." He motioned to the man on his right, the smaller one in the gray suit. "Silvio, go downstairs and call my accountant. Make sure Mrs. Rossini's pension is restored starting today. Family is everything, my boy. I should know. I've outlived three wives."

Word on the street said he'd killed the first one himself when she wouldn't give him a divorce. The second might be dead to him, but she was alive somewhere in Europe with instructions never to set foot in this country again.

Only the last one had died a natural death. Maybe.

"And you." He pointed to Nick. "It's a shame you can't stay for breakfast. Gena will be so disappointed. She was hoping to see you again. You two were such good friends in school."

His daughter? They were never friends. For laughs, or to prove she was her father's daughter, she had intentionally dumped Kool Aid in his lap in fifth grade, then told everyone he wet his pants. He only attended her birthday parties because his mother made him. What was this, the carrot and the stick? Screw up again and join his father in a watery grave. Dispose of the problem and win the prize, Mr. A's demanding daughter, until he disappointed her, which was likely to happen all too soon.

The boss must be desperate to get Gena married off before he died if he'd reached down the list to him.

Avendondo leaned back in his chair and pointed to the

door. "Now get back to Houston and finish the job. I'll expect to hear good news since your mind is clear and you can concentrate."

"How do you want it handled, sir? Leave the bodies where they fall or make them disappear?"

Avendondo's hand fluttered as if shooing away a fly. "At one time it mattered. Not anymore. Not after you shot the wrong FBI agent. The new one. The one I expressly told you not to harm."

What the hell? He'd said take out the old one. The guy he shot had to be in his fifties. Unless he meant old as in had been on the case for a long time. Shit. The boss was losing it. He couldn't give clear instructions. How much trouble was he in for that error?

Avendondo sank back into his chair. "What's done is done. As long as no one is left who can tie anything to me, I'm satisfied. This is your area of expertise. You handle it however you want."

Nick held back the sigh of relief itching to escape. *Show no weakness.*

He started for the door when Avendondo stopped him. "When I say go back to Houston, I mean it. Do not take any detours. Do not stop to visit friends. Do not change your ticket. Your return flight leaves in one hour and forty-five minutes. If you hurry, you can make it. Do not, under any circumstances, miss that flight."

Nick spun around. He ran for the door and down the

stairs. He threw himself into the car and slammed it into gear. Luckily, the gate was opening as he tore away, missing the wrought iron by inches.

He took time to make one call as he raced through the countryside. Thank goodness he'd paid the guy the extra hundred. Turned out he still needed him. When the familiar voice answered, he shouted instructions as he sped around slow-moving traffic. "The cop you found for me. You told me his wife was dead, yet some woman is living with him. Find out who she is and everything about her. If he's not home, maybe they've gone to her place. I'll call you as soon as my plane lands."

CHAPTER TWENTY

Lincoln propped his bare feet on the coffee table and flipped through the TV channels. Sweet Pea snuggled deeper into his lap.

This was the most relaxed he'd felt since he could remember. Long before this ridiculous chase across Texas started. His last girlfriend had accused him of having a stick up his ass. He wasn't surprised. He'd been hearing similar versions of that song since middle school.

The same traits that made him the darling of the debate club drove those around him crazy. He could never figure out what was wrong with wanting things done correctly.

He'd longed to join the FBI since he was a kid. While other boys were playing at Teenage Ninja Turtles or superheroes, he was reading about Elliot Ness and Donnie Brasco.

He'd never broken a rule in his life—until he met Jax Duncan.

No, that wasn't true. There was that six-week period when *The Tornado* blew into his life and he'd briefly lost his mind. That only made him double down on the rule-following obsession.

Now suddenly, following rules felt like a prison sentence and breaking them like a weight had been lifted off his shoulders. Like, for once, he didn't have to prove anything. Like he'd already failed, so he might as well go for it.

Sweet Pea lifted her head as Jax wandered through the room, a severe case of bedhead spoiling the effect of the clean clothes she wore. A maroon blouse set off her fair complexion.

"You look nice. Is that something new?" He'd searched her backpack when they first got into his car at the diner. She had one pair of jeans, two sets of underwear, a pair of socks, and three black T-shirts. Other than that, the only thing he'd found was a toothbrush and a photo of two young girls, approximately fourteen and sixteen years of age—the younger obviously Jax and the other most likely her sister, Krista. The photo also had a ragged tear down one side, leaving only a woman's hand visible on Jax's shoulder.

He recognized the background as Gavin Duncan's pool and patio.

"My clothes are all dirty. These are probably Laurel's. I don't think she wants them. They were in the back of a closet, and this shirt had a hole under the sleeve." She lifted her arm and pointed to a spot. "I sewed it up, but Lord knows I've worn worse."

"There's coffee ready in the kitchen if you want some. I've already had two cups." His clothes were dirty, too. There was a washer and dryer in the laundry room. Maybe they should do a load.

If he and Jax had been on the run long enough to go through all their clothes, it was time to wrap up this case. They had thirty-six hours before Conner's deadline, but he didn't want to wait that long.

Jax must not have wanted to wait, either. She came back with a mug of coffee and settled onto the sofa next to him. "I turned the oven on to preheat. When I finish my coffee, I'll put the sweet rolls in to bake. Have you called Earl yet to see what he can find out about Rossini and his Littlefield alias?"

"The guy doesn't get in till ten. I didn't want to take a chance on leaving a message. Right now, I'm searching for the weather. I think it's supposed to rain this afternoon."

He caught the tail end of the forecast, which showed a line of red moving in from the north. He switched channels to see if he could get more information and hit on a lifelike drawing of Jax, thinner, with short, blonde hair and glasses.

She sat up, spilling her coffee. "Shit! I guess Dwayne got back from Mexico and went to the police when he discovered I didn't work at Denny's. Now I won't be able to go out at all. I hope he had to explain how he knew me to his wife."

Sweet Pea gave a start at the commotion. Lincoln stroked

her head while he waited. They didn't show his photo or mention his name. He wasn't sure if that meant his superiors were giving him a chance to close this case or were expecting him to self-destruct and finish off what was left of his career.

He slipped a hand under Sweet Pea's tummy and sat her on the floor. "I'm going to take the dog outside to do her business before the rain starts. When I get back, I'll try Earl. See if he's in yet. I don't know what he can find out—I'm sure the address is a fake—but we need any information we can get. We've got to do something besides sit here and wait for Rossini to try to kill us again."

Noah got away from Austin later than he planned. He and Laurel had celebrated her success late into the night and then again in the morning, barely making the eleven a.m. checkout time.

He drove most of the way home with his left hand, clasping Laurel's with his right. They left the radio off and talked for two hours straight.

They discussed the meal they'd shared the night before and if the waiter had been peeking down her dress or filling her water glass.

She explained one of the questions on the exam she was sure she'd missed.

He listened without comment while she debated whether

to sell her townhome or rent it.

He asked her to remind him to get a haircut before he went back to work.

They laughed about the dismal view from their room.

She wondered if Harvey had missed her. He lied and said the cat hadn't noticed she was gone.

They were approaching home when he brought up Jax's case and his worries that he and Lincoln wouldn't be able to prove her guilt or innocence, one way or the other.

"You've been around her for a couple of days. What do you think? Did she do it?"

Noah let that roll around in his head for a minute. Had he reached a decision yet? "I think she got caught up in something she wasn't expecting and didn't know how to handle it. Unfortunately, every move she's made since makes her look guilty. Even if we catch the guy who's been chasing them, unless he's willing to turn, she's not out of trouble."

Laurel patted his hand. "Then you need to make sure you take him alive."

Twenty minutes later, under heavy, gray skies, they pulled into their driveway. He unloaded their bags while she unlocked the back door.

The house felt wrong. Too quiet without Sweet Pea running to greet him. He needed to head over to Laurel's townhouse, see what Lincoln had learned, and pick up his dog.

He rolled Laurel's bag through the kitchen and into the bedroom, where he found her kneeling on the floor beside the bed. "What's wrong?"

"I can't find my turquoise ring. My dad gave it to me and I wanted to wear it during my exam for good luck, but I forgot to pack it. I'm sure I left it on my nightstand but I don't see it. Maybe it rolled under the bed. Can you look on that side?"

Noah went around to his side, pulled out his phone, turned on the flashlight, and stopped. "Have you already searched over here? The spread is folded back."

"No. I came straight to my side. It shouldn't be over there unless it rolled."

Noah stretched out flat on the floor and shone his light under the bed, but found nothing except dust bunnies and one missing sock. "It's not here. Are you sure you didn't pack it?"

"I'll go through my suitcase again, but I don't remember putting it in. I took it off the night before I left and set it right here, meaning to get it in the morning. Then we . . . ran a little late and I forgot it."

Noah smiled. They had been later getting out of bed than intended that morning. He pushed up off the floor. "Well, the good news is you didn't need it for luck. You aced that test on your own merits. It'll turn up somewhere in this house. Do you mind if I run over to your townhouse and check with Lincoln to see if he's made any progress on the Duncan case? I'm anxious to finish things and have them out of your house."

"I don't mind them using my place. They're welcome to stay as long as necessary. I just don't want you to get in trouble if something goes wrong."

Would he get in trouble? Probably. But he had before and likely would again. Although, harboring a fugitive was right up there on the department's list of no-nos.

"You want me to come with you? I wouldn't mind meeting the famous Jacqueline Duncan or seeing Lincoln. He's one of my favorite people."

"Five minutes ago, you were telling me you couldn't wait to get home, unpack, take a long soak in the tub, play with your cat, and chill for the rest of the day. Why don't I go alone this time and save your visit until things are settled?"

The look on her face said he'd made the right decision.

THE KITCHEN CHAIR squeaked as Lincoln pushed back from the table and carried his plate to the sink. He'd learned a few things from his mother.

Jax stopped him as he turned on the water. "Don't worry about that. I'll clean up the kitchen and put in the wash. You call Earl again. I'm getting a funny feeling in the pit of my stomach. The one I always get when it's time to run. We're sitting ducks here, waiting for something to happen."

He had to agree with her on that. His flight instincts might not be as fine-tuned as hers, but the longer they waited, the more likely Rossini would find them.

He started for the den when Jax stopped him. "There's one thing I've been wondering about." She swung around, leaning her back against the sink, a dish towel in one hand.

Only one thing? He had a laundry list of things he wondered about. "What is it?"

"You told Noah how you found me the other times. None of them were a surprise. I kind of knew what went wrong. But who tipped you off in West Monroe? I was extra careful and didn't make any mistakes I knew of. And I never had that *ants crawling in my stomach* feeling like the other times you were onto me."

"The librarian lady, Mrs. Reynolds."

"What?" Jax's eyes doubled in size, and tears formed at the edges. "I thought she was my friend. I can't believe she double-crossed me. I never had a clue."

"She didn't turn you in. Not intentionally. There's some kind of newsletter for small-town libraries so they can help each other out. They run a contest every year. Nominating someone from the community who volunteers their time. The winner gets a certificate, and the sponsoring library gets three hundred dollars for books. She sent in your name and a photo of you teaching kids how to use the computer."

"I didn't know anything about it. I would have stopped her. So what happened? How'd you figure it out?"

"It wasn't me. A guy showed up from Dallas. Stu, the one who got killed in your trailer." Damn, he shouldn't have said that. He could see how much it upset her. Didn't make him too happy, either. "He brought a message from the head of the Dallas office that you were in West Monroe, and we should pick you up immediately."

"How did he get a small-town library newsletter?"

"Seems the name you chose—"

"I got it off a tombstone in Tulsa. I was careful not to use it in the same state. I learned that trick after the disaster with the forger in Albuquerque. Find someone close to your age who died as a baby or toddler. I sent off for the birth certificate and *presto*, I'm legal."

"Well, the name you chose was a bit unusual. Not too many Sandy Crawford Hoffbergs running around. Turns out, Sandy's mother is the librarian in charge of putting the newsletter together. She mentioned the coincidence to her father who, being a retired sheriff's deputy, knew about people taking names off tombstones and thought it was suspicious. He talked his old partner in Dallas into using the face-recognition software on the photo and your name popped up. My old boss, Darrell Byrne, works in Dallas and is still listed as officer-in-charge of that case. He's out with heart problems, so he sent Stu to Houston to get me and bring you in."

"Okay, so Hazel Reynolds didn't turn me in. I guess that makes me feel better. I hate it for Mrs. Hoffberg. I bet it was a shock to see her dead daughter's name turn up that way."

Jax always surprised him. He hadn't thought how hard it would be on Mrs. Hoffberg.

"Maybe I can call her later. After this is all over. Promise her I didn't do anything to dishonor her daughter's name. There is something else I'm curious about. How did my face end up on the local news in Houston?"

"A total screwup. My boss likes to leak selective things to the news media. Things that make the FBI look good. And nabbing you would not only make the FBI look stellar, it would make the Houston office into a star. Wouldn't hurt his promotion chances, either. Only problem was, the idiot newscaster pulled up your file and left it on his desk, and it got run *before* you were captured, not after."

Jax grabbed a dish rag and scrubbed a coffee cup hard enough that Lincoln worried she might break it. "*Soooo* sorry arresting me didn't go as predicted and messed up his plans for promotion. I'd really like to screw them up further and get myself out of this fix. You think Earl is in by now?"

"I'll see." He tried the number Noah had given him and Earl's familiar voice answered.

"Yo, Hoss. That you?"

Lincoln pictured the tall, skinny, black man hunched over his phone. It was hard to imagine how someone that frail could have such a powerful voice. A cross between Barry White and Martin Luther King.

"It's Lincoln Montgomery. Did Noah tell you I might call?" He flipped the phone on to speaker so Jax could hear.

"Sure he did. Only I didn't recognize this number."

"Were you able to find anything on the two names he gave you?"

"Some, but still working on a few things. Your Mr. Brandon Littlefield died twenty years ago, at the age of five. Yet, he amazingly has a California driver's license and a passport."

Lincoln glanced at Jax and nodded. She wasn't the only one to discover that method of creating a new identity.

Earl's voice filled the room. "The address is a fake, however. So is the company he supposedly works for."

Lincoln wasn't surprised. He figured that would be a dead end.

"Now for the other guy you asked about. Dominic Rossini, age twenty-nine, height six feet four, brown hair, and green eyes."

They already knew that much, but at least he was sure Earl had the right guy.

"He grew up in New Jersey. Father missing, but no record of his death. One brother and one sister—brother younger, sister older. He's listed as living with his mother in Jersey, but any record of him stops after high school. He doesn't work, or at least doesn't pay taxes. He has a Jersey driver's license but no record of owning a car."

"So he's a ghost?"

"I didn't say that. About the time he drops out of view, here comes a guy named Nick Ross. Same height, weight, etc. Photo looks the same. The birthdate is different by one year, one month, one day."

Jax squinched up her eyes in a puzzled look. "Isn't that kind of dumb and easy for someone like us to figure out?"

Lincoln scooted the phone an inch closer. "Maybe, but it's also easy for him to remember if a cop stops him and he gets nervous."

Earl gave a short laugh. "Changing your birthdate is essential on fake IDs, but you'd never believe how many mopes forget what they put or get tripped up when asked how old they are and what year they were born. Nick Ross has a California license. Looks like the same photo, but with another fake address. This one goes to a business that holds your mail for you or forwards it to a P.O. Box. An entrepreneur who figured out a way to help scumbags hide their real address. Say the word, and we'll get the Sacramento PD to bust the place and find out where he really lives."

They'd have to do that eventually, but for now, Sacramento was the one place they knew he wasn't. "Let's wait on that. We should go through the FBI, not HPD. I don't want to get Noah into trouble for helping me."

"Give me an hour. I might have something good for you. Then you can decide what to do."

Great, because what they had so far, while solid information, didn't help them find Rossini.

CHAPTER TWENTY-ONE

The sky was so dark, Nick needed to turn on his headlights. The breeze picked up, and the temperature dropped below what it had been when he left at midnight. He'd barely slammed the car door when the rain started.

Before leaving the lot, he called his contact. "You get that information for me?"

"Cop has a girlfriend named Laurel Bledsoe. Some of our mutual friends have done a bit of business with her ex-husband from time to time, but he's not in good standing at the moment so you don't have to worry about that. Since her divorce, she bought a townhouse—I'll text you the address—about a year ago. However, she's recently filed a change of address and has her bills sent to the cop's place. She works for a real estate agency. I'll text you that address, too. You need anything else?"

"Her cell phone number?" If worse came to worse, he could call and threaten her. Tracing her location through her cell was possible but required better contacts than he had available right now.

By now, the rain was coming down so hard he could barely hear. He covered one ear and waited.

"That'll be an extra fifty. I'll send it when I get it."

Fucking a-hole. Nickle-and-diming him to death. But what could he do? He needed the info. "I'll expect to hear from you sooner rather than later."

He flicked on the wipers before backing out. Low spots in the parking lot were already full of water and splashed when he drove through. He paid cash when he reached the attendant, not wanting a record even on his fake card.

Driving away from the airport, the rain came down in sheets. The car in front of him sent up a rooster tail of water, almost blinding him. A bolt of lightning hit the roadway, and he felt a tingle travel through his body.

He hated this damn state. The faster he could get away the better.

And to that end, what should he try first, the cop's place or the girlfriend's townhouse?

NOAH WAS AT the door when his cell rang. He considered

ignoring it until he saw the caller ID. His neighbor wouldn't phone him unless she had a problem. "Hi, Mrs. Powell. When did you get back? Your sister doing okay?"

"My sister's improving. She can manage alone now with one of her daughters stopping by every day. I got in about twenty minutes ago. I saw your truck in the driveway and thought you must be home. Can you come over for a minute? I have something I need you to look at."

Most likely a dripping faucet or broken chair. A spider in the kitchen she could handle herself. He didn't mind helping her—was happy to—but now wasn't a good time. "I was about to head out the door. Could I come over this evening?"

Mrs. Powell hesitated for a long minute, and something felt wrong in Noah's chest. She didn't ask for help unless she needed it. Finally, she answered, "Yes, that will be fine. I won't touch anything until you get here."

"Why don't I do it now?" He called to Laurel over his shoulder, "I'm going next door for a minute," then into the phone, "I'm halfway there already."

She met him at her back door. An egg carton sat on her counter, the lid open. "I felt tired and hungry when I got in, so I thought I'd fix myself some eggs and then lie down for a rest."

Okay, so what was the problem.

"I had six eggs when I left for my sister's. I know because I worried about them spoiling before I got back. Now there are only three."

Three missing eggs, that's why he came over? "Could you

have decided to eat something before you left?"

"I don't think so because I was in a hurry. And I would never have eaten three at a time. I couldn't possibly eat more than two."

He studied her thin frame. Imagining her eating three eggs at a time was tough, but maybe she broke one and forgot about it. He'd always marveled at how sharp she was, but she was in her eighties, after all, and worried about her sister when she left.

"That's not all. There's something strange in the back." She started down the hall toward her bedroom and Noah followed.

"The first thing I did was roll my suitcase back here, and I didn't notice anything right away. Then the sun broke through the clouds for a minute, and I saw this indentation on the bed."

His parents, grandparents, and every relative except his sister and her family were long gone. He considered Mrs. Powel his surrogate grandmother.

How many times had she showed up at his back door with soup or cake or whatever she cooked for herself after Betsy died? Without her, he might have starved because he didn't have the energy or interest to eat.

His sister brought over vegan casseroles, but he didn't consider that food.

The thought of losing Mrs. Powell—mentally or physically—broke his heart.

He squatted to study the bed. A cloud passed by and he saw it. Not a wrinkled area when she might have sat to tie her shoes, but a full-length indentation over six feet long, reaching from the pillow to the foot of the bed.

Mrs. Powell couldn't be more than five feet tall.

"And then I found this." She lifted a long, brown hair from the pillow. "My hair hasn't been this color for twenty years and hasn't been this long since I was a teenager."

"Do you think that's what happened? Some teenager came in while you were gone and got comfortable?"

"Broke in here, cooked three eggs, cleaned the kitchen, and took a nap? Unlikely. Besides, how many teenagers do you know who add garlic, onion, and bell pepper to their eggs?" She pointed to the trash can under the sink. The green core of a bell pepper stared back at him.

"I have to leave for a while, but I'll stop on my way home and buy you better locks." He'd been telling her for a year her locks weren't any good. He should have fixed the problem before now. "Until I get back, turn on all your lights and TV so anyone passing will know you're home. And keep your door locked."

Noah hurried across the grass as the first few fat drops of rain fell. He needed Laurel's advice. Something was wrong, and he didn't know what. She hadn't known Mrs. Powell long, but maybe she saw her with fresh eyes.

Because if it wasn't her mind slipping, it was something else. Something dark and dangerous. Something he wasn't ready to accept.

He let the door slam behind him. "Honey, I'm home.

Where are you?"

"Back here." Her voice floated from the far end of the house.

She had her back to him, her hands on her hips, facing down the hall to the front door. "I was searching for Harvey. You know how that cat can hide when he wants to. But he's usually glad to see me when I first get home, then decides to get mad at me later."

"Did you find him?"

"Yes. He's cowering under the sofa. Won't come out. But look at our front door."

A thin line of light showed around the frame. Noah stepped closer. A sliver of the frame was broken and sticking out, like a two-inch-long spear.

He had to yank at the door to get it open. Outside, more of the frame was splintered.

"Don't unpack your suitcase. Grab what you need. I'm going next door to get Mrs. Powell. Y'all aren't staying here while I'm gone."

CHAPTER TWENTY-TWO

Lincoln paced a line through the kitchen, into the breakfast room, and back, phone in hand, when he saw a black vehicle pull into the driveway. Noah in his beloved truck, Lola. He stepped into the laundry room where Jax was changing the clothes from the washer to the dryer. He didn't want her startled when the back door opened. "Noah's here."

She glanced up and nodded. "Good. We can get to work on a plan."

The door opened and Noah came in, followed by two women and their rolling suitcases. He recognized Laurel, but not the white-haired lady, and had no idea why they had brought suitcases.

Sweet Pea ran in, her tail wagging like a whirlybird. Noah scooped her up in one hand but didn't say a word.

"Hey, Noah. Hi Laurel. It's great to see you again. Have you met Jax? Jax Duncan, Laurel Bledsoe." When all else fails, make a proper introduction. His mother—Manners 101.

Somehow Jax managed to look surprised, puzzled, and happy all at the same time. "Hi, Laurel. I'm really glad to meet you. Thank you so much for letting us stay here. I absolutely *love* your house. It's exactly what I've always dreamed of. Especially the rose garden in the back and the little gazebo."

"Thank you, Jax. I'm happy I had it available when you needed it." Laurel seemed frazzled but still managed to be gracious.

Okay. Enough of the chitchat. There had to be a good reason they were here.

Lincoln stepped back and motioned with his hand. "Come on in. Let's go to the living room where you can get comfortable." Inviting Laurel into her own home was awkward, but the little laundry room was getting crowded as everyone pushed inside to avoid the rain.

Jax slammed the dryer door and turned it on. The roar prevented any conversation as all traipsed through, rolling their luggage behind them.

Once Lincoln had everyone in the living room, he wasn't sure what to do. Noah was busy checking that the doors were locked, and he still didn't know who the gray-haired woman was or why they were here with their suitcases.

Jax took over. "Laurel, I heard you passed your Broker's Exam on the first try. That's great."

"Yes. My boss helped me study. He knew the type of questions they often asked." Laurel moved from one foot to the other and fidgeted with her hands. Her picture could be under the word *nervous* in the dictionary.

Not the elderly woman. She went for the overstuffed chair and made herself at home.

Lincoln was getting as nervous as Laurel. Something was wrong, and he hadn't a clue what.

Jax plucked at the shirt she wore and turned toward Laurel. "I hope you don't mind that I borrowed your blouse. I found it upstairs. All my clothes are in the wash."

"Not at all. Take anything you want. Have you *seen* the closets at Noah's? I've lived in dorm rooms with more storage space."

Lincoln bit back a scream. His mother would have loved the two women who were able to chat about clothes and closet space while waiting for the world to explode. The epitome of Southern hospitality. He, on the other hand, considered grabbing Noah by his shirt and shaking him until an explanation fell out.

Finally, Noah quit messing with the locks and faced the others. "Mrs. Powell is my next-door neighbor, and she's been away taking care of her sister in Portland."

"Oregon or Maine?" Jax asked.

Who the hell cared? He wanted to know why she was here.

"Oregon, dear. The weather was lovely. I usually visit in the summer, but spring was delightful."

"Is your sister better now?"

Please stop, Jax. Please. Please. Please.

"Oh, much better. Thank you."

"Anyway," Noah broke in. "When Mrs. Powell got home a little while ago—"

"Noah, dear. If we're all going to be staying here together, you have to start calling me Elaine."

That explained the suitcases. Five adults and a dog in a two-bedroom townhouse? Good thing he was used to sleeping on the sofa. Now if he could only find out why.

"So Mrs. Powell—Elaine—got home from her visit, and a few things didn't seem right. She noticed three eggs were missing from her refrigerator."

All this to-do over three eggs? Lincoln managed an Oscar-worthy look of concern. He couldn't have said how many eggs were left in his mostly empty refrigerator if someone held a gun to his head.

"Then she went into her room, where it appeared someone tall had lain down to rest on her bed and left behind a long, brown hair. Her bedroom faces my house. If someone were to open her curtains and lie on her bed, he'd have a perfect view of my driveway and would know immediately when I came home."

That didn't sound good.

"Meanwhile, Laurel discovered my front doorjamb was splintered, as if someone had forced their way inside. You can see why I didn't think it safe to leave either of these two ladies alone."

Lincoln wasn't surprised by the fire in Laurel's eyes. He'd seen it before. "If you guys would hurry up and catch this prick, I could go home and do my laundry in peace. As it is, I need to put in a load of wash here. Everything I have with me is dirty."

"Let me know when you finish, dearie," Elaine called from her chair. "I have the same problem."

JAX'S HEAD SWIRLED. Each breath sent less air to her lungs. An image of Ponytail's giant hand clasped around her wrist, blood dripping from the dead body on his shoulder, filled her mind. Only this time, tiny Elaine Powell took her place.

Noah was a cop with a gun. He knew how to take care of himself. Laurel wasn't any larger that she was, but she'd managed to face down a serial killer and live to tell about it.

Elaine would be utterly defenseless.

Death and destruction had followed wherever she went over the last four years. She couldn't live with herself if anything happened to this little, white-haired lady.

Lincoln held up the phone in his hand. "I've got some news of my own."

She'd heard his phone ring a few minutes before the house filled with people, but she hadn't had time to ask who called.

"Earl and Conner have been trying to locate our missing

Mr. Littlefield. It seems someone using that ID caught a flight from Houston to New Jersey at midnight last night."

He was gone. The weight of a 280-pound hit man lifted from her shoulders, then crashed back again. How were they ever going to catch him now? She was doomed to run the rest of her life.

Noah seemed surprised. "Earl was able to dig up that much information? He's better than I thought."

"No, this is Conner. And he says to tell you he was always that good. He discovered the same Brandon Littlefield was booked on a return flight at 11:30 this morning. He couldn't determine if our guy was on that plane without an official FBI inquiry, but the flight had a rain delay of half an hour. It landed thirty minutes ago, and all passengers have deplaned." Lincoln lifted the phone to his ear and listened for a moment. "Thanks, Conner. Let me know if you learn anything else."

A chill started in Jax's chest and spread through her torso. "Then he's back in town. And looking for us."

Laurel voiced everyone's concern. "What now?"

Noah looked around the room. "The three of you need to stay here where it's safe. Finish washing your clothes. Lincoln and I will go back to the house and wait for him to make an appearance."

Lincoln started shaking his head before Noah finished. "He found your address. How do we know he hasn't found this one? You have to stay here. I'll go back to your house alone. I'll take your truck in case he knows it, turn on the lights, then wait for him to show up. He won't have any idea we're onto him. I'll ambush him the minute he comes through the door."

Heat boiled up the back of Jax's neck. They were talking about this as if she didn't have any say in the matter. "I'm not staying here *doing laundry* while you run around, risking your life." Her voice rose with every word. "There's no way you can take him alone. He's not going to stroll in like he owns the place. He'll be expecting a cop and an FBI agent. It's me he's after. I'm going with you. I'll stay in the kitchen or somewhere visible and act as bait. When he comes after me, you can surprise him and take him down alive so he can clear my name."

Because all this was for nothing if the guy died without a confession.

CHAPTER
TWENTY-THREE

Rain still fell in torrents, and water collected in the street. Nick pulled up to a drive-thru to get something to eat and think about his situation. He'd eaten a bag of pretzels on the plane, but nothing else since he'd fixed an omelet the day before.

He sat in the car, rain drumming on the roof, and downed two burgers, fries, and a drink without tasting them. What he needed was a workable plan so he could finish this damn problem.

Water had already reached the curb in front of him, and drivers were pulling into parking lots and leaving their cars. One car tried to follow a truck through an underpass near him and flooded out. He drove a Toyota. If that Subaru couldn't make it, neither could he.

Even if it could, two bodies might fit in the trunk if one of them was a small woman. But three? Never.

Add the problem of getting in a house when the occupants were already suspicious.

He could wait until everyone was asleep and slip in quietly. He knew the layout of the cop's house, but not the townhome if he had to go there. The boss wouldn't like the delay, but he wouldn't complain if the job was finished with no additional screwups.

On the other hand, if he did screw up, Mr. A might take the hinted hookup with Gena off the table. Prison might be preferable to a shotgun wedding with that bitch, Gena, although probably not the best solution.

For now, he needed a different ride, and he saw one across the street. An abandoned plumbing company truck. It offered everything he needed—a higher ride, large storage area, innocent-looking tools that could be used as weapons, and an excuse to knock on the front door.

"Incoming." Jax watched as Lincoln slipped away from his post at the front window and positioned himself in the pantry. "A plumbing truck stopped in front. I don't know if it's real or fake, but be ready."

"Okay." She took a deep breath and adjusted her earbuds. The cord trailed down into her pocket but attached to nothing.

They were a prop to explain why she wouldn't hear the door open.

Noah's small, backup revolver rested under a dish towel near her right hand. That had been her biggest fight with Noah and Lincoln. She convinced them she knew how to shoot. If only she remembered now.

She had given in on the bulletproof vest worn under Laurel's loose-fitting robe. It offered some degree of comfort, but she had to fight the urge to wear a heavy saucepan on her head like an army helmet.

After much discussion, they had decided to turn on all the lights and TV at Elaine Powell's place with Noah's truck parked in the drive and leave Noah's house dark. That way, if Ponytail did come—she'd been calling him Ponytail for too many years to stop now—he would try Noah's house first.

There was a hard knock on the front door. She turned on the water and began to rattle plates and utensils, as if washing dishes.

Could she hear Lincoln breathing, or was that her own ragged breath that sounded to her ears like a dragon belching fire? Would Ponytail be able to hear it? She clanked a spoon against a glass so hard it broke.

THE RAIN HAD stopped, and the sun now shone in a bright-blue sky. Like someone had turned off the spigot and everything had returned to normal.

Nick carried a clipboard with his gun underneath, hidden from prying eyes.

He had come up with an idea on the drive over, but if there was one thing he'd learned the hard way during the last four years, it was that no plan is foolproof. Plan for the best, prepare for the worst, his father used to say. Too bad he hadn't paid attention earlier.

If everything went right, he wouldn't need the truck.

Even if things went wrong and he had to dispose of the bodies, the truck looked less suspicious parked in front of the house and gave him a reason to be at the door.

He'd been careful not to leave a fingerprint anywhere. He'd worn skin-colored gloves everywhere he'd been. The cop had never seen him, so if he wasn't here, he was home free. Even if the woman had given a description, it wouldn't be enough.

If the cop *was* here, he could kill three birds with one shot.

The trick was to work it right. Make it look like a shoot-out. They had killed each other. No honor among thieves, so to speak. He had bought two guns on the street the first day he hit Texas. He left one in his pocket to keep his hands free. He might be able to finish off the woman with the heavy wrench he'd hooked through his belt.

After all the trouble she'd caused him, she deserved to see it coming.

Nick knocked a second time. The doorjamb was still splintered. Either no one had been home in the last twenty-four hours, or they used the back door. The only people who came to his mother's front door were salesmen or service people.

He eased the door open. It squealed slightly, but not enough to carry far.

The living room was in a deep shadow. He wasn't surprised. He could tell on his first visit the room was seldom used. The back part of the house was brighter, as sunlight spilled in through large windows he'd seen when he was here before. The sound of water running and a woman humming drifted down the hall.

Good. She was here. If nothing else, he could dispense with the one who had caused all his problems.

He eased down the hall, his rubber-soled shoes making no sound. He caught her reflection in a mirror. It only showed her back, but he'd know her anywhere, from any angle, with any color or style of hair.

The door to the pantry stood halfway open. It had been closed before. He couldn't see any movement, but it made an excellent place to hide.

Nick took a breath, sprinted down the hall, and body-slammed the pantry door. Jax screamed and swung toward him, a broken glass in her hand.

Lincoln realized his mistake when he heard running

footsteps. He braced himself as the door slammed into his shoulder. He took one step back but held his ground.

The pressure on the door eased and he shoved back. The door moved a few inches and he jumped out to see Ponytail stumble forward, the gun in his hand pointed at Jax.

Jax swung her arm, and blood appeared on Ponytail's shoulder.

Lincoln hadn't noticed the broken glass in her hand until it turned red. She gagged and spun back toward the sink.

With Jax leaning over the sink, Ponytail aimed the gun at Lincoln. He didn't have time to think, just react. Ponytail held the weapon in his left hand. Lincoln threw his right arm up as hard as he could. The blow knocked Ponytail's arm up, causing him to fire into the ceiling.

Ponytail drew back his right fist and punched Lincoln in the gut. All the air left Lincoln's lungs in a loud *woosh*. Try as hard as he could, no air seeped back in. How the hell did the guy pack such a punch with his non-dominant hand?

He stuck out a weak foot to trip the guy. It didn't work. Ponytail brought the gun around, and Jax slashed at his arm again with the broken glass, opening a gash that spurted blood like a water fountain. He dropped his gun. Lincoln kicked it to the side before the big man could reach it.

Lincoln drew his own gun, but Ponytail swatted it aside like a Tinker Toy, then grabbed him around the throat.

Lincoln watched as a Taser barb flew through the air and stuck into the side of Ponytail's neck. The big man growled and yanked it out. Noah stood in the doorway, disbelief plastered across his face.

What was this guy made of?

Lincoln's feet skidded on a pool of blood. He went down but swiveled as he fell, taking Ponytail with him. He tried to pin the man to the ground, but Ponytail outweighed him by thirty pounds.

From the corner of his eye, Lincoln saw a blue dish towel fall to the floor. What the hell was he supposed to do with that?

The barrel of a gun appeared, pressed to Ponytail's right eye. Another barrel pressed to his left eye.

Noah's voice came over his left shoulder, cool as if he'd been sitting in a lounge chair, watching. Maybe he had been.

"Dominic Rossini, you're under arrest for the murder of Special Agent Stu Hawkins, Stella and Craig Barker of Lake Conroe, and Mrs. Fran Clark of Target Realty."

"Don't forget Senator Cory Sheppard." Lincoln's throat felt like gravel as he forced the words out.

"We'll get to that. Right now, I'm only concerned with the people he's killed in Texas."

Lincoln trained his weapon on Ponytail as Noah slapped on the cuffs and frisked him, taking out a second gun, a Crocodile Dundee knife, a five-pound wrench, and two phones. The guy had come ready for a fight. Thank goodness Laurel had insisted she and Elaine would go to a movie so Noah could join them.

There must have been a bulge in Ponytail's side pocket because Noah reached in and pulled out a turquoise ring.

"Asshole," he muttered and gave him a halfhearted kick in the leg. He set the ring on the kitchen counter.

While Noah was busy, Jax slipped her gun into the pocket of her robe, out of sight. Lincoln sighed. He'd have to get that back from her, but breathing was all he could manage for now.

CHAPTER TWENTY-FOUR

Jax stepped back as Noah and Lincoln pulled Ponytail to his feet. Noah wrapped the dish towel around the worst cut, then secured it with duct tape. Ponytail ignored him.

How could he stand there, unfazed, after all the harm he'd caused?

She couldn't decide if she wanted to cry or scream. Heat rose in her body until it overpowered her.

What she wanted to do was shoot him. She slipped her hand into the pocket of Laurel's robe and felt the weight of the gun.

She couldn't do it. Not while he was handcuffed and bleeding. Life wasn't fair.

She ran at him and beat on his chest. "You killed my cat," she screamed.

"What? Princess? No, I didn't."

"Don't you dare call me Princess." That's what her stepfather had called her. Right before he groped her next to the Christmas tree. That's what men always called her before they did something they shouldn't.

"Cleo. Her name was Cleo." Jax socked Ponytail in the arm. "She was only a kitten." She hit him again. "She never did anything to hurt you."

"The cat? I didn't kill her."

"Then you let her out to die in traffic." She socked him once more, but the steam had run out of her anger.

"I would never hurt an animal. I gave her to my niece for her fifth birthday. She named her Princess. They've slept together every night for the last four years. I can get her back for you if you want."

A low moan started deep in her throat. Lincoln took her arm and led her into the guest bedroom before it turned into a scream.

She hung her head, fighting for control. Lincoln stood with his hands in his pockets like he was unsure how to proceed.

"Do you want me to get the cat back for you?" His voice was raspy, painful to hear.

"You don't understand."

"You're right. I don't. Explain it to me."

She sat on the edge of the bed. Lincoln knelt in front of her, his hands sliding up and down her arms, warm and comforting. It had been four years since anyone touched her like that. Maybe she could tell him. If she could find the words.

"Everything is so screwed up. Watching Senator Sheppard die and Ponytail chasing me and being so scared. It was all mixed up together, and I couldn't think about it or I'd break down. I couldn't grieve for him, so I grieved for Cleo instead. Only now I find out Cleo was alive this whole time. And belongs to a nine-year-old girl. I can't ask her to return the cat. Cleo didn't even like me, not really. Yet it feels like I lost the cat twice. Now I can't take the cat back. I can't get my relationship with my mother back. All those people who were collateral damage can't get their lives back. Even with Ponytail arrested, I can never get my old life back. And despite everything, no power on heaven or earth can ever bring my sister back. I think it would have been better if Ponytail had caught me in Sacramento and killed me."

Lincoln tightened his grip on her arms. His eyes bore into hers. "You didn't harm those people. Ponytail did. Everything he did was his own choice. He chose to work for the mob. He chose to follow their orders. He chose to murder Sheppard and dispose of his body. Do you think Sheppard was the first person he's killed? No. He chose to become a hired hit man."

"My sister. . . ." She took off her glasses and wiped her eyes.

"I can't imagine how hard it would be to lose a sibling. I can only guess what a hole it's left in your heart, but I do know it wasn't your fault."

"But what if it was? I knew she was unhappy. Yes, Mother disappeared into her room sometimes, but life was good. Or at least I thought so. I was busy with gymnastics and dance and I had my friends. I was selfish. I should have done something. She was my sister."

"You were what, fourteen when she died? You weren't responsible. I promise."

He didn't understand. How could he? That was only half the story.

LINCOLN LEFT JAX washing her face. She seemed stronger, and he didn't want to leave Noah alone with Ponytail too long. He rubbed his throat. The guy was tough and slippery.

Noah had pulled out a kitchen chair and had Ponytail sitting in the center of the room. "Everything okay with Jax?"

"Sure. She just needs a minute. This has been a long time coming. After four years of running, she finally figured out catching this guy wouldn't solve all her problems. Well, we've got him. What do you want to do now?"

"I want to call a wagon to take this scumbag off our hands while you phone your office and explain what you've been doing for the last five days."

"Unless he's willing to confess, that won't get Jax off the hook." He couldn't let this end with Jax still in trouble. A good lawyer might get her off, but that could take years and thousands of dollars. Money she didn't have.

"We've got him cold on trying to kill a cop, an FBI agent,

and a witness." Noah swung around to face Ponytail. "You'll sing, won't ya?"

Ponytail glared back. "I ain't a snitch."

Jax strolled back in, looking cool and calm and in control. Unless you knew better. He kept a close eye on her to make sure she didn't hit Ponytail again. Although he wouldn't have blamed her if she did. He had to get the guy to talk.

"Let's take a minute to think about this." Lincoln stood over Ponytail. He tried to sound strong, but his voice didn't want to cooperate. "What are you afraid of? Benedetto Avendondo? With your help, we'll take him down. He won't be able to hurt you."

"I'm not afraid of that old fart. If he's not dead in six months, I'll kiss your ass."

Lincoln's FBI antenna perked up to hear Avendondo was on his way out, but not so much at the ass-kissing prospect. "Really? We've been hearing those rumors for years. Have you seen him lately?"

Ponytail's refusal to answer was as good as a confession of where he'd been for the last fifteen hours.

"You might as well tell us. We already know what flight you took to New Jersey, when you got back, and what car you rented. By the way, Hertz isn't too happy about the condition of the car you returned. Your Brandon Littlefield credit card is going to have a huge repair charge. I've been driving for more than twenty years and never did that to a transmission. Not even when I was a hot-rod-loving teenager." He'd never been a hot-rod-loving teenager. He'd been a home-ten-minutes-before-curfew teenager, but Ponytail didn't need to know that.

Jax shrugged. "I tore up a transmission one time in Santa Monica. I was racing some dweeb on the beach. Sand got into everything. My stepfather yelled at me, but bought me a new car. You got a rich stepdad?"

Noah chuckled. "I had to work construction all summer to pay for the car I tore up. Nearly killed me but taught me the value of a dollar. Your father ever teach you morals and work-for-your-money type shit?"

That obviously got under Ponytail's skin. His face turned red and his lips curled out, but he didn't answer.

All this irritate-the-suspect crap had its own page in the FBI interrogation manual, but that wasn't where Lincoln's mind went. What kind of screwed-up kid had he been that he never broke a rule? That he was—as Jax so aptly put it—a dweeb.

Well, he'd made up for that now. He'd broken more rules since the day he picked Jax up at the diner than most kids did in a lifetime.

Noah's phone rang, and by the smile on his face, Lincoln knew Laurel was calling.

"Hey, sweetie, y'all out of the movie? What'd you see?" He nodded twice. "Really? I wouldn't have guessed. Everything is good here. We've got him, so it's safe to go back to your place. It's likely to be crowed here for a while. I'll ring you when everyone leaves. Why don't you take Elaine out to eat first?"

He nodded a couple more times and shut off his phone. "Laurel offered to take Elaine to see *Casablanca* at the River Oaks Theater, but she wanted to see the new *Star Wars*. Let's finish up here. I want this guy sitting in a prison cell instead of my kitchen. You gonna call your boss or shall I call mine?"

"Wait. Wait. I can't go to prison. I wouldn't last a day." Ponytail's eyes widened to the size of dinner plates.

That didn't make any sense. "A guy your size? You're who the other convicts are afraid of. If you're not worried about Avendondo, what is it?"

"I'm gay. Do you know what they do to gays in prison?"

Lincoln sat in the only empty chair. "What if you don't tell them?"

Noah glanced up. "Or we could tell the judge and ask for protective custody."

"Then my mother would find out." His voice held an edge of panic. "And the Family."

The man murdered people for a living but was afraid of his mother? "Why don't we not say anything at first and see how it goes? You really ought to tell your mother. It's not healthy to keep that a secret. She loves you. She'll understand." He couldn't believe he was giving gay life advice to a killer.

"Are you kidding? She'd never understand. She considers it a crime against God."

Lincoln put his head in his hands. He needed some way to convince the guy to talk, but he never expected this would be it. He felt dirty, but this was Jax's only chance. "Your choice. Talk, and we'll do everything in our power to protect you. Don't talk, and we'll drop you in the middle of general population with a sign around your neck. Then your mother *and* the Family will know everything. I've heard they're not that broad-minded, either."

"If you promise not to tell *anyone*, I'll cooperate. Jax Duncan didn't have anything to do with the senator's death. Benedetto Avendondo ordered the hit. He shouldn't get to live out the rest of his life in luxury while causing grief to so many people. I'll help you take him down, but I want a good lawyer. One who'll get me the best deal possible."

Lincoln sat back, exhausted. "Good lawyers are expensive. You got any money?"

"I have enough, but I don't know anyone in Houston."

Noah rolled his eyes. "Fuck. I'll have to call Tom Meyers."

CHAPTER TWENTY-FIVE

Jax watched Noah reach for his phone and stopped him. "We can't. Not yet." Ponytail had cleared her, but would that be enough?

"Why not? He offered to cooperate."

"I know you and Lincoln don't want to believe this, but the mob had help finding me. Our friend over here"—she nodded at Ponytail—"claimed Avendondo has snitches all over the country, both local and federal. Once you make that call, the news of his arrest will spread like a flu epidemic, only faster. Avendondo will know before you put the phone down."

Noah threw up his hands. "What do you want me to do? Lock him in my bathroom for the rest of his life? Slip him food through the window?"

The color in Lincoln's face had returned to normal. His

breathing no longer sounded like a steam engine heading uphill. "It kills me to admit it, but Jax is right. If we want to catch the one who is responsible for this mess, we have to keep this low-key. We call in a few people. Only those with enough clout to make things happen and who you'd trust with your life. Who would that be in HPD?"

"My boss. He'll give me a hard time, but he'll do the right thing. The District Attorney is a hard-nosed bitch who knows how to play politics, but in this case, that's a plus. She'll recognize the need for secrecy. What about on your side? Some of these charges will be federal."

"There's an agent I know who's made his bones chasing the mob. He'll know exactly what needs to be done. We'll have to call the lawyer you mentioned. Rossini needs representation."

Lincoln and Noah were concerned with convicting Ponytail and his cohorts. That was important, but it didn't solve her problems. "Once you have them, can you guarantee no one will come after me? Not in California or Texas or the FBI or the mob?"

Lincoln and Noah glanced at each other but didn't answer.

Jax sagged in her chair. Her heart decided to try break dancing against her ribs. No one could guarantee her that. Noah's truck was in the driveway next door. She could slip away, hide out until she read in the paper her name had been cleared.

She stood. Lincoln immediately went on alert and she knew—this was her life from now on. People would stare and wonder what she'd gotten away with.

"Where're you going?" he asked.

"I need to get out of Laurel's robe and put on my regular clothes before people start coming over."

Lincoln eyed the debris on the kitchen table. Ponytail's weapons, wallet, keys, a handful of coins, and two phones. A light blinked in the corner of his brain. He needed more than Ponytail's questionable offer of cooperation to guarantee Jax's safety.

He picked up one of the phones and tried to switch it on. No luck. The thing was locked.

"That's personal," Ponytail complained.

Did the fool still think he was in charge? Lincoln carried the phone behind the thug's back and pressed his thumb on the fingerprint pad. The phone unlocked.

"Hey. Wait. I said that's personal."

Lincoln scrolled to contacts. Not many listed. He tried one number. Over a cacophony of background noise, a male voice answered. "Frankie's Pizza. Will that be delivery or carry-out?"

"Sorry. My other line's ringing. I'll call you back in a minute." He'd have someone check. Make sure it was a real pizza place, but he'd ordered enough pizzas in his life to recognize the sound. He could practically smell the garlic.

Jax wandered back in wearing jeans and one of her black

T-shirts. Her face was washed and her hair combed. You'd never know she'd slashed a guy with a broken glass and cried over a missing cat.

She shot Ponytail a glance full of daggers and he winced.

"Don't call my ma. I don't want her to hear about this from just anyone. Call my brother. He's on there. Robby. Let him tell her. It'll be easier on her."

"I can't call him. Not right now. How do I know you don't have some kind of coded signal?"

"Robby's not in the life. I made sure of that. He's a civilian. Got a good job with Synergy Power. Works on the electronics for those big wind turbines. Really tricky work."

Maybe that was true, but he still wasn't placing the call. Not yet. "Who are the rest of these?"

"My sister. My landlord. My gym. A Chinese take-out place that delivers."

"How about this one?" He lifted the other phone. "If the first one is personal, I guess this one is business." He unlocked it with Ponytail's thumb.

Recent calls showed a variety of numbers with different area codes but no names. "Which one is Avendondo?"

"You don't call Avendondo. He calls you. See that third number? That's Mr. A's man, Lester. Messages go through him. He's a complete moron, but he does what he's told. The next two numbers are airlines, and the one after that is the car rental."

"I'm interested in this number. You've called it several

times. Who is it?"

"I don't know his name or where he lives. He's my information guy. Mr. A set it up. I call the number. Ask for information. He gives me a price. I pay it. He calls me back. Usually within the hour. He's good."

Now they were getting somewhere. A direct link. Plus, a good guy to take out of the equation.

Noah looked over his shoulder. "Wanna try calling him?"

Lincoln studied Ponytail. The guy didn't look sufficiently defeated. The call could be a signal to Avendondo and his pals. "Not yet. I want to check him out first. I've got a guy."

Noah turned toward Jax and made air quotes. "He's got a guy."

Let them make fun of him. He'd been an agent for five years. He had contacts. He settled into a vacant kitchen chair and dialed a number. His phone clicked and beeped as the connection jumped from one place to another. Finally, a woman answered. He'd never been able to place her voice as to age or nationality. In fact, he wasn't absolutely positive it was a woman.

"I've got a phone here with a number on it I'd like traced. Who does it belong to and where is he located? Can you do that for me?"

"Does the Pope shit in the woods?"

Not as far as he knew, but he didn't plan to argue. "What do you need from me?"

"First, turn on the phone you'll be calling from and give

me the number."

Lincoln held his phone in front of Ponytail and had him repeat his number. Several minutes went by as Lincoln heard only the click of a computer keyboard.

"Okay. Got it. I'm in your phone. Now dial the number and keep the guy talking as long as possible."

Lincoln leaned closer to Ponytail. "You screw this up, and I'll personally call your mother and describe every shithole thing you've ever done. You understand?" He wanted to add he'd out him to his family. One look at Ponytail's face, and he knew he couldn't do that.

"Yes, but what am I supposed to say?"

"You're looking for this guy." Lincoln wrote a name on a pad of paper. "He's a forger someplace in the Houston area. You need his location."

Noah uncuffed Ponytail's right hand, attaching the left one to the refrigerator. As if that could stop the big man if he tried to make a break.

Lincoln dialed the number, hit record, and put the phone on speaker. He glanced at Noah and Jax and put his finger to his lips. Not that they needed the reminder.

Noah pulled out his phone and put it on video.

Ponytail's phone went through a series of beeps and clicks, much like Lincoln's had, before stopping. Ponytail punched in a code, which caused more beeps and clicks.

"Talk to me." The voice was young, male, arrogant.

"I need everything you can tell me about a guy. He calls

himself John Hancock. He's a forger, operating somewhere in the Houston area. I need his location."

"It'll be an extra hundred due to the fake name. I can have it for you in an hour."

"Keep him on the phone," Lincoln mouthed.

"Any way I can get that now? I'm in a bind. Got to move fast. I'll pay extra."

"You're in luck. I don't usually do this, but your guy's such an amateur, I have him already. Name is Troy Wagner. Age fifty-two. Operates Pawn O Rama on West Gray. If you stiff me on this, I'll see to it your life is miserable."

Lincoln made a draw-it-out motion.

"I won't. Consider the money on its way. Hey. One more thing. I might have been a little testy last time. Things aren't going well around here. Mr. Avendondo is climbing up my butt to finish off the Duncan woman so he can relax."

"I heard you left the senator's door open and she walked in on you. Not professional, bro."

"It wasn't me. I was already inside. Sheppard came home with his arms full. Maybe he kicked at the door and it didn't shut. I don't know. All I know is I closed and relocked the door when I got there, then searched the whole house. She wasn't there. Anyway, if I gave you some attitude earlier, I'm sorry. No offense meant."

"None taken. To prove it, I'll give you a piece of advice. Your guy's second-rate. Try Andy at Print on Demand, near the corner of 249 and Mischke Road. He'll give you quality J.

Edgar himself couldn't spot."

"Thanks, man. You'll be hearing from me. And I'll recommend you to anyone I trust."

"I may need that if the boss is as sick as I hear."

Noah took the phone from his hand and switched it off.

The woman on Lincoln's phone said, "Got it. He's good. Not as good as me, but good. You may have trouble bringing him in. He is a US citizen, but he lives in Brazil. I'll text you the address. You need anything else?"

Lincoln glanced at Jax. Would this be enough to help her? They had Ponytail recorded and on video claiming Jax was an innocent bystander. "Yeah. One more thing." He slipped into the other room and shut the door behind him before continuing his conversation and telling the woman what was on his mind.

He held his breath and waited for her answer.

He'd never heard her sound surprised before. "Whoa. That's a big-time crime. Not my thing. I'll tell you what. My curiosity is piqued. I might poke around a little. Nothing too deep. Just to see if I can do it. Who am I kidding? I can do it, but . . . I won't go back in time. If anything new shows up, I'll ding you."

"I couldn't ask for more. Thanks."

He stepped back into the kitchen to find Noah and Jax staring at him.

"I don't know where to start," Noah said. "What was that all about?"

"We had to give the guy something to work on. Might as well be the case I was assigned to when I got pulled off to pick up Jax. Now we have them both admitting on tape that Avendondo wanted Jax dead. That's got to help her case."

"I understand that." Noah paced the room. "I was talking about the little stunt you pulled when you left the room."

"Only a farfetched idea I had. I'll let you know if anything comes of it."

"Hey guys?" Ponytail spoke up. "I have to pay that guy. Doesn't matter if I go to jail or not. He'll find me."

Lincoln pulled out his wallet. "How much?"

"Four hundred."

Lincoln lay down two hundreds. "Worth it to me to get two forgers off the street and clear my latest case." And to have the recording of Ponytail confirming Jax's innocence.

Noah opened a coffee tin in the pantry and brought out a hundred. Jax reached into her pocket and added five twenties.

Ponytail stuffed the cash in his wallet and dialed a number he probably thought Lincoln didn't memorize.

Lincoln and Noah nodded, and each reached for their phones to call their bosses.

PONYTAIL SAT AT the kitchen table, his hands now uncuffed so he could sign whatever agreement they came up with and talk on the phone. Noah stood inches away, his hand on the guy's shoulder.

Lincoln stood a few steps back. He wanted room to maneuver if Ponytail made any unexpected moves. The hit man's shoulders slumped, and he gave every appearance of being broken. Maybe, but Lincoln didn't trust him.

The Crime Scene techs had come and gone. So had his boss and Noah's. They must have attended the same boss school because they both fussed and bitched about their underling going it alone, or as Noah's boss called it, *playing cowboy*. In the end, they didn't cause any trouble.

Why would they with one of the biggest busts in the country going down in their jurisdiction?

Ponytail's lawyer, Tom Meyers, wasn't a large man, but he managed to project an aura of strength. Could come from his perfectly groomed, silver hair. Could be his expensive suit and tie. Could be his oversize ego.

Or it could be he was just that good.

Whatever the cause, he'd managed the best plea deal Lincoln had ever seen for a confessed killer.

And one look at Noah said it chapped him big time.

Meyers glanced at the District Attorney who glared at the Chief of Detectives. The Chief of Police was conspicuously missing. He would distance himself from this case, unless and until it proved beneficial to his career.

That left the FBI's top local lawyer, who had wanted to put Jax in handcuffs the moment he walked into the room and saw her. Noah had flat-out refused, surprising everyone, including

Lincoln.

Meyers tapped his pen on the table. "If everybody's ready, we need to get started. Avendondo is a sick, old man, and if we wait too long, he'll have gone to bed and we'll have to wait until morning. By that time, it will be impossible to keep this thing quiet."

The two men and one woman gave barely perceptible nods. As if not agreeing out loud meant they could deny responsibility if it blew up in their faces.

Meyers looked each one in the eye. "Remember, not a sound no matter what happens. My client is risking his life here. I don't even want Avendondo to hear your breathing."

Meyers and the FBI lawyer sat on either side of Ponytail. Each with his own recorder.

Ponytail picked up his phone and put it on speaker. Three recorders clicked on. The Chief of Detectives was above such menial tasks.

"This is Rossini. I need to speak to the man."

Say his name, the FBI lawyer wrote on a notepad in the middle of the table.

Ponytail ignored him. "No. I need to speak to him directly."

A full minute went by before a shaky voice answered. "Dominic, my boy. Have you got news for me?"

"Yes, Mr. Avendondo. I think you'll be pleased. I took care of our problem, and it shouldn't bounce back on you in any way."

"Were you able to dispose of all three so they won't be

found?"

"I tried something you taught me. I shot the cop and the Fed immediately, and then used my backup piece on the girl. With a little maneuvering, I made it look like she shot them and they shot her. Case closed. No point searching for anyone else."

Avendondo's laugh turned into a cough. "Excellent job. We could have explained away the Fed as dirty, but once that fucking cop got involved, I was afraid it would get too complicated. Maybe taking out the wrong Fed in that shithole town wasn't such a big mistake after all."

"Yes, sir, and I apologize again for misunderstanding your directions. My fault entirely."

Ice pellets formed in Lincoln's gut. That was him they were talking about. Stu Hawkins died in his place.

"I hope you won't have any trouble replacing him. I know you were counting on him in the future with your local man considering retirement."

"That fucktard better not retire until he finds me a new replacement. He's as much to blame for this screwup as you are, so he owes me. Texas is getting too important not to have eyes on the ground. I'm going to bed now, but I'll look forward to the morning news."

"I wouldn't count on seeing it tomorrow, sir. The cop is off work this week and his girlfriend is out of town, so you might not hear anything about this until she gets home and discovers the bodies."

"The longer it takes the better. Hard to pinpoint a time of death or who shot first, etc. when the bodies have been hanging around for a while. It took some time, but you've done well cleaning up this mess. Sorry I had to sanction you for the Philly debacle. You let that woman walk right past you without noticing her. I couldn't let that go by without a punishment. Now come on home. Gena is anxious to see you."

Three sets of eyes widened in surprise. Lincoln was afraid someone might blurt out a question. He grabbed the notepad and scribbled *daughter.* Nobody bothered with research anymore.

"I totally understand, sir. I won't be able to get there for a few days. I have to go back to California first and clear out my apartment. It would look suspicious if I didn't. Tell Gena I'm looking forward to seeing her again soon. I don't think I've seen her since she was about seventeen, but she was already on her way to becoming a beautiful woman." Ponytail rolled his eyes and made a gagging motion.

Tom Meyers scribbled *Is that enough? Need anything else?* on the notepad and held it up. Everyone shrugged, whatever that meant. No one wanted to take responsibility.

Ponytail hung up and sagged back, exhaustion covering his face. Meyers, the DA, and the federal attorney clicked off their recorders.

Lincoln glanced around the room. He, Noah, and Jax had risked their lives while everyone else in the room had sat in their air-conditioned offices. If all went well, and they were able to take down Avendondo and his associates, these people's careers would take off. If anything went wrong, his and Noah's would be over.

And Jax could still end up in jail.

CHAPTER TWENTY-SIX

The FBI lawyer, Peterson, got under Nick's skin. Too bad he wasn't the one in the trailer in West Monroe.

Nick had answered questions for hours. Now this Peterson guy was angry he'd left out a few details. He couldn't remember everything that had happened over the last four years.

The only one in the room he had any respect for was Jax. She had shown guts and talent, evading him for so long. If things had been different, he wouldn't have minded working with her.

On the other hand, she was the reason he was in this jam. If she'd stayed home where she belonged, he'd be attending culinary school by now.

Everything was winding down. If he wanted to make a

move, this was the time.

It had taken three of them to subdue him earlier. There were seven in the room now, but four were worthless.

He eyed the recorder sitting in front of him. He could scoop it up in his left hand, use it to crush Peterson's windpipe, then hurl it at the fat detective standing across the table like he was better than everyone else.

The DA would be no problem. She was a large woman, but out of shape. She'd go down easy.

There wasn't much to his own lawyer. That neck would snap like a twig. But the man had done his best for him and deserved to walk away. If he didn't give him any trouble.

The cop and the Fed were the problem. They each knew what to watch for and had the moves, if in different ways. Too bad because the cop should be the first to go after the crack he'd made about Pops not teaching him anything.

And then there was Jax, who sat out of reach, never taking her eyes off him while her hand rested lightly on the gun in her pocket no one seemed to realize she had. She was too good to be an amateur.

"Tell me again how you pay for the information."

Nick's eyes drifted back to Peterson, the asshole. "I gave you the number. I don't know who he is. He doesn't know who I am."

"How do you pay him?"

"He texts me a number. It changes every time."

"What about when you get orders for a job or information

on where to find Miss Duncan? Does Avendondo call you direct?"

"Occasionally. Usually it's his flunky, Lester."

Peterson's eyes lit up so bright, Nick worried he might be having an orgasm. "And you could swear in court it was Avendondo you talked to?"

His heart sank. Going to jail was bad enough. He hadn't realized he'd have to go to court and testify. Sit there, facing Mr. A and all his men. Men who had known his father. With his mother, brother, and sister watching.

He couldn't do it. He'd rather be dead than turn rat.

The DA gathered up her recorder and copies of the plea deal. "I think I have all I need for the moment. I'm sure we'll talk again soon." She turned and headed for the door. The fat Chief of Detectives in the cheap suit followed her.

Too bad. He'd have liked to take out that guy, along with Peterson.

On the good side, that only left the cop, the Fed, and Peterson to deal with. Jax was too far away to be an immediate problem, while both lawyers were too wimpy to be any problem at all.

He could use Peterson's own recorder on him, flip the table to keep Jax occupied, slam his chair into the cop, and shove him into the Fed. If the cop went to the floor, he could get his weapon easily. If not, he'd improvise.

Nick leaned back in his chair and took a deep breath, relaxing his arms, getting ready. He'd make his move when

Peterson looked down at his notes.

A soft, warm hand took his and rubbed a thumb gently across his fingers.

Whoa. Was that his own attorney making a move on him? The man was good looking in a sissified kind of way. Much younger than his white hair led you to believe. Too bad he didn't have time to start anything now. Maybe in a year or two he could swing back by Houston and look him up.

A sudden shaft of pain shot up his arm as Meyers bent his fingers back almost to the breaking point. He leaned over and whispered, "Don't even think about it. You'll end up dead, and I won't get paid."

LINCOLN HAD SEEN Ponytail's eyes sweep the room. Judging distances. Making plans.

He'd taken a step back, putting more distance between them, before unsnapping his holster. He wasn't sure if Noah had recognized Ponytail's plans, but with his hand on the guy's shoulder, he would have felt it when he started to move.

Meyers was a surprise. He wouldn't have expected the lawyer to be that observant. He didn't know exactly what Meyers had whispered, but he saw the trick with the fingers.

Peterson, the idiot, didn't have a clue how close he'd come, and the whole thing had been his fault. Ponytail was still adjusting to the idea of squealing on people he'd known all his life. He wasn't ready to accept the natural progression of his choice . . . that one day he'd have to face them in court.

That needed to be brought into the conversation slowly, one step at a time.

Lincoln unhooked the handcuffs from his belt. "Now that you've finished talking on the phone and signing papers, let's put these back on."

For a moment, he thought Ponytail might fight him. Instead, he stiffened, then held out his hands.

Peterson questioned him for another half hour about what he'd personally seen or heard Avendondo say.

When he finished, Lincoln had a question. "What's the best way to get into Avendondo's compound without being seen?"

"Are you kidding me? That place is a fortress. You can't break in there."

"We don't want to break in. We want to serve a warrant, and we don't want to get shot or let them destroy evidence while we're doing it."

Noah leaned down. "Come on, man. You know you've done it. We all do. It's a game we play whenever we go to some place that's supposed to be impenetrable. *How would I get in if I needed to?*"

"Not by the front gate, that's for sure. You'd need a tank to ram through that, and you'd still have to drive half a mile of winding road to reach the house. Maybe from the back. The ocean side. And don't come in straight. Dock at the neighbor's, wait until dark, and walk in. There's a five-car garage behind the house. It'll shield you from view most of the way. The maid lives upstairs. Sometimes she runs back and forth from the house to her place. She might leave the back door unlocked, but I wouldn't count on it."

Peterson looked interested again. "How many people in the house?"

"Besides Avendondo? At least two at all times plus the maid, who ain't armed. Often more. Higgins acts like a big-shot butler with his coat and tie and *Yes, sir. No sir.* But don't underestimate him. He's packing. There's a goon they call The Goose who's usually close by. He's young and stupid. The numbnuts don't know how to position himself correctly. But he won't hesitate to shoot if he thinks the boss is in danger. Lester is usually close by if not in the room. Really, I wouldn't do it. Phone ahead and tell 'em you're coming. Or ask him to meet you downtown."

The light went out of Peterson's eyes. He'd been looking forward to a showdown, a gunfight. Of course, as a lawyer, he'd be waiting in the back. Where it was safe.

Peterson turned off his recorder and gathered his notes. He stepped toward Jax. "You'll need to come with me, Miss Duncan. I know Mr. Rossini claims you had nothing to do with any of the murders, and that may well hold up. But until then, you have a history of running. You need to be locked up until an official determination is made about your responsibility in all this. Leaving the scene of a crime, evading arrest, obstructing justice. These charges are still undecided."

Lincoln's jaw dropped. He couldn't be serious, could he?

Noah stepped forward. "Miss Duncan has had every opportunity to flee over the last several days. She has chosen to stay. She put her life at risk to help solve these gruesome murders, and I won't repay her by placing her in jail where Benedetto Avendondo's men can get to her. She'll stay with us. Agent Montgomery and I will keep an eye on her."

Two uniforms came to take Ponytail to the hospital to have his arm stitched up, and Peterson left in a huff, shooting Lincoln a frosty glare. There might be a bill to pay later, but Lincoln had solved the murder of a state senator and three other people. The cost wouldn't be too high.

Silence filled the house after all the activity of the last several hours.

Noah strolled to the kitchen counter and picked up the turquoise ring, studying it in the light. He tried it on his little finger, but it barely fit past the first knuckle. He shrugged and slipped it into his pocket. "I need to call Laurel and tell her it's safe to come home. And to please bring my dog. You two don't mind staying at the townhouse for a few more days, do you? I said we'd keep an eye on you but I didn't say where, and you'll be more comfortable there. We'll try to get this straightened out as quickly as possible."

Lincoln dropped into a kitchen chair. His own apartment waited on the other side of town. He'd planned to be gone overnight. He'd been gone almost a week.

He should have been ready to get home. He wasn't. "I don't mind if you don't, Jax."

Jax glanced up from the chair where she'd been sitting for the last hour. Her eyes, which should have been filled with relief at being cleared, held an aching sadness. "I don't have any other place to go."

He crossed the room, took her hand, and pulled her from her chair. "Then let's go home. Tomorrow, if you feel like it, you can make me those *huevos rancheros* you claimed to be an expert at."

NICK WATCHED AS houses and cars and trees and tall buildings zipped past. Overhead, a quarter moon hung in a sky too full of ambient light for stars to show through. As a kid, he'd driven his car an hour east of town to a deserted beach, stretched out in the sand, and watched the stars. That's where he did his best thinking. How long would it be before he was outside again?

He glanced at the downtown skyline. He might not be that familiar with Houston, but he knew where the medical center was and this wasn't it. He beat on the heavy-gauge, wire partition and yelled at the driver. "Hey. What're you doing? I thought I was supposed to go to the hospital."

"Cool your jets and stop beating on the partition, or I'll have to come back there and make you behave. You're going to the hospital, just not the one you think. We've got great docs in the county jail. They stitch up cuts all the time. They may not be plastic surgeons, but they've had plenty of practice and get the job done. If you end up with a scar, I suspect it won't be your first or last."

Asshole must think his uniform made him bulletproof. He'd remember that face when he got out, although this put a crimp in his plans.

Regular hospitals weren't prepared for someone like him. There'd be lots of ways out. He'd palmed a letter opener before they shuffled him out of the cop's house. Not the best weapon, but useable.

If they searched him at the jail, they'd take it away.

At a hospital, you walk out the door, you're home free. You can grab a car and be halfway to the next county before they know you're missing.

In jail, getting out of the hospital ward was only half the battle. You still had guards and bars and barbed wire between you and the street.

The patrolman pulled into the prisoner drop-off area and the process began. He was photographed, fingerprinted, frisked—where they found the letter opener immediately— and given papers to sign. It felt like he'd signed his name two dozen times between here and his plea agreement.

He was ushered through halls that smelled of steel and concrete and unwashed bodies. Doors clanged, and the sound traveled down his spine like an electric current. In the hospital ward, he was undressed none too gently and his wounds examined for pieces of broken glass.

While he waited for a doctor, a trustee brought him a plate of cardboard turkey with a brownish sauce the consistency of paste. He pushed it away in disgust.

If this was what they called food, he might starve to death and save them the trouble of keeping him locked away.

A middle-aged man with a receding hairline and pronounced paunch came into the room and sat on a stool in front of him. "I'm Dr. Garza. I'll be taking care of you tonight."

The gash on his left arm needed twelve stitches. The one on his right got only butterfly bandages. He wasn't given a numbing shot or offered pain meds.

"What's this one, an old gunshot wound?" The doc cleaned it with antiseptic.

Nick shrugged.

"Looks like you've had a rough couple of days." The doc rolled his stool back and snapped off his gloves. "I'm going to put you on an IV antibiotic for tonight, plus a saline solution. You might be a touch dehydrated. We'll reevaluate your arm in the morning. Unless I see signs of infection, you should be okay to go back into regular population tomorrow."

"Wait a sec, Doc. I'm supposed to be in protective segregation."

"I only sew them up. I don't decide where to put them." The doc dropped his gloves in the trash and stopped at the only other occupied bed. "How ya doing tonight, Jerry?"

A skeleton of a man nodded. "I reckon I'll live, Doc."

They both laughed, and Nick figured it wouldn't be for too much longer.

Fifteen minutes later, he had an IV in his arm and his leg chained to the bed. The doc had flipped off the overhead lights on his way out. Now it was only bright enough to read by, not land an airplane.

How was he supposed to get any sleep this way?

He'd have to learn to. Escape seemed impossible.

Prison wasn't known for its quiet nights and comfortable beds. And he'd have to master what it took to get along in a different world.

Depending on where they sent him, he'd be able to see his family occasionally. His sister wouldn't be able to visit often, not dragging three little kids across the country. He might get to see her if she came home for Christmas. Robby would bring Ma whenever she was up to it.

Robby. That was the one thing he'd done right. His brother was young when their father died and thought *the life*, as Pa called it, was romantic. Swashbuckling. It had taken years to convince him that was a lie.

Realizing the pain Ma felt when she wasn't able to bury Pa in the churchyard helped.

Now Robby was an honest, respectable citizen. An electrical engineer. Not the job he'd wanted at first, but he'd learned to love it. He swore he could wire anything from a gigantic turbine to the smallest computer chip, no matter how complicated.

All the running around and worrying, plus loss of blood, must be catching up with him. His eyelids felt like they weighed ten pounds each. He drifted off and didn't know if it had been five minutes or five hours when the rattling of a chain pulled him toward the surface.

His eyes fluttered open, then closed again.

The IV attached to his right arm jiggled, then fell still.

A voice whispered in his ear. "Night night, Mr. Rat. My wife and kiddies thank you for your service."

CHAPTER
TWENTY-SEVEN

The townhouse felt empty after being around so many people all day. Lincoln was used to spending much of his time alone. These last few days with Jax had felt oddly comfortable—even if she was a murder suspect.

Truthfully, he'd never believed she had anything to do with the murder or the money laundering. The scene in her apartment had felt staged from the beginning.

He bore some responsibility for the subsequent events, and he'd have to live with it. If he'd spoken up more forcibly, maybe he could have changed his partner's mind. But he was a Probationary Agent, and Darrell Byrne was his boss. And Byrne had his mind made up from day one.

He flopped onto the sofa, kicked off his shoes, and propped his feet on the coffee table.

Jax stood on the bottom step. "I'm exhausted. Think I'll go on to bed. You know you don't have to sleep on the sofa any longer." She paused as if realizing what she'd just said. "There's a perfectly good bedroom down the hall. I'm sure Noah and Laurel wouldn't mind if you used it."

He watched her, standing on the step, waiting for a response, and something stirred inside him.

She wasn't a suspect anymore, or even a witness. But there was no guarantee Avendondo wouldn't decide to come after her, if only for revenge.

And he was still responsible for her safety.

"I think I'll stay here. I'm used to this sofa. It feels like home. You sleep well, and I'll see you in the morning."

His eyes followed her every step until she disappeared into the guest room.

He spent the rest of the night listening to the house settle, wondering if he'd made a mistake.

JAX STUMBLED DOWN the stairs like a zombie, searching for coffee instead of brains. She knew there was some close by. She could smell it.

She'd been lying in bed, watching the ceiling fan turn in lazy circles as she had most of the night, when the aroma drifted upstairs.

Like she had every night for the last four years, she'd

hooked a chair under the doorknob and set up a warning system in the windowsill. Ponytail had been caught and put away. Her name had been cleared.

For some reason, she still didn't feel safe.

Probably because Avendondo and his cronies were still out there.

That was definitely part of it—a big part. Her conscience was the other part. How many people had died, had she lied to, disappointed, all because she hadn't driven directly to the police station when she saw Senator Sheppard's dead body.

As Scarlet O'Hara said, she'd think about that another day.

Lincoln hadn't been awake for long. His hair stood up in black spikes, as if he'd run his hand through it.

More than once.

The man must have had as rough a night as she had. She'd spent the first half worrying he might follow her up the stairs and knock on her door. She'd spent the second half wondering why he hadn't.

"Morning, sunshine," he said as he hooked a thumb over his shoulder. "There's coffee in the kitchen."

"Thanks," she mumbled. Her voice came out an early morning croak.

She grabbed a cup and joined him on the sofa, letting the hot liquid clear the hoarseness from her throat before speaking.

He beat her to it. "I know we need to keep this quiet for a couple of days until we round up Avendondo. I was wondering if you'd decided what you want to do once this is all over?"

She hadn't expected *that* question.

"I haven't even thought about it. Not yet."

"You need to call your mother. She's worried about you."

"I don't think so. She didn't exactly stand by me when everything fell apart. I watched her interview on TV the next day, and it felt like a knife in my back. I did call her once. Did she tell you that?"

"Yes, but not until years later. She didn't want to give me any clue where to find you."

"Ha. I doubt that. More likely, she didn't want to get herself in trouble. Did she tell you what she said? I called her at her beauty shop, where she went every Tuesday. I knew she wouldn't miss an appointment no matter how much trouble I was in. She told me I'd embarrassed my stepfather, and I should turn myself in right away."

"Which you should have. She's been through a lot these last years. She's not the same person she was then."

"Neither am I. There's something else she probably didn't tell you. Remember when I said I left our house on Christmas Eve and cut off all communication with my family because my stepfather tried to stick his hand up my dress and his tongue down my throat, and told me I had to be the woman of the house because my mother wasn't available to him anymore?"

Lincoln's mouth gaped open and closed, as if he didn't know what to say.

Okay, maybe she hadn't actually told him that part. It felt

too personal. Too dirty.

"That's not completely true. I went to my room and locked my door that night. The next morning, I told my mother about it. She yelled at me. Told me I didn't appreciate all he'd done for us. How we'd been almost starving when he took us in. Said I was ungrateful. Making up stories. Just like my sister. In other words, my sister wasn't a drug addict who overdosed by accident. She took drugs to blot out what had been happening to her for years. She committed suicide to make it stop. And my mother knew about it and did nothing."

"Some of that is true, Jax. A lot of it, but not all. Soon after you left, your mother was diagnosed with breast cancer. Her doctor liked to send his patients to a therapist to learn how to handle the stress of the treatments. He felt it helped in their recovery. The therapist took one look at your mother, heard her history, diagnosed her as bipolar, and put her on medication. She claims getting cancer was the best thing that ever happened to her."

Jax sagged back into the sofa cushions and blew out a long breath. "That explains so much. I knew she was depressed, but . . . is she okay? Did she get over the cancer?"

"Yeah. The treatments were really rough, but she made it. The day she rang the bell and the doctor gave her the all clear, she divorced your stepfather. Don't know if it was karma or possibly your mother ratting on him. Soon after she left him, the I.R.S. came for him big time. He's broke now with his reputation in tatters. She took her settlement and bought a little house close to the beach in Carlsbad. Last I heard, she was volunteering at a thrift store three days a week."

Wow. That was a lot to absorb. It might take some time to adjust to that information. She couldn't simply flip her feelings on Lincoln's say-so.

Lincoln wandered into the kitchen for another cup of coffee, giving Jax space to think. Changing your mind about someone you'd hated for years would be tough. She might never manage it completely, not after some of the things her mother had done.

He should have told her earlier, but it never seemed the right time.

A tap on the kitchen door made Lincoln jump, spilling coffee on the counter.

Noah's face stared at him through the window. He wasn't smiling the way he should have been after all they'd accomplished yesterday.

Lincoln flipped the lock off and motioned him in. "You want some coffee?"

"Nah."

"Jax is in the living room. Head on in. I'll be right there."

"Okay."

Noah had never been exactly chatty, but these one-word answers were out of character. And he'd never known the man to turn down a cup of coffee.

Lincoln swiped at the counter with a paper towel and followed Noah into the other room. A knot threatened to form in the pit of his stomach. It always showed up when someone acted out of character.

Noah was pacing, chewing on a thumbnail. "You guys have breakfast yet?"

"Not yet. We haven't been up long." It was after ten o'clock, and they'd been moving like a Monday-morning hangover.

"Grab your things and come with me. I'm treating."

Jax slipped on her shoes and stood up.

Noah shook his head. "Get everything. We might not be coming back here."

What now? Lincoln didn't like this at all. He grabbed his go-bag, which he'd thrown in a corner. Jax went upstairs to get her backpack. Too bad. She'd only now started to leave it in another room.

NOAH DROVE TO a pancake house he knew of and ignored his passengers. Jax sat in the back seat. Lincoln tried to start a conversation, to no avail.

He wasn't ready to talk yet. He needed to decide what to say and how to say it. He'd tried on the drive over. It hadn't worked.

He ordered Belgian waffles. Lincoln ordered a three-egg

omelet. Jax stuck with toast and coffee.

He'd start with the easy stuff first. "Conner called this morning. A federal judge signed a warrant to search Avendondo's estate in New Jersey. It took a couple of hours to get everyone gathered up. They're over there now. Two guys tried Ponytail's system of going through the back door. They opened the front gate for the rest of the team."

Lincoln nodded, looking more relaxed than he had since he'd spilled his coffee all over the kitchen.

"There's one problem." Probably more than one, but why worry them any more than necessary? "No one was home. Not even the maid. Rumor has it Avendondo has gone to some cabin in the woods for rest and relaxation. Only no one knows what cabin. Or which woods. Or who owns it. Until then, his place is being searched down to the bare floor."

Lincoln slammed down his coffee. "Son-of-a-bitch." People in the restaurant turned to look and he lowered his voice. "Someone warned him. We should have started searching for the leak last night. I'll bet Ponytail knows more than he admitted. We need to get right over there and question him about this."

"I guess that's our second problem. Ponytail died last night while in the jail hospital ward."

Lincoln shoved his cup away. That man was a serious threat to a cup of coffee.

Jax had been picking at her toast, turning it into a pile of crumbs. "Do they know what happened?"

"Not without an autopsy. The doc is trying to say natural causes. Raise your hand if you believe that. The only person in the room with him was a prisoner dying of cancer. Doc swears he isn't strong enough to stand up, let alone kill a guy like Ponytail without leaving any marks."

Lincoln reached for his phone. "Let's call up there right away. Tell them to save any IV tubing. An air bubble injected into his IV would enter his bloodstream, make its way to his heart, and *boom*—instant, untraceable heart attack."

"Too late. When they found him, they ripped out the IVs and started giving him CPR. They've stepped all over those tubes and kicked them out of the way. Even if we could find a tiny hole, how would we prove where it came from?"

Jax tore her last piece of toast into long strips. "So Ponytail is dead. Avendondo is missing. We have no idea where the leak is coming from. And I'm still in danger."

He knew she was smart. He'd kind of hoped she wouldn't figure out that last part. "And that's our third problem. With Ponytail dead, unless we find something incriminating at Avendondo's estate, we won't be able to hold him even if we find him. That means you're back to being the only live witness against him."

"Wait a minute," Lincoln hissed, his voice low but angry. "Her testimony is hearsay. Without hearing Avendondo issue the orders herself, nothing she overheard Ponytail say can be used in court."

Noah leaned closer. "You know that. I know that. Every

lawyer in creation knows that. Even Avendondo probably knows that. Are you willing to risk Jax's life that he won't want to tie up that loose end?"

"We could put her in Witness Protection."

"Possibly. They don't pass those things out like candy. That's federal, the U.S. Marshals Service. You'd have to ask them. With what she knows, they might go for it."

She shook her head. "No. I couldn't see my mother. I couldn't use my real name. I'd have to lie to everyone I met. I wouldn't be any better off than I was the last four years."

Lincoln placed his hand on top of Jax's. "We'd supply you with a name, social security card, driver's license. All that stuff. We'd get you set up in an apartment, help you find a good job with decent pay. You wouldn't have to live in the shadows."

She pushed her plate aside, the food destroyed but uneaten. "Like prison but with better food."

The next words were gonna hurt Lincoln. Noah had to say them anyway. "I know you don't want to believe your FBI is involved. I don't blame you. I would feel the same way about the HPD. We both know Avendondo was getting help from someone on the inside. Until we find that source and plug it, Jax isn't safe. The leak's still there, and we still don't know who it is."

Lincoln hung his head. "I asked my guy to work on it, but I don't know when or if I'll hear anything."

So that was the secret conversation Lincoln had with his hacker. Nice to know he'd finally accepted that someone in the

FBI was dirty. That didn't make them any safer.

Jax took a last sip of her coffee and stood. "I don't have any choice. It's time for me to run."

CHAPTER
TWENTY-EIGHT

Jax took her usual seat in the back of Noah's truck. It felt almost normal. Three friends going out for a ride. Except that one of them had a target on her back.

Lincoln waited until Noah pulled onto the street, then turned to face her. "Give the search team a couple of days to see what turns up at Avendondo's place. They may find all we need to put him away for good."

Had he waited to suggest she stick around a little longer because he was worried she'd jump out and run away? "How will we know? I doubt they'll put it on TV."

Lincoln and Noah spoke at the same time. "Conner."

They were asking her to put a lot of faith in Noah's ex-partner. A man she'd never met. "Let's see where we are at this time tomorrow. That'll give them twenty-four hours."

Lincoln seemed to relax as he turned back toward Noah. "Are we going to pick up Laurel now?"

"No. I dropped her off at her office before I came over this morning. She needed to put in a few hours' work and pick up some files. She wasn't too happy about taking Harvey to the kennel—the cat had barely forgiven her for going to Austin. But she wasn't willing to risk leaving him at home if there was any possibility of someone else breaking in."

"Then what's the plan? Where're we going?"

"If I'm not mistaken, Lincoln still has the key to the safe house on Lake Conroe."

Oh no. She did *not* want to go back to that awful place.

Lincoln gave a huge smile. "That's a great idea. I do have the key, so we don't have to check in with anyone. No one will know we're there. That place is a bunker. We can wait there for the search team to finish. Conner can keep us up-to-date using our burner phones."

"I've got one errand I'd like to run if y'all don't mind. Then we'll swing by my house and pick up Sweet Pea before getting Laurel."

The knot in her chest loosened. She'd missed that little dog. Having something warm and furry around would brighten up that gloomy place.

They drove for about twenty minutes before reaching an upscale shopping area. Noah cruised until he found a parking spot. "You can wait here if you want. I won't be gone long."

Not hardly. She didn't plan to wait out in the open when

she'd just been told people might be after her. Plus, she wanted to know what Noah was up to in this ritzy place.

Lincoln must have agreed—about the not staying in the open part, not the being nosey part—because he spoke up. "It's too hot to sit here. We'll come with you."

Noah's flush of embarrassment surprised her. She thought nothing could fluster him.

Noah strode into a jewelry store like he'd rather be any place else in the world. She wandered around, looking at rings and necklaces, while Noah searched for the manager.

A tall, dignified, African American man came out from the back. "Noah, how good to see you again." His voice flowed, deep and mellow.

He reminded Jax of someone she couldn't place. Barry White? James Earl Jones? She shook her head. The guy had really missed his calling. He should be in show business with that voice.

"What can I do for you?" he asked. "Someone's birthday? A little early Christmas shopping?"

"I'm not shopping today. Could I ask you for a small favor?"

"Anything. I owe you big time for giving me a heads-up when this place came on the market."

"Is there some way you can tell me what size this is?" He reached into his pocket and pulled out the turquoise ring.

Jax stifled a laugh. She should have known.

The man measured the ring and smiled at Noah. "A perfect

size seven. Always good information to have . . . for the future."

Noah flushed slightly and started out.

Jax motioned him over to where she was standing. She pointed to a ring. "That one. For when you're ready."

"How do you know?"

"I've met Laurel. I've seen how she decorated her house, what type of clothes she wears. I know her style. And I know jewelry. Get her that one or something similar. It's good quality but not too flashy. She'll think you're a genius, I promise."

The owner smiled and waved as they made their way to the door. "Say hello to my Uncle Earl for me. Remind him he's got a job here if he ever wants to stop working for HPD."

BY THE TIME they picked up Sweet Pea and Laurel and drove to Lake Conroe, the sky had turned a soft pink around the edges. Laurel and the dog had taken his seat in the front, and Lincoln had moved to the back, next to Jax.

He didn't mind. He'd come to enjoy her company. If things were different. . . .

The garage door of the safe house hung at an odd angle. Jax must have done that in her haste to get away. No need to worry about what the top of his government-issued SUV looked like. That car sat totaled behind a shot-up motel room.

Noah stopped and stared at the crooked door. "I don't like the idea of leaving Lola out here and announcing to anyone who passes by that the house is occupied. Plus, it would be easy to slip inside the garage and work on opening the side door in secret."

Jax leaned forward. "We could park next door. Sort of like Ponytail did when he was waiting at Elaine's house."

Lincoln shuddered as he glanced at the yellow crime scene tape, its ends flapping in the breeze. The memory of bullets flying past his ear all too vivid. "First, let's see if Noah and I together might be able to maneuver the door back onto the rails. If not, we can probably lift it high enough for Laurel to drive inside, then let it down easy. We wouldn't be able to use the automatic opener to get out, but our weakest point of entry will be protected."

The door squealed like a kitten being given a bath. Only ten times louder. Laurel pulled Lola inside, and the door squealed again as they lowered it. Lincoln prayed none of the neighbors looked out their windows.

Inside, everything was just as they'd left it four days ago. Hard to believe so much had happened since he got the call to drive to West Monroe and arrest Jax. He gathered up the dirty coffee cups and carried them into the kitchen.

Noah hauled his and Laurel's suitcases upstairs to the extra bedroom. Sweet Pea trotted up the stairs after him.

Jax paced like a lion in a cage—up one side of the room, down the other. Her hands rubbed together in a washing motion.

Laurel didn't exactly look relaxed. No wonder, the way Jax

was acting.

Jax swung around and faced him. "Could you check the back deck and see if there's any blood? I don't want to come across it unexpectedly. If I know it's there, maybe I can prepare myself. Picturing it out there is driving me crazy."

That didn't make any sense. She was fine earlier. "I don't understand. How can a few drops that have probably been washed away by the rain upset you this much, but you didn't blink when you knocked me out with a toilet tank lid, leaving me in a pool of blood?"

"How would you know what happened? Rumor has it you were asleep at the time."

Still with the hypotheticals. This was getting old. "What about yesterday at Noah's? You managed to slash Ponytail's arm—twice. Once after he was gushing blood all over Noah's floor."

Shit. He was nervous and worried and upset and taking it out on her. And maybe still a little embarrassed that she got the best of him four years ago. It might be time to get over that. "Sorry. I was being a jerk. I'll check the deck as soon as we have the house secured and the motion detector cameras running."

"I was plenty upset yesterday, but the blood was fresh and didn't have an odor. Plus, the kitchen still held the faint aroma of coffee and bacon. That's the worst part—the smell. Everything can be fine, but if I get a whiff of blood, I'm back in Senator Sheppard's house all over again. His sightless eyes staring at me. His blood, warm and slimy, dripping on my hand. Ponytail gripping my arm and threatening me. As real as the day it happened. Frozen in one spot with my heart hammering and tears in my eyes and my mouth too dry to speak. Back in my apartment, I scrubbed my hands until the water in the sink turned red and finally pink, but it was still there, under my nails."

Yep. Definitely a jerk move on his part. "Don't worry. I'll clean it up. I didn't have any idea it was that big a deal."

"I hate to be this silly. I know there can't be but a few drops out there, and like you said, dried up and likely washed away by the rain. It's just that I thought I was through running. Yet here I am again. Exactly like that first time, with a voice in my head saying, *Run. Run. Run.*"

Laurel wrapped her arm around Jax's shoulders. "That's not silly at all. It's perfectly understandable. Seeing the senator shot and that man coming after you has given you a first-class case of PTSD, and that sucker picks its own time to reappear, like a punch in the gut."

"What? No. I was never in a war or anything like that."

"Doesn't matter. Trauma is trauma. It can happen to anyone. You can keep it hidden for a while, but sooner or later, like it or not, it's going to come roaring out and stop you in your tracks. You should talk to someone about it once you get settled."

"Maybe I will. I thought it was getting better. I've gone months without an episode. That is, until these last few days. I came close when we crashed in the woods and even closer yesterday. Somehow, knowing I was the one in charge—that I cut him, not the other way around—helped. Either that or the bacon. I don't know which."

Lincoln flipped on the deck lights. "I'll go out and check before it gets dark. If I see any spots, I'll clean them up." He swung back around to face her. "Unless you want to do it. Like scrubbing them up would put you back in control."

Jax's smile was tentative. "I think I'd like that."

CHAPTER
TWENTY-NINE

Jax didn't sleep well despite the comfortable bed. All the moving around, sleeping in a different place every night, was getting to her. Although that had been her life for years, settling in only when she reached West Monroe.

There weren't any blood drops on the deck to scrub away. Maybe that would have helped. Maybe it wouldn't. Maybe she was too damaged for anything to help.

One thing for sure, if she ever got any place steady where she could use her own name, she would take Laurel's advice and look for somebody to talk to. Considering her screwed-up childhood, her relationship with her mother, her sister's suicide, and the trauma of watching Cory Sheppard die in front of her eyes, she had enough baggage to keep a professional busy for years.

At five a.m. she gave up, kicked off the covers, and tiptoed downstairs.

All the lights were off, but a glow from the living room said the TV was on. Lincoln was on the sofa, playing a video game. A set of headphones muted the sound.

Jax flopped down beside him. "Who's winning?"

"I'm playing some guy in Florida called DragonLair2. He's whipping my ass. He says he's a twenty-one-year-old man who needs to leave for work in ten minutes. I'm pretty sure he's a twelve-year-old kid whose mother just told him to get ready for school."

"What's your . . . handle? Is that what it's called?"

"For tonight only, I'm CentOfRain. Cent. With a C. Like a penny. You know, Lincoln."

"Yeah. I got it. Have you slept any?"

"No. I felt like somebody ought to keep an eye on things even though the alarm is set."

Lincoln began slamming the joystick from side to side. An explosion filled the screen. "Damn it. He got me. I hope the little turd flunks his algebra test or whatever they have at that age." He gave her the side-eye. "You want to play?"

"Nope. I'm too uncoordinated. Or is that what you were counting on?"

"Me? Certainly not. I'm guessing you couldn't sleep, either. I'll call Conner at eight and see if they've learned anything. Until then, want to watch a movie?"

Jax looked around. A few lights twinkled in the distance,

but the sky was still dark. Lincoln was right. It was much too early to call Conner. "Might as well. Comedy, action, or sci fi?"

"I think we've had enough action for a while, and this whole thing is beginning to feel other-worldly?"

"A comedy it is."

Lincoln reached for the remote and jerked back. Had the thing shocked him? Could remotes do that?

"The alarm." His voice was low, hushed.

"I don't hear anything." For some reason she whispered, although she'd been speaking normally only seconds before.

"I have it set to sound through my headset. I didn't want to wake anyone if the damned possum came back."

He ripped off his headphones and a soft *beep, beep, beep* came through.

The door to the security room stood open and they rushed inside. The computer monitors gave off an eerie, green glow. He started at one edge, and she started at the other end.

"There." He tapped on a screen. "Behind that tree. That's no possum."

"Here's another not-a-possum." She pointed to a different monitor.

"Go upstairs. Wake Noah. You and Laurel take Sweet Pea, lock yourselves in the bathroom, and call 911."

Like hell she would.

She ran up the stairs and tapped on Noah's closed door. "Noah. Noah. Wake up." She turned the knob and pushed the door open far enough to lean inside. "Someone's sneaking around outside. Two someones. Lincoln needs you downstairs. Laurel, he wants you to take Sweet Pea into the bathroom and stay there with the door locked. You can call for help once you're inside."

"Like hell I will," Laurel whispered.

Jax knew she liked that woman.

She raced down the stairs, Noah close behind her, pulling on his pants. Sweet Pea yelped excitedly when Laurel exiled her to the bathroom, but the sound faded as she closed the door.

Lincoln had unlocked a panel in the wall, exposing an array of weapons. His eyes traveled up the stairs to her and Noah and Laurel, in that order.

"Don't you ever follow instructions?"

LINCOLN WATCHED IN disbelief as the trio traipsed down the stairs. Noah had on jeans but no shirt. Laurel was pulling a sweatshirt on over her pajamas. Jax was wearing yoga pants and no shoes. Bright-red toenails winked up at him. She must have painted them while they were staying at Laurel's.

Why would he notice a thing like that at a time like this, and why did people seem more vulnerable without the protection of their normal clothes?

All three rushed to the arms cache and chose weapons.

Noah already had his Glock and a backup piece. He took

one look at the Taser and shook his head. "I made that mistake once before," he said before selecting a lethal-looking knife. He stuck a pair of zip-tie handcuffs in his back pocket.

Laurel chose a mini version of Noah's Glock. "I think this is the one I have at home."

Jax looked puzzled. "I don't see one like I used to have."

Lincoln handed her a small revolver. It was lighter, easier to use, and less likely to jam than the semi-auto, with less danger of going through walls if she shot and missed. "Let's try to take these guys alive. Don't shoot unless you have to. And especially, don't shoot me. I've had a hard week already."

Everyone seemed to be looking to him for instruction. "Jax, I need you to go into the security room and watch the monitors. I want to know every move those mopes make."

"Don't try to stick me in a back room. I want to help." Jax took off her glasses and cleaned them on the hem of the T-shirt.

"You will be helping. I can't work blind, and I sure as hell don't want someone we didn't know about sneaking up behind me."

Noah backed him up. "It's important, Jax. You're our eyes in this. We're counting on you."

Now, what to do with Laurel? He took her by the hand and led her to a spot in the corner, hidden by a tall bookcase. "Stay here." He handed her the Taser. "If anyone gets past me or Noah, shoot them with this. I know it didn't work too well at your place, but neither of these guys are as big as Ponytail.

He was a mountain."

"They've gone around to the front. They're checking out the garage door," Jax called from the security room.

Lincoln switched off the TV, plunging them into darkness. A light from the upstairs bedroom offered enough illumination to maneuver by . . . if you knew the layout of the room.

"Shit," Noah muttered. "I couldn't get that door locked. It was too bent. If they get inside the garage, they'll see Lola and know we're here, plus have access to whatever tools they need to force the side door open."

Jax stood in the door to her little room. "Do you want me to sound the alarm?"

"No. They'll take off running and disappear. Then we'll never be able to prove who sent them. Did anyone call 911?"

Laurel's voice floated out of the darkness. "I was busy trying to grab Sweet Pea before she hid under the bed. Sorry."

"Can you do it now?"

"My phone's upstairs, charging."

"I've got mine." Noah patted his pocket.

His was on the coffee table, next to the video controller. If he went for it now, he'd be exposed if they decided to simply kick down the door and rush in.

A soft glow appeared as Noah switched on his phone. "I could call now, or we could wait here in the dark, let them come in, close the door behind them so they can't get away, and take them down. There's four of us and only two of them."

He'd agree with Noah if it weren't for Laurel and Jax.

Unfortunately, that seemed to be their best option if they wanted to take them alive. And alive and testifying against Avendondo was the only way to insure his whole operation was shut down.

"Guys?" Jax's voice came from the security room. "I think I see another not-a-possum behind a tree on the far side of the house."

CHAPTER
THIRTY

Lincoln glanced around the room. Two cops and two civilians against three armed assassins. "Change of plans. Quick, Noah. Move that bookcase in front of the door. Don't let them get in."

Noah slid the bookcase while Laurel guided it.

"Jax, keep an eye on our friends outside. I need to know exactly where they are at all times. Have they gotten into the garage yet?"

Jax swung around and raced back into the security room. "They have the door up a foot or so. The first guy is crawling in."

"Okay. Noah, you and I will head out the back door. Give me three minutes. I'll take out the guy on the side of the house. You keep the two creeps penned in the garage until I get there to help you."

"Will do." Noah grabbed his shoes from under the coffee table and jammed his feet into them.

"Laurel, you stay to one side. Don't get in front of the door. It's steel, but I don't know how thick. They may try to shoot through it, and I don't know what type of weapons they have. If they do manage to get in, don't think twice. Shoot the hell out of them."

He didn't want either of the women to have to live with taking a life—no matter how much the assholes deserved it—but if they got in, they'd use the women to force him and Noah to drop their weapons, then kill all four of them. He couldn't let that happen.

He looked at Noah. Noah nodded and started for the back door.

"Jax, where are they now?"

"The guy on the side is at the edge, peeking around the corner, watching the front door. He has his back to you. The other two have made it into the garage. If you leave now, they won't see you."

Lincoln slipped out onto the deck. That left the back door to worry about. It would lock automatically if he let it close, and they would be trapped outside if things went wrong. If he left it open a crack, and there was a fourth man they hadn't seen yet, the women would be in danger.

He pulled it shut behind Noah.

He pointed to himself and around the corner, then held

up three fingers.

Noah tapped his own chest, pointed the opposite direction, and gave a thumbs-up.

Lincoln hugged the edge of the house and eased to the corner. He bent low and took a quick look. Yep. The guy was there, all right. Much taller than he thought from the video. Getting a choke hold around his neck would be tricky.

Avendondo must think hiring giants gave him an advantage.

Didn't matter. He'd done the maneuver hundreds of times in the gym. Of course, his life hadn't depended on it those times. He rolled his shoulders and shook out his arms.

He'd need both hands. That meant holstering his weapon.

The ground was covered with dried brush and twigs. Reaching him without making a sound would be tough. He could run and take his chances. Nope. The guy already had a gun in his hand. He'd never make it unless he shot him in the back.

Tempting as that was, he couldn't do it.

A motorboat started up across the lake, and Lincoln used the noise to cover his steps. He was two feet away when the guy sensed his presence and glanced over his shoulder.

Lincoln turned on the speed and leapt at him. He got his arm around the guy's neck, but it wasn't a clean hold. They both fell to the ground, the big guy on top. The air whished out of Lincoln's lungs, but he didn't loosen his hold. The guy's face was turning purple. All he had to do was outlast him.

Instead of fighting, the guy waved his gun and attempted to aim at Lincoln's head. He fired one shot, and the bullet kicked up dead leaves two inches from Lincoln's ear.

Time to finish this off.

Lincoln heaved and rolled the guy over, burying his face in the dirt. The guy tried to move his arm, but Lincoln pinned it with his knee.

JAX HEARD THE gunshot and felt something freeze inside her chest. The camera angle was poor, and the eerie, green glow kept her from seeing exactly what was happening. She couldn't tell which figure was Lincoln and which was the other guy, but one wasn't moving.

Noah's head snapped up at the sound of the gunshot, and he seemed to consider leaving his post. He may have yelled at the two men in the garage, but the video didn't have sound and she couldn't be sure.

Whatever set them off—Noah's shouts or the gunshot— the two men in the garage began to beat on the side door.

Laurel cried out as the bookcase vibrated. Books tumbled out onto the floor.

Another crash against the door, and the bookcase moved an inch.

Two more crashes. Each time, the bookcase moved forward.

Every fiber inside Jax screamed for her to go help Lincoln, but she couldn't leave Laurel.

She flew into the room and helped Laurel flip a heavy, oak coffee table on its side. They both crouched behind it as the door opened a few more inches. A man's arm, dark from a thick coating of hair, snaked through. The hand clutched a weapon, waving it wildly, searching for a target.

Jax kept her gun pointed at the opening, waiting for a face to appear. *Deep breath*, *squeeze the trigger* she repeated over and over. What else had the guy told her the day she bought that piece-of-crap gun from him?

Laurel pointed the Taser at the arm. Blue light and a zapping sound spewed from the barrel. Its barbs buried themselves in flesh. The smell of burning hair filled the room.

A man bellowed in pain. The arm dropped the gun and disappeared.

Jax and Laurel rushed forward and shoved the door closed. Jax picked up the gun and raced for the back door.

LINCOLN LIE ON the ground, panting, when he heard the back door slam. A quick glance told him Jax was headed his way.

Running.

With a gun in her hand.

He had to secure this piece-of-shit fast. He forced the guy's arm back and slapped the cuff on one wrist, then grabbed the other hand and did the same. "I've got him. You can relax. Quit running with that gun in your hand, and for God's sake, take your finger off the trigger."

Amateurs. More likely to kill you by accident than professionals on purpose. Ponytail had tried to kill him four times, and this guy had tried once. Yet, here he was, living and breathing with Jax his biggest danger.

Jax halted long enough to move her finger off the trigger, then came nearer. "Are you sure you're okay?"

"I'm fine, but I need to go help Noah. You sit on this guy for me. Make sure he doesn't move."

Jax lifted the gun and pointed it at the man on the ground.

"No. Put the gun away. I meant sit on him. Literally. Sit on him. If he moves, hit him in the head with this rock. But not hard enough to kill him."

She settled herself on the man's back, and he handed her a rock the size of a tennis ball. Surely she couldn't do any lasting damage with that.

Her determination to be in the thick of things might actually drive him crazy. On the other hand, he'd never had anyone willing to rush into danger for him before.

His mom and dad would jump into a fight for him, but carrying legal papers, not guns.

He sped around the corner of the house in time to see Noah on his knees, peering under the garage door. "Drop your weapons and come out with your hands where I can see them."

A voice called out from the back of the garage. "Kenny

can't move. That bitch shot him with something."

"That's my bitch you're talking about so watch your mouth. You come out with your hands in the air, and we'll take care of Kenny."

"I can't put my hands in the air. I have to use them to crawl under the door."

"Figure out a way because you don't want me coming in there after you."

Lincoln wasn't sure Noah was capable of crawling under the two-foot-wide opening, so he grabbed a corner of the rolling door and shoved it up higher. "Try it now, asshole."

A kid who couldn't be more than nineteen duck-walked out, his hands in the air. Noah had him on the ground with his hands cuffed behind him before Lincoln could close the gap.

Lincoln sprinted into the garage to find Kenny doubled over in pain. The kid looked up at him with tears in his eyes.

"That lady hurt me."

Lincoln might have been rougher than necessary putting the cuffs on him. "Good. You're lucky she didn't kill you. It wouldn't be her first time."

He had no idea if Laurel had ever killed anyone. He doubted it, but in the short time he'd known her, she'd tracked down a serial killer, shoved him into the path of a copperhead, and now Tased a hit man. Nothing the woman did surprised him.

He just hoped Noah was strong enough to handle her.

Noah stood in the driveway, gripping the arm of the young

kid. "Let's take these nimrods around to the back. I don't want to risk Laurel or Jax shooting us if we tried to go in that door."

"Jax is in the back, sitting on hoodlum number three, but you're right. I don't want to take a chance of surprising either of those women. Ever."

CHAPTER THIRTY-ONE

Noah and Lincoln marched the three would-be hit men into the house. They sat them on kitchen chairs and draped their arms over the back before duct taping them to the chairs.

Noah smiled to himself as he secured the last shooter's leg to the chair. *Ah, duct tape. It can't fix stupid, but it can make sure it doesn't cause any more trouble.*

When Noah was satisfied they couldn't move, he motioned Lincoln to follow him out onto the deck where they could keep an eye on things but not be heard.

"Is this something we'll have to worry about for the rest of our lives?" He couldn't ask Laurel to live that way. It would kill him to break up with her, but that might be the only way to keep her safe.

"Not if I can help it. I'd like to check with Conner and see what he's learned before we get the sanitized version from the suits."

Noah pulled out his burner phone. "I'll be glad to get rid of these things. They make me feel dirty."

Conner answered on the first ring. Noah flipped on the speaker so Lincoln could hear.

"We've caught three more assholes trying to kill us. These are babies, amateurs. But the next ones might not be. Have you learned anything that could help us? Have they found Avendondo or figured out who killed Rossini?"

"Sorry partner. The only news I have is bad. Avendondo showed up at his compound with his lawyer in tow about fifteen minutes after we found out Rossini died. The local branch was only half through searching his place. The lawyer is screaming the search warrant is no good now because it's based on the testimony of someone who is no longer alive."

"Doesn't that just chap you? Kill off the witnesses and walk free." Noah wanted to throw the phone against the wall, but what good would that do?

"Rossini's brother showed up at the hospital, yelling and making a fuss. He wants to know why his brother wasn't protected and who killed him. He's threatening to sue the State of Texas, the doctor, the guards, and anyone who saw him in passing."

Lincoln leaned toward the phone. "Can't say I blame him.

Why wasn't he being protected?"

"He was on an IV, so he couldn't be moved to a cell. The only other patient was a sick, old man dying of cancer, and he passed away this morning."

"What about the doctor?" Noah asked.

"He was eating dinner with friends in a public restaurant when Rossini died."

"Well, isn't that convenient. Any money show up in his account lately?"

"Not yet. He's on paid leave while the case is being investigated."

"And Avendondo?"

"Everything's on hold until a judge rules on the search warrant."

"Did they ever find out where the old fart had been hiding?"

"This one is rich. He was in a cabin in Upstate New York. The reason no one knew about it is because it was registered in the name of Rossini's father—a man who disappeared ten years ago, yet has never been reported missing. The place was purchased two years ago with a cashier's check from Avendondo's bank."

"If his lawsuits are a bust, maybe young Mr. Rossini can make a claim on the cabin. Somebody ought to come out ahead because the only thing we've got is a boatload of shit."

THE SAME TEAM that had met at Noah's house was on their way to the safe house. Lincoln's boss. Noah's boss. The Chief of Detectives. Much like the first time, the Chief of Police wouldn't make an appearance until he was sure nothing could go wrong to blow back at him.

The only difference was that the DA, the Assistant DA, and the uniformed officers would be from Montgomery County.

Lincoln glared at the three douchebags sitting in front of him. "I want to know who sent you."

The one he'd caught outside was older and appeared to be the leader. "I want a lawyer, man. I'm not talking without one."

"I don't care about lawyers. This isn't for trial, and what you tell me won't leave this room. I need to know who's behind this. Tell me, or my friend here will give you a dose of what she gave Kenny."

He glanced toward Laurel. "You may need to goose up the voltage a bit. This one's bigger."

Laurel picked up the Taser and rotated the dial.

"Hey, man. You can't do this. That's police brutality."

"Who do you think they'll believe? All my reputable friends here or some little turd like you?"

Laurel shook the Taser and it emitted a short *bzzz*.

"My uncle Lester, okay? I've run a few errands for him from

time to time. Nothing like this. He called me from New Jersey and gave me this address. Told me to round up a few friends, so I called Troy and Kenny. They're brothers who live down the block from me. We weren't supposed to kill you. I promise. Just shake you up a little. Tell you to drop your vendetta and go home. Forget any of this ever happened. I don't know what happened, but there are people out there you shouldn't get in fights with. And if you do, apologize and walk away while you can."

Lincoln didn't believe for an instant they weren't ordered to take out everyone in the house. The question was . . . how did they know where they were?

"Who does Lester work for, and who told him how to find us?"

"I don't know, man. Mom's never said. It's all a big secret. I'm not supposed to ask any questions. He sends her money sometimes, when she falls behind on things."

Red-and-blue lights flashed against the walls, and a series of car doors slammed.

"I'll give you pieces of dog shit one word of advice before the rest of your world tumbles down around your ears. Tell the guys coming in everything you know. Don't hold back and don't lie about anything. It's your only chance. Don't try to protect Lester. He's the one who got you into this mess. You're about to go away for a long stretch, and it won't be any country club prison. I'll ask you one more time to answer my question. Do it, and I'll put in a good word for you. Who does Lester work for, and where did that guy get his information?"

Jax slow-walked to the front door to answer the insistent knocking.

Kenny's eyes filled with tears. "Tell him, Marcus. I don't want to lose my virginity in prison to some bruiser named Butch."

His brother hissed at him. "Shut up, you pussy."

None of this mattered to Marcus. He'd made up his mind. "I only ever heard him call the guy Mr. A. I don't know his real name. Lester said they knew you were here when you turned on the alarm."

Jax tried in vain to delay those at the door. It didn't work. These were people used to getting what they wanted. And they wanted in.

Within two minutes, the house was swarming with law enforcement personnel. The sound of cars in the driveway meant more were on their way.

Soon it became a replay of the night before at Noah's times three. Only the color of the uniforms was different.

Eventually, the trio of losers was taken away to be questioned further at the Montgomery County Jail. There'd be a custody fight over them later, but Lincoln didn't have to be involved in that.

He and Noah and Laurel and Jax were questioned and requestioned and questioned again.

Each had to show their position and the position of everyone else, then write down what they'd said and sign it.

They weren't allowed to speak to each other.

Lincoln's boss took him to the side. "Are you finished playing cops and robbers? I never pictured you as the reckless type. I want you back in the office first thing Monday morning."

Other than the fact he believed he deserved some time off, the thought of sitting at his desk, chasing down leads on the computer, sounded like heaven to him.

If he never had to stare into the barrel of a gun again in his life, that would be too soon.

NIGHT HAD FALLEN before the house was quiet again. A quarter moon peeked through the clouds.

The whole place was surrounded by yellow crime scene tape. Jax, Lincoln, Noah, and Laurel sat silently on the back deck, each with their own thoughts. Sweet Pea curled up in Noah's lap, and he absently stroked her head.

Jax wasn't sure about the others, but she didn't seem to be able to concentrate. Her mind wanted to leapfrog from one disaster to a worse one.

Lincoln slapped his knees and sat up straight. "We can't stay here tonight, and we can't stay at Noah's. If it's all right with you, Laurel, why don't we head back to your townhouse?"

Laurel stifled a yawn. "That's fine with me, but only for tonight and only because I'm too tired to argue. Tomorrow, I'm going by the kennel to pick up my cat and take him home.

This isn't fair to him after all he's been through. He must be scared to death I've left him back at the pound."

"How about we get a good night's sleep and talk about it in the morning. For now, Laurel, Jax, why don't you go upstairs and gather your things. Noah and I will lock up the house."

The fact that she knew Lincoln well enough to recognize when he was hiding something disturbed her. He wanted her and Laurel out of the way so he could talk to Noah.

That wasn't going to happen. She didn't plan to toddle upstairs like a good girl and let the big boys decide what to do. Not when it concerned her future. "My stuff is all gathered. I never bothered to unpack."

Laurel stopped at the door and swung around. "Mine's pretty much together, too."

Lincoln shrugged. "Okay then. Let's talk about this. What do we know that we didn't know before?"

Jax knew the answer to that question. "That Avendondo will never give up as long as he's alive. I'm the one who saw Ponytail shoot the senator. The case is weak without Ponytail. Without me, it's finished. If I disappear again, you'll all be safe. Lincoln, I hope you remember your promise to me."

She didn't want to say it out loud in front of Noah. He'd been a big help so far. Who knew if he'd draw the line at helping her vanish?

Lincoln gave the briefest nod. "I remember. Let's not rush into things yet. Marcus said Avendondo knew where we were because I turned on the alarm."

Noah's eyes brightened. "Is there a specific person who would be in charge of keeping that up to date?"

"Maybe some tech. I don't know. It's all automatic. It covers dozens of safe houses in every state. However, anyone with enough clearance could check who's used it and when or where. I probably couldn't, not without asking permission. My boss could. And anyone above him. Although, I doubt the bigwigs at the very top have enough computer savvy to know how to do it."

"Are you saying you suspect your boss?"

"No. He's as straight as they come, but someone like him."

"So a fairly narrow field of people. High enough to have access and low enough not to depend on secretaries or assistants to do the grunt work for them. Do you have anyone in mind?"

A light went on in Jax's brain. "Ponytail said he was in trouble for killing the wrong agent. He was supposed to kill you. I thought it was because you might recognize him. What if it was because your partner was one of them?"

"Exactly. There's not much we can do tonight. First thing in the morning, I'll make a couple of calls. One to my boss to ask that your house be released by Crime Scene so you can go home."

"Thank you, Lincoln. I appreciate that." Laurel's face was still tired, but not as stressed.

"Then I'll call Conner. See if he's heard anything new on Ponytail's death or whether we'll be able to use any of the information the search team uncovered against him in trial. Tell him what we've figured out and see what he can find out about Stu Hawkins and how he ended up riding to West Monroe with me. I'd do it myself, but I'm under strict orders to stay away from this case."

If Conner could answer those questions by midmorning, great. She'd love to know. Any later than that and she was gone. Lincoln had promised to help her disappear, and she planned to hold him to it.

Somehow, he, Noah, and Laurel had become the best friends she'd had in years—maybe ever. And as long as she was around, they were in danger.

CHAPTER
THIRTY-TWO

Noah and Laurel had taken the master bedroom, a spot they seemed intimately familiar with. Jax had returned to the bedroom she'd used before. Leaving Lincoln to sleep in what he'd come to accept as his usual spot—the downstairs sofa.

Logically, he knew Avendondo wouldn't have learned his rent-a-hit man trio had failed in time to find new ones or send his own crew to Houston. That didn't stop him from floating half in, half out of sleep. Keeping alert for any strange noise during the night.

Noah came down at seven with Sweet Pea at his heels, looking as haggard as Lincoln felt. "I must have gotten up a dozen times during the night . . . any time a dog barked or an owl hooted. I don't know what to do about Laurel. This is the safest place I know of, and I don't want her staying here. And I certainly don't want her staying at my house."

"Doesn't her mother live in town?"

"The only person she'd hate to stay with more is her sister."

Family fighting was an enigma to Lincoln. Sure, his brother drove him crazy with his constant jokes about the FBI and J. Edgar Hoover. His mother's not-so-subtle hints about finding a girlfriend were getting old, but since his sister got pregnant, she'd eased up on those.

"I believe you and Laurel are safe. Why would Avendondo want to come after you? You didn't see Ponytail murder the senator or hear Ponytail admit who hired him. He wanted me out of the way to make killing Jax easier. Jax is the only one who could conceivably be of any danger to him."

"Deep down in my toes, I think you're right. It's that one percent chance you're wrong that keeps my stomach in knots. Not for me—I can take care of myself—for Laurel. She can't go back to my place when there's even a remote chance of danger, but the only way I can come up with to keep her away is to pick a fight with her and break up. Then hope she'll take me back when this is all over."

A heavy, black cloud filled Lincoln's chest. What had he done, getting them involved in this mess? He should have taken Jax straight to the FBI immediately, no matter the risk. "Don't do anything rash. We've got a few hours to come up with something."

"You think we can solve this in a couple of hours when we

haven't accomplished squat in a week?"

Lincoln didn't have an answer for that. Luckily, Jax and Laurel came down the stairs, Laurel smiling. Jax, not so much.

"I don't suppose either of you made coffee," Jax said.

"In the kitchen." Lincoln held up his half-full cup.

Laurel kissed Noah on the forehead. "I've got everything packed whenever you're ready."

"I have to get clearance from Crime Scene before we can get back in the house, and they're not in the office yet. Plus, we need to check in with Conner and see if anything new has turned up. I wouldn't want to call him too early."

"He's at Quantico. That's an hour later than here."

Lincoln stood and headed for the kitchen. "How about we get a little something to eat first? Give Conner time to check out the latest news."

"You can only stall me for so long. I am going to pick up my cat and go home today, so you do whatever you need to do to get clearance."

Noah looked defeated. "I'll do what I can, but the kennel doesn't open until nine."

"You've got one hour. Use it well."

EVERYONE HAD PICKED at their breakfast. Noah had called Crime Scene about releasing his house. They promised to call back as soon as their boss gave the okay.

One look at Laurel said they had delayed as long as they could.

Lincoln reached for his phone, unsure if he should call his boss or Conner. Conner would be a friendlier conversation, but his boss was . . . well . . . his boss. Any trouble he was in at work came from not including his boss in every decision he'd made over the last few days.

His phone rang before he made his decision.

The caller ID listed Conner.

"Hey, Conner. How are things in Virginia?"

"Interesting. It's been an eventful morning, or night."

"Interesting good or interesting bad?"

"Not sure I've had time to process it enough to decide."

That sounded like things leaned more to the bad side. "What happened?"

"Remember I told you Avendondo and his lawyer went to court yesterday to have the search warrant declared null and void since Rossini died and couldn't be cross-examined?"

"I remember, and I called bullshit. He gave a taped confession, was questioned about every incident, and signed an affidavit."

"The judge must have heard your argument. He agreed with you. The search and everything it uncovered stands. With all the evidence of money laundering, bribery, intimidation, and organized criminal activity, the government plans to file for a RICO judgment."

"So he'll lose everything? Bank accounts, property, boats?"

"Almost everything. He's got some stock that's been a good investment, and he'll get to keep that. He's set up trusts for his kids and a college fund for his grandkids. Anything that belonged to his wife is off limits, even though he probably bought it with stolen money."

Lincoln had the phone on speaker and Noah joined in. "Good, because without Ponytail's testimony, the murders might be hard to prove."

Conner broke in. "Who?"

"Rossini. We started calling him Ponytail before we knew his name. Now Avendondo will be too tied up in court cases to worry about any of us and too broke to hire others to do it for him."

"That's the rest of my news. The part I'm ambivalent about."

Just when things were looking up. If this was good news/ bad news or just good news/not great news, it didn't bode well for them.

"Yesterday, Avendondo and his lawyer were in court all day. His bodyguard went with him, and the maid wasn't back yet from wherever he sent her during the raid and search. An electrician showed up with a work order to fix some wiring. The idiot watching the house let him in without checking."

Lincoln's heart froze. He knew what was coming. He felt it in his bones. He gave a quick glance over to Jax, not sure how to prepare her.

"Late last night, no one is sure what time because everyone had gone to bed, Avendondo reached over to turn off his bedside lamp and received an electrical shock. Maybe it wouldn't have killed a stronger man, but he was old and sick. When the maid went in with his coffee this morning, he was dead."

"Are they sure it was the lamp, not his heart?"

"The doc could tell. Also, the local M.E. sent for an electrician. The wiring to that lamp was rigged. So far, no one can trace the repairman."

Jax's eyes filled with tears. "Then we're free. All of us."

"Yes. I suppose you might be asked to come back for some type of hearing, nothing else. I'm relieved you don't have to hide any longer and that Lincoln, Noah, and Laurel don't have to watch over their shoulders, but I hate the old bastard got off that easy. He should have had to answer for his crimes."

Lincoln could barely speak over the knot in his throat. "He'll have to answer, all right. Just to a higher authority."

JAX AND LAUREL sat at the kitchen table. Lincoln had gone into the other room to check in with his boss. Noah was calling Crime Scene for the third time to see if they had released his house.

Jax twirled her empty coffee cup. "I don't know how to feel. I've spent so many years hating Ponytail and Avendondo. I don't think I've slept a night through without being afraid. I should be happy they're gone. Relieved. But I'm just . . . numb."

Dark circles showed under Laurel's eyes. "I can't begin to imagine how you feel. I've only been hiding from them for three days, and I'm exhausted, angry, and confused."

"I know Ponytail was a bad man. He killed Senator Sheppard, the old couple at Lake Conroe, and the lady at the vacation rental place. And that's only the people I know about. Now I find out he had a mother he hadn't seen in four years. That's as long as I've gone without seeing mine. He had a brother and sister who cared about him and a niece he must have loved because he gave her my cat. A cat that is probably happier than if she had stayed with me."

"Noah told me Ponytail wanted to get out of the business and become a chef. He asked Noah to try to pull some strings and get him a job in the prison kitchen."

"I didn't know that. And now his brother came all the way to Texas to arrange for his funeral and to try to find out who killed him. They may never figure that out with Avendondo dead."

Laurel got up to pour herself more coffee. She held up the pot to see if Jax wanted more, but Jax shook her head. "Noah always says people aren't just one thing. A killer can love animals. A crook can appreciate art and music. A man can give to charity and still beat his wife. Their actions are the only things we can judge them for. The rest is up to God. I'm not confused about Avendondo. That man wasn't just bad. He was pure evil. He ran an organized crime family that specialized in drugs, violence, and murder. He'd killed one wife. No one in his family would speak to him, except his daughter."

A fist-size rock sat in the pit of Jax's stomach. How could she have abandoned her mother for so long, leaving her to fight breast cancer alone? There were opportunities over the years. She could have at least tried to contact her.

She knew her mother's marriage was rocky and that Gavin isolated her and kept her supplied with pills and alcohol until she didn't have the strength to stand up to him. He had brainwashed her into believing everything he told her.

Noah came in with a big grin. "That dorky, little techie I always complained about is walking the papers over to his boss now. He'll text me the minute they're signed. Shouldn't be long. Guess I'll have to be nicer to him in the future."

Laurel jumped up and gave him a kiss. "That's wonderful because I was about to grab a pair of scissors and cut that damn yellow tape myself." She swung toward Jax. "You're welcome to stay here as long as you like. Don't rush making any decisions. You've got your whole life ahead of you. In fact, we'd all love it if you'd consider staying. Houston is a great town, and you already have friends here."

Three friends. That was more than she had anywhere else. Although Lincoln felt like something more than a friend. She just couldn't decide what. Certainly not a brother.

Noah bent to give her a hug. "Bye, Jax. You keep in touch with us, okay?"

She hugged back and whispered in his ear. "I will. And you call me when you get up enough nerve to do something about that ring."

Sweet Pea came to her for a tummy rub. She would miss that little dog.

After a flurry of activity—grabbing bags, hugs, kisses, handshakes—they were gone, and she and Lincoln were left alone. After all the time they'd spent together, this felt different. Awkward.

Lincoln glanced around the strangely silent house. "If you don't feel comfortable staying here, we can go to my apartment. It's not too far. It's only a one bedroom, but I'm used to sleeping on the sofa. Laurel's right. You should take some time. See what you want to do. I'm kind of hoping you'll stay in Houston. Or better yet, come to Alabama with me."

Alabama? Was he serious?

"Whatever you do, you'll need a car. My dad is an economics professor. I call my brother The Car Whisperer. They went in together and opened a used car lot. Dad can look at your finances and tell you within a nickel how much of a monthly payment you can afford. My brother can sit in a car and know if anything is wrong with it. Together, they'll fix you up."

Tears welled up but she fought them back. That might have been the nicest offer she'd ever had. She was deeply tempted to accept. "I don't have a job, Lincoln. I can't afford any car. I can't stay with you, either, but there is something you can do for me."

"What? Just name it." The look in his eyes almost broke her heart.

"Drive me to the airport. I need to see my mother."

CHAPTER THIRTY-THREE

Carlsbad, California
Four months later

Jax propped her feet on the railing of the deck at her mother's tiny house, three blocks from the beach in Carlsbad, California. If she sat in the far corner, she could see the ocean.

The sea breeze and the rolling waves calmed her better than any drug. A yellow tabby eyed her from two feet away, its tail flicking in time to the music drifting out through the open door.

The ringing of her phone startled her. So few people ever called. Lincoln's name in the caller ID made her smile.

"Hey there, Special Agent man. How are things in Houston?"

"Hot. Hot. And more hot. It's August. What can you expect? I saw Noah today at the courthouse. He said you talk to Laurel once a week or so."

"Yes. It sounds like she's been busy taking over her old boss's business. Her first job as a new broker was to sell her own townhouse. Not sure why that made me sad. Felt like I was losing an old friend."

"That's funny. I couldn't put my finger on why the news bothered me, but I think you hit on it. I wanted to tell you how sorry I was to hear about your mother's passing. Are you doing okay?"

"Yeah. It's been six weeks. Every day is a little different. Two steps forward. One step back. We had three good months before the cancer came roaring back and took her away. We were able to work through and settle a lot of issues during that time. The last two weeks were bad, but I'm glad I could be here for her when she needed me."

"I am, too. That must mean a lot to you."

"I know she loved me and regretted the way she'd acted. I've been working with a counselor for several weeks. The rest I'm learning to deal with."

The cat crept a foot closer. If Jax stretched out her arm, she could scratch its ear with one finger. Silky fur ruffled in the breeze.

"I worked with her at the thrift shop while she was able. When the manager left, they offered me her job. It doesn't pay much, but you know I don't need a lot. I love the job. It feels like I'm doing something worthwhile. Paying back people who helped me along the way."

A low vibration traveled up her fingertips as the cat began to purr.

"So you're managing okay there, by yourself?"

"Turns out, when Mother had her right mind, it was a sharp one. She knew to take an up-front settlement from Gavin before his business crashed. Then she paid cash for this house. It was old and needed lots of work. She did some herself, and I'm learning to do the odd repairs. I even have a sort-of cat now."

Lincoln's laugh rolled across the miles. "How can you have a sort-of cat?"

"She's feral. Shows up when she wants to. Doesn't if she has somewhere else to go. She does allow me to feed her. If I stay on my side of the deck and don't watch her eat. Lately, she stops by every day. She won't come in the house—not yet. But she will let me touch her. When I leave the door open, she peeks inside as if she's thinking about it. I'm starting to come to terms with everything that's happened. I'm not going to let it define me."

"I can tell by talking to you. You sound more relaxed than I've ever heard you."

"What's going on there? Were you able to prove that someone at the FBI or police was helping Avendondo track me?"

"Funny you should ask. You know my old boss, Darrell Byrne? He's the one who pushed for you as the lead suspect. I always thought he did a piss-poor job of investigating. Then he sent Stu Hawkins down from Dallas to help pick you up. We know Ponytail fingered Stu as one of Avendondo's men."

A chill raced up her spine. "I remember. He was supposed to shoot you instead."

"I got a call from my hacker a week ago. She found some odd messages between Darrell and Ponytail's information guy both times we went to the Lake Conroe safe house. A series of numbers and symbols she couldn't decipher."

"That's it. Can you go after him now?" The cat eased closer than she'd ever come before. Jax stroked her head and neck, waiting to see if she would bolt. She didn't.

"Doesn't work that way. What she did is illegal and wouldn't hold up in any court."

"So he gets away with it?" Every time she got close, they moved the finish line.

"Not really. Darrell retired. Put in his papers the day Avendondo died. He was only fifty-seven. Never came back to the office after his heart surgery. His wife left him, and he bought a cabin way out by itself on a lake in the Ozarks. Said he planned to spend the rest of his life fishing."

"It's supposed to be beautiful up there. A popular place to retire." Some people loved the mountains. She preferred the freedom and openness of the ocean.

"Maybe. Except he hated fishing. Told me it was the dumbest waste of time he'd ever heard of. Spend thousands of dollars to catch a fish you could buy for $3.99."

That didn't make sense . . . unless he had a reason. "Did he have family there?"

"Nope. All his family, kids included, live in New Jersey."

The chill in her spine turned into an icicle.

"A few days ago, his cabin caught fire. Went up like a torch. Took Darrell with it. Barely enough left of him to identify."

"But they are positive it was him?"

"Absolutely. Dental records. A pin in his left arm where he broke it as a child. They'll have the DNA by the end of the week, but yeah, they're sure."

"So what happened?" Jax stood and started into the house. The yellow cat followed as far as the door, stopping half in, half out. Maybe it was time to move the food and water bowls inside. See if the cat would come all the way in.

"The fire marshal said it had something to do with the wiring. The thing is, the cabin was brand new. The nearest neighbor is a quarter of a mile away. He says he might have seen an electrician poking around the day before when he was out on his boat. Didn't think anything about it at the time. Could have been a different cabin. It's hard to tell from the water. If so, Darrell was in town getting groceries at the time."

Jax sank into the chair she and her mother had dragged home from the thrift shop, laughing as they tied a scarf onto the legs jutting out of the trunk of the car like a demented sculpture. "Is anyone investigating?"

"They're calling it an accident. Nobody is looking at anything. Nobody *wants* to look at anything. Whatever happened to Darrell, he deserved. With him gone, so is any

Bureau tie with the mob.

"What do you think?"

"The doc who treated Ponytail in the jail infirmary was out fishing when the motor on his boat caught fire. He's not dead, but he'll never practice medicine again. All that's left is a few old men who play cards on Tuesdays, drink coffee at Starbucks on Thursdays, and go to Florida in the winter. There is no more Family, and no one wants to start it up again."

"And you're okay with that?"

"Avendondo, Darrell Byrne, the doc. What happened to them didn't have anything to do with the Family. If it had, they'd have come in shooting. It's the only way the mob knows. Those guys were taken out for revenge, and by someone smart enough to rig the wiring and leave no trace."

Jax sucked in a breath. It was right there in front of her, but she hadn't seen it. "You're right. I never thought of it that way."

"I've got a brother, too, and I know how I'd feel if someone harmed him. I'd go after them with everything I had, but not that way. Not stone-cold murder. But as long as the asswipe behind all those mishaps stays on his side of the country and doesn't cause any more trouble, I can live with it. What I do care about is you. Any chance you would consider coming to Houston?"

There it was again. That tug. "Not yet. I need more time to heal. You know, planes fly in both directions. You could come here for a visit."

She held her breath.

"It so happens I have vacation time coming up next month. My mother wants me to come home to see my sister's new baby. But lately, I've had an urge to learn to surf."

She looked at the framed family photo over the mantle. Not the torn one she'd carried for four years. The original. With her mother, sister, and herself, their arms around each other. Smiling, laughing. Was Gavin already abusing Krista? She'd never know.

"I'll tell you what. Go home to Alabama. Give your mother a kiss. Meet your new niece/nephew?"

"Niece. Named Kennedy. Following a family tradition instituted by my civics-teacher mother of naming us after dead presidents."

"And your sister is?"

"McKinley. My brother is Harrison. Unfortunately, my nephew is Roosevelt. Why anyone would do that to a poor child is beyond me."

Jax's smile made her cheeks hurt. The first time in weeks. "Family is important. Keep yours close. Then come see me in the fall, when it's not so hot. My house is the fourth one from the corner. The one with the red door. I'll be here. I'm through running."

ACKNOWLEDGMENTS

A special thank you to my son, Ron Muller, and my friend Bobby Squire for beta reading this manuscript. Your helpful advice and sharp eyes are much appreciated.

To my daughter, Angela Rehm, my son-in-law, Jason, my daughter-in-law, Karen Muller, and my grandkids, Andrew, Sam, Caroline, and Bode. You are in my heart at all times.

A great big special thank you to Maggie, who is always by my side, rain or shine (especially during thunderstorms!), keeping a sharp eye out—when she's awake—to protect me from marauding squirrels or possums or the FedEx guy.

Thanks to Carla Rossi Editing, Joyce Mochrie of One Last Look, E.M. Tippetts Book Designs, and Najla Qamber Designs for making me look good.

Thank you to Shauna Allen for spurring me onward and helping with my blurb.

Thanks to my friend Christie Craig for more things than I can mention.

Thanks to Kimberly Dawn for all your help.

Thanks to all the members of Susan's Clue Crew. You're the best!

Thank you to my fans, supporters, and to you, the reader.

Dear Readers,

I hope you enjoyed reading this book as much as I enjoyed writing it. If you did, please consider taking a moment to leave a review. Authors live and die by reviews. Reviews don't need to be long. A single paragraph works better than a long retelling of the story. Just say what you liked about the book. How it made you feel. Did it offer heart-racing excitement or heart-tugging emotions? Did the characters come to life? Were you invested in the outcome? Did the villain give you the creeps?

If you want to see more of Noah, Laurel, and Conner, check out my *Seasons Pass* series. If you want to see more of Lincoln and Tom Meyers, *Time for Justice*, the next book in my *There's Always Time for Murder* series, will be out soon.

Facebook:

https://www.facebook.com/SusanCMuller/

Webpage:

http://www.susancmuller.com/

Newsletter:

https://susancmuller.us14.list-manage.com/
subscribe?u=627d3abeb080863cd3d5ec388&id=ee87633272

BOOKS BY
SUSAN C. MULLER

Occult Series

The House on Forest Bend

The Witch on Twisted Oak

Voodoo on Bayou Lafonte

Seasons Pass Series

Winter Song

Spring Shadow

Summer Storm

Autumn Secrets

"Tis the Season

Time's Up Series

Time to Run

Other Must Read Books

Redeeming Santa

Circle of Redemption Anthology